By A. J. Langguth

JESUS CHRISTS 1968
WEDLOCK 1972

Wedlock

Wedlock

A. J. LANGGUTH

 *New York*

Alfred A. Knopf   *1972*

Wedlock

Bᴙ ᴛʜᴇ ᴛɪᴍᴇ the bus reached the terminal in downtown Los Angeles, I was on my feet pulling my raincoat off the overhead rack, more than ready to separate myself from the face in the window. For three days and nights we had traveled together, and though he took himself away for hours at a time, I was aware of his presence beside me. On the January morning we left New York he had shown up in the glass, the whites of his eyes, and his teeth when he yawned, bright against the gray buildings. The whole of that first night he rode with me through Ohio, vanishing only when I blinked from the lights of an all-night diner.

The next day either the sun was striking the window at angles that discouraged him, or the cornfields and low wheatland deprived him of the backdrop he needed. I opened my French-English dictionary and faltered through half a chapter of *La Chute* without his keeping watch. I ate a cheese sandwich. In New Mexico I woke up to a raw daylight with no dark places for his image to collect.

He rejoined me for our final three hundred miles across the Mohave. The sun was down, and over a sea of sand my dim reading bulb was the only light. This time he smiled, to assure me we had done well to board this bus and set off to live in California; to try to live in California. Long before San Bernardino he was wiping his face with his shirt sleeve, brushing

3

at his hair, making himself presentable for the welcome he expected.

He peered at me, anxious for approval. I don't think it was vanity that made him smooth his dark blond hair one more time and bite at the dirt under his thumbnail. Certainly it wasn't pride or even curiosity—rather, mistrust—that had kept me staring at him. For this specter was husky, when I thought of myself as slight. He was blond—unsuitable coloring for a man—while in my mind my hair was dark and my skin swarthy, possibly brown. The glass couldn't show the exact color of his eyes, only that they were a drained and vacant shade, not dark, as mine were. In all, a specimen behind glass that was perfect for California—blond enough, healthy enough, careless if not actually cruel, one of life's idlers, with routine oppressive hands. I who observed him was a man he would mark out as a victim—intelligent, gentle and kind, sad-hearted, the only sort of man who might still, in a century such as this had been, lay a modest claim to virtue.

Inside the bus terminal they were already waiting: three tall men and one short girl carrying a dog. The girl bounced on her toes in a show of excitement. The fat Pekingese in her arms stirred from its usual torpor to bark twice at the bus. Without a trace of self-consciousness, the tallest of the young men waved a hand-lettered poster, BRAD FELL DAY IN L.A.

Until the time I was drafted two years before, I had been called Bradley Fell, but only on sufferance. By then I was twenty-two, yet I still believed that one day a better name would present itself and I would take it for mine. I waited all through school in Northern California, and later in Philadelphia and New Haven, using the name my parents had thought to give me. Then, on my first day in the Army, this temporary name was abruptly cut short. I had looked down at the green fatigues I was wearing, the rifle in my hand, and answered to Brad.

Tonight, with a flicker of disgust but no surprise, I realized

4

how much the man in the glass liked the name his friends were calling. There was no mistaking either, as I shrank back and hoped the other passengers wouldn't guess this spectacle had been staged for me, what delight he took in their banner.

But at least the four of them, the friends, were on hand as they had promised. I was grateful for that, even as I reminded myself that things between us couldn't be as they were when we first came together in France. Then we were conscripts making the best of it. Now, our freedom had been restored to us and we had the world to choose from. Why pretend those makeshift friendships were worth preserving?

And of the pretenders I was the worst. Coming here I had forced the others to assemble tonight. It was I who insisted that mufti changed nothing, that freedom couldn't separate us.

The bus driver remained behind the wheel completing his paperwork before he opened the door, and I had time to inspect each of the four, to smile, wave, look impatient for them. At that moment, standing in the aisle of the bus, I did not regret having come. The decision had been made for me by the enemy in the glass, and he was untrustworthy in all things but this.

A paradox, an irony, a twist of fate usually irritates me because it makes its point by taking two truths that are complementary, if only we understood the way they mesh, and then demeans or simplifies them until they can be pitted against each other. So to say that I was aware of a paradox in my nature is only to admit that I understood that nature very little.

All the same, I found it strange that I, this man I knew myself to be, should feel a compulsion to understand others—not only understand, but help and serve. Yet my good intentions made me stilted and I'd stammer and fall short, while my body was left free to promise friendship and draw attention to it. Warming indiscriminately, exuding fellow feeling, the body somehow did what I could not do, and succeeded against my will, since I knew it was too profligate to honor any of the vows it was making.

In France I had fallen in love, and the twenty-year battle I had been waging with my body ended briefly in an honorable truce. The love escaped me, and when it did my body showed compassion beyond anything I could have expected. It led me here, to let these friends set about consoling me. Not with words—I am too reticent to invite expressions of sympathy—but by reminding me with their presence of a time when I was happy.

The bus door opened with a snort, I stepped out, and they were all over me. Jenny threw her arms around my neck, Doug Goodwin and Josh Black each pumped a hand, and George Ranchek, whose poster had fallen from its stick, pinned a piece of yellow cardboard to my lapel. "It's a safe conduct pass," he said, "to assure you unmolested travel off Main Street."

"You must be tired." Jenny Black had mastered twenty or thirty phrases that she thought appropriate for a young wife coping with her husband's friends. Bundle up! she had cried to us in France whenever it rained. Drive carefully! Every mild exhortation a sisterly concern. I believed that because Jenny was incapable of taking an interest in anyone but her husband she had turned gratefully to these counterfeits of feeling.

"A little tired," I said. "I didn't sleep much on the bus."

"Why didn't you fly?" As he asked, Josh Black was hoisting my duffel to his shoulder. Doug Goodwin had scooped up the smaller bag, and they marched me across the dirty lobby toward an exit. The large poster was cumbersome for Ranchek, but he refused to give it up, hoping, I suppose, that I would ask for it later as a souvenir.

"When I went home for vacations I always flew," I said. "I thought the bus would give me a chance to see the country and think."

6

"Did you?" Goodwin's unassertive drawl sounded good to me. "Think?"

"Do you ever, when you're trying?"

"I never tried."

Outside the terminal, the undercurrents of night air were warm in a way that would have meant early April in New York. "The fifth of January," Black said. "You can't complain about the weather."

"Is a native son to be lectured on California by two Hoosiers and a redneck?"

Jenny, always literal, said, "George is from Long Beach. And anyway you're from Northern California. That might as well be another state."

"I've never believed," Josh Black said, "that Ranchek grew up out here. Say something in Southern Californian, George."

"Property values."

"You swore you'd never come west to live," Goodwin reminded me, not accusingly.

"That's right," Josh agreed. "I remember that. Never, you said. Never."

"Never ended."

"You have come, as our brochure puts it, to spend the sixties in the sun." Ranchek was the manager of a suburban chamber of commerce.

"The sixties," Josh repeated. "It sounds funny."

In the parking lot, Black let down his station wagon's rear gate for Goodwin and Ranchek. I rode in front with the Blacks. By the time we reached the Hollywood freeway, the wind was strong enough for me to roll up the window, and as I cranked the glass I again confronted the imposter. A crack in the window had severed him from eyes to chin, and his badly joined halves were held together entirely by his eager expression. I looked past him to Los Angeles.

If cities have gender as folk wisdom claims they do, if New York and Chicago are male and Boston and Washington ma-

tronly, I was hard put, at first sight, to assign a sex to Los Angeles. It was supple and smooth, androgynous as its name, an
entire city reclining on its side, like a hermaphrodite I had
seen in the museum in Naples.

Since it wasn't quite midnight, Black took us high in the
hills above Hollywood, where the roads wound and twisted
but inclined so gradually that his old station wagon strained
and slipped to low gear only once, for a wracking boost to
the crest of Mulholland.

"Our house is out there." Black pointed to the far end of
the San Fernando Valley. At our back, the older half of the
city spread a cover of rich and variegated lights. The Valley
had less to boast—isolated white pearls, unstrung and
scattered across its floor.

We drove west to the ocean, down a wide street of Tuscan
villas and English manor houses. A blowsy scent of flowers
stirred my misgivings. I wanted to be among clean grass in a
northern valley or to smell damp leaves smoldering in the
gutters of Philadelphia.

By my watch I had been in Los Angeles for seventy
minutes and could wait no longer. "And Ann?" I asked
offhandedly. "Do any of you see her?"

"I saw Ann in Santa Monica a few weeks ago." Ranchek's
voice was very serious; he wouldn't make a joke now. "She
didn't seem especially happy. She was talking about signing up
to teach overseas again."

"I've heard from her since then," I said. "She's getting
married."

"To the same fellow she was engaged to when she came to
France?"

"Yes."

"She's a beautiful girl." Goodwin had never thought so and
didn't think so now. But he had found a less portentous way
than Ranchek to express his sympathy.

We had agreed that until I found a job and my own apartment I would stay with Ranchek in West Los Angeles. For anyone without a car, the Blacks were too rural, and Goodwin was renting a single room in a boardinghouse near the factory where he worked. We drew up in front of Ranchek's building, which turned out to be gold-colored and a block long. The words "Isle of Eden" were carved in wood and illuminated by a spotlight. "A street number wouldn't suffice?" I asked cautiously, as befit a guest.

"There's a number, too," Ranchek said. "The name is just an elegant touch."

Again I wasn't allowed to carry my bags. Black lugged the duffel up a flight, puffing and swearing when it caught on the railing. "What've you got in here? A corpse?"

"A few books."

Ranchek obviously considered his overhead fixture harsh and uninviting, so he ran ahead to switch on a ceramic lamp on his end table. "Why, George, this is nice," Jenny said, stepping inside. "From the way you've been talking, I thought it was a dungeon."

The apartment was really one large room with two single beds that masqueraded beneath orange corduroy spreads as twin couches. The beds were shoved together at right angles, a corner table between them concealing one end of the second bed. Around the room I recognized Ranchek's mementos from a six-day leave in Spain—a wine bag, stained from repeated poor marksmanship, a woman's black plastic fan, open and intertwined with red roses, also plastic. On one wall hung an immense poster advertising a forgotten afternoon in the Tijuana corrida.

Ranchek hurried to his tiny kitchen and returned with an array of glasses and a bottle of cheap rum. "Rum is good at night, don't you think?" he asked. In France, where it had cost a dollar a bottle, Ranchek had ordered cognac.

We sipped dark rum and by default let Black hold forth. Asleep with my eyes open, I dreamed myself out of that strange room, away from the sound of Josh's voice, back to an apartment built over the camp school where I had drunk coffee for hundreds of hours and studied a woman's face with such care that I could conjure it up now while I looked toward Jenny Black and erased her.

Across the room, Goodwin had tilted back on a kitchen chair and closed his eyes. He could claim the excuse of working an early shift, but I knew that even wide-awake, he found Josh's stories resistible. Jenny, though, was listening enrapt, and her expression reminded me that before I ever met her I felt I knew Black's wife intimately.

In France Josh would get drunk at the Enlisted Man's Club every Saturday afternoon and then, back at the barracks at suppertime, he would stand on the footlocker next to his bunk and read aloud the latest love letter from Jenny. The other men tried to ignore him, but he demanded attention from Doug Goodwin and me, especially for the gamier passages. I doubted that Jenny Black, who was due shortly in southern France, to join her husband at our camp, wished his friends to hear that she was counting the hours until she could once again slip his cock into her mouth. That shriveled organ was on display nightly in the shower room, wedged between fat white thighs and overhung by a soft round belly. Even allowing for peculiarities of taste, it was hard to understand how so little provocation could arouse such unrelenting desire.

But Josh's reading of his wife's letters aloud did serve one good purpose: it put to rest the suspicions that his pretty profile had engendered when he first arrived at the post and announced that in civilian life he had been an actor.

When Jenny finally stepped off the train in Bordeaux, Black's makeup kit under one arm, a fat Pekingese squirming in the other, she was hardly what her letters had led me to expect. A withdrawn girl, absorbed in her husband so completely that the mere effort of being civil to anyone else seemed a strain for her, she let herself be dragged directly to a welcoming party in her honor. There she watched miserably as Josh danced and flirted with the French farm girls. She tried to appear indulgent and only looked tense. Ranchek found her immediately attractive, as did Doug Goodwin, who was widely regarded as the handsomest man on the post and from that eminence set standards of female beauty for the younger recruits. If Goodwin said a woman was good-looking, three or four eighteen-year-olds would be moaning over her that night on their bunks.

In her way, a grainy, whittled way, Jenny was pretty, I suppose. Her skin was white, unblemished, but somehow clotted, as though a light cloud of fine dust had settled over her. She was lithe and light on her feet. Her figure was trim. Yet the way she moved made her seem wooden, and she took an instant too long deciding whether to smile.

To all of us in turn that night, Jenny was distractedly polite. She danced when she could think of no excuse. Trapped, she talked.

Because Josh lavished love on his Pekingese bitch, Jenny was coddling the spoiled dog with an extravagance that wasn't natural to her. Now a year later, here she was in Ranchek's apartment, still clutching the animal to her breast, treating it to inattentive hugs and pats and other spasms of affection that the dog ignored.

We would still be sitting there, such was the power Black's voice exerted over his wife and himself, if Goodwin, nodding into a deep sleep, hadn't almost fallen from his wobbling pink chair face forward to the floor. Even Black was forced to acknowledge the growing restiveness. "I guess it's time to go." He waited for an argument, but Ranchek, though he never got tired, had been watching his rum disappear. Now he nodded briskly, stood up and yawned. Goodwin hauled himself off the chair and tottered for the steps. Our goodbyes, because of the hour, were muffled grunts and hisses.

Back inside, Ranchek was making up both beds, mine with

new linen straight from their plastic wrappings. The sheets were aflame with red rosebuds. "That isn't necessary, Ranchek," I said. "Old sheets would be fine."

"Never mind, never mind." Ranchek could dismiss my protest and let me know at the same time that he agreed the sheets were a remarkable luxury.

Army training had impressed on me the wisdom of sleeping in underwear, but Ranchek disappeared into the bathroom and emerged in gold silk pajamas with a charging bull woven over the pocket. "Do you like them?" he asked. "Dawn bought them for me in Ensenada."

They had not been designed for a gringo of Ranchek's proportions. The jacket gaped open, the drawstring barely knotted around his waist. From the age of sixteen, Ranchek had lifted weights to offset a frail physique, and seven years later he possessed a body that looked as though it had been inflated, biceps and thighs, with an airhose.

"Dawn? I had forgotten Dawn. Now that you're back do you see her?" In France Ranchek had regaled us with stories of a bosomy girl who had pursued him all over Southern California. He was tempted to marry her, he said, only when he was in his cups, or hers.

"Now that you're here," Ranchek said, "I guess I'll have to make a clean breast of it."

He told me he had married Dawn twenty months ago, on the day he was sent to France. She had awakened him that morning to say she was pregnant, and from somewhere in Oxnard an older brother had materialized to drive them the two hours to Tijuana for a six-minute ceremony. That same night an Army transport plane carried Ranchek to Paris. Two months later Dawn wrote to say she had suffered a miscarriage.

"Then you've never lived together?"

Ranchek had turned out the light, and the couch creaked as he stretched his legs. I could see his feet extending far into the room, a sheet draped over them like the towel on a waiter's arm.

"I stayed at her apartment the first weekend I got back," he said. "Now we see each other once in a while. We go to the movies." He paused coyly. "Or something."

"Why don't you get a divorce?"

"Please!" In the dark, not seeing his face, I could almost believe Ranchek was offended. "This is a Catholic home!"

"You can't let it drag on like this, Ranchek. You've been out of the Army four months. Either get an annulment or try living with her."

"You're absolutely right," Ranchek said and then was quiet. I tensed the muscles in my calves, hoping to convince them that I wasn't huddled for another night in a reclining chair, that this room wasn't hurtling westward at seventy miles an hour. When I was almost asleep, Ranchek stirred and sat up on an elbow. "I almost forgot to say it," he whispered. "Welcome to Los Angeles."

My first civic duty, outranking even the finding of a job, was to buy an automobile, but when I set out to look for one I wasn't happy about it. The one day I had really enjoyed in the Army was the morning I left training school and embarked for France, carrying everything I owned in the world in my own hands.

Boarding the bus in New York had given me that same sense of compactness, and I had wished I didn't have to consign my duffel to the hold of the bus. I would much rather have piled my few goods around me, at my feet or on the next seat, not because I was worried about anything being lost or stolen—I had nothing of value—but because my baggage had become an extension of me. As was an automobile. It might belong to me, but parked on a street, it would be exposed to the view of any chance passerby. That person looking at my car, however safe I had made myself in an apartment two blocks away, could intrude on my privacy.

My apprehension was nothing I could confide to Ranchek. I let him steer me to the nearest used car lot. Once there, I ignored his clamor to buy a red British sports car and picked instead a battered family sedan in something like working order.

Ranchek then took me on another tour of the city, this time with me at the wheel, to acquaint me with the main avenues. "An occidentation course," he called it. To discourage more jokes, I looked baffled.

We drove that afternoon for more than one hundred miles and seldom left the city limits. The day was sunny and clear. Whenever we passed a famous landmark, the twenty-foot plaster dog atop a hamburger stand, for example, Ranchek either pointed out a diversion across the street or praised the sunshine more fervently. His chauvinism went for nothing. I may not have been in a mood to like Los Angeles—or any place—but I was prepared to stay.

In Brentwood I'd begun to coast slowly down a street of yellow apartment houses when Ranchek said, "Isn't this where Ann lived?"

"Is it?" I hadn't expected him to remember. Accelerating, I turned on Wilshire toward the beach. By the time we parked on the Santa Monica pier, it was late afternoon, and the sun was going down straight ahead of us. Its fading gold light was more than I could tolerate. I started up the engine. Plaintively, Ranchek said, "I'd like to stay and watch the sun set." I knew he had never come out on this pier, had never sat still five minutes for any natural phenomenon, and such was my pain—or egotism—that I wondered if he was trying to hurt me. "Another time," I said.

We were strained together on the ride back and began to reminisce about the Army. We needed the guarantee that whatever doubts were arising today we had once been friends.

Ranchek exhumed a story about my going-away party in Biarritz: the next afternoon I was to board a military plane in Paris that would fly me to a post near Brooklyn where I would be released from active duty. I had no idea I would soon leave New York to follow the Blacks, Ranchek and Doug Goodwin to Los Angeles. For all we knew that final night in France was our last together. I had been subdued for three weeks, since the girl had returned to the United States; Goodwin and Jenny never raised their voices at any time. But Black and Ranchek were so boisterous over champagne that the restaurant owner threatened twice to turn us out.

We stumbled to the street well past midnight and realized for the first time that we had forgotten to book rooms for the night. It was early October, but a humid weekend had lured hundreds of Frenchmen into Biarritz, and we lurched from one small hotel to the next, suddenly timid as we asked whether there might be *chambres* for us. At last we found one room with two beds. Ranchek, Goodwin and I crowded into one sway-backed double, the Blacks into the single near the window.

Ranchek remembered the dinner and our search for a room but my memory continued past that. As soon as the lights had gone out, the springs of the bed across the room began to twang. I thought Black and Jenny were adjusting themselves to the narrow mattress, until the noise grew louder, irregular, then rhythmic, then frenzied. Black was showing off, and I resented being made an auditor to his exhibition. Goodwin lay motionless on my left, giving no sign that he heard. On the other side, Ranchek was snoring. After a time—a very short time, I was grumpy enough to notice—the creaking ended.

During a week of inquiries, the best job open to me was editorial writer for a small morning newspaper in Hollywood. At high school in Philadelphia I had contributed occasionally to the Friends' journal, but the editor who hired me mistook those clippings as being from Philadelphia's leading newspaper, and I did not embarrass either of us by correcting him.

He wanted me to start work immediately and led me to an isolated desk next to an oak coatrack. I might hang my jacket, he suggested, before attacking my first subject. I asked what topic he had in mind and he started fumbling through an apologetic speech to the effect that while the publisher wanted provocative editorials, he saw no reason to alienate potential advertisers with belligerence or bad temper. Bearing that in mind, the editor suggested an essay on the charm and utility of the month of January.

I did my best, completed the column within an hour, and was sent back amid smiles and congratulations to ponder another, perhaps somewhat less plainspoken than the first, on moral values in the space age. To another man the writing of editorials might have seemed a drab pastorate. For me it reawakened an enthusiasm that had first stirred during my years in a Friends' school.

Shortly before their divorce, my parents had sent me to Philadelphia, less from religious promptings than because it had been the only school they could agree upon. Though he was a democrat, my father took pride in being descended from Thomas Fell, an Englishman who had contributed to the founding of the Society of Friends by dying and leaving his widow free to marry George Fox. My mother simply hoped that the Quakers' social concern would prove the antidote to a hedonism already on the rise in postwar California. "We don't want him growing into a savage, after all," I overheard her telling my father's sister. It may have justified her forebodings that at fourteen I was more flattered than hurt.

The Friends' example touched me deeply. Without accept-

ing the faith I was entirely persuaded by their ethic. Four
years later when I went to New Haven, my first priority was
the living of a good life, by lights revealed to me in Philadelphia. Yale put no conspicuous obstacles in my way. I carried
my virtue through four uneventful years, spilling very little.
Given the limited moral range of the fifties, that meant that I
lied sparingly, never cheated on examinations, and assured
myself that I intended to marry each of the three girls I slept
with.

I was ending the second editorial with an exhortation to
spare the moon our lunacies, Mars our wars and Venus our
lechery when a small young man with an animated face approached my desk. He introduced himself as Billy Stein, another reporter on the paper, and promptly invited me to
dinner that same night to meet his wife.

My instinct then was to say no. But I had come to California, after all, to be cosseted and reassured about my worth. So
after formulating a few tentative excuses I reversed myself,
thanked Billy Stein and accepted.

From the several words we exchanged, Billy seemed to
know everything about me there was to know. Since he was,
as I discovered, an inveterate gossip, he may have already
gleaned what the editor could supply from my résumé. However much he knew, he looked even more knowing because of
the way he grinned as we talked. No matter what he said, he
grinned. Over the weeks, I would compare him to a variety
of sprites—elf, leprechaun, troll—before hitting on genie.
Billy Stein was a genie who would grant your wish, knowing
all the while that you have chosen as foolishly as everyone before you.

By seven o'clock that evening I had located the address
Billy had given me on La Brea and, squaring my shoulders,
straightening my tie, I rang the bell. A plump black-haired
girl opened the inner door and looked out curiously. "You're
wearing a fucking coat!" she said.

"No, no," I said, "I was only invited for dinner."

She kicked open the screen with a bare foot and let me pass inside. Billy Stein was sitting on the floor in front of a portable television set. "Look at this, Margo." He waved to me, grinning. "They've got ballet dancers on."

If I had known that first night that, chunky as she may have been, Margo Stein had trained for years as a classical dancer, I'd have been less surprised when she crouched and stared intently at the screen. While the dancers twirled and tossed each other through the air I stood ignored against the wall. Finally, after seven or eight minutes, I pointed at a woman leaping from one pair of arms to another. To say something, I said, "She's good."

"She's shit," replied Margo Stein, pushing past me for the kitchen.

That first evening with the Steins, glum in every respect, was followed by others no happier. Billy invited me; Margo, except to put a plate of fried chicken within my reach, ignored me. After dinner the three of us would watch television. Billy sat directly in front of the set, paging through magazines by its flickering blue light. Margo loved to watch a local dance program in which members of the audience were dragged on stage and coaxed into stumbling through the new steps. She turned her back on competent performers, but when an awkward or elderly woman lurched and threatened to fall, Margo's interest revived. "Off the stage, stupid!" she would shout at the set.

After five or six insults, some of her hostility reached to me, and I would rise and bid them good night. Just when I had decided that Margo had taken a dislike to me and I should outrage her no more, Billy confided the real reason for his wife's bad temper: "She's pregnant."

"I thought you were newlyweds," I said, not considering that I might be embarrassing him. But he grinned cheerfully.

"We've been married three months. The doctor says she got pregnant on our honeymoon."

"It's nice to have children while you're young enough to enjoy them." It was a commiseration I had heard.

"Tell me about it," he jeered. "Margo is eighteen. Her ballet teacher doesn't think she can ever get back in shape. She's not a natural. To be allowed in class, she's had to diet and exercise harder than any of the other girls."

"Would it bother her if she couldn't keep on?"

When his grin did fall away, Billy could look like his own sorrowing grandmother. "I don't know much about what bothers her," he said.

＊＊＊　　　＊＊＊　　　＊＊＊

As my official welcome, the Blacks invited me on my second Sunday in Los Angeles to join Ranchek and Doug Goodwin for dinner at the ranch house they had rented in the San Fernando Valley. By that time I had chafed Ranchek into telling them about his wife, and I said I wouldn't go unless he agreed to take Dawn. After three days of argument and excuses, he consented to call her. As the church bells were striking noon we left for her apartment a few blocks away in Westwood.

When Ranchek led her to the car to meet me, Dawn was wearing a short white linen jacket over a black dress from which, despite a decorous neckline, her breasts bulged out like knapsacks. On the long ride to the Valley, I found myself studying them with increasing fascination and deciding at last that for all of their enormous size, little about them was erotic. Dawn was only four or five years older than Ranchek —twenty-eight at the most—but the size of her bust had conferred on her an air of age and responsibility. She could not tilt or flash or flirt with her breasts as less encumbered women might. For Dawn, they served on the sidewalk as ballast for those moments her heavy buttocks threatened to rock her off her heels, and then as she climbed into the front seat, they became unruly presences, each with a will of its own, defiant within her brassiere and bent on finding ways to embarrass her. I watched as she planted herself stiffly between Ranchek and me, turning her neck with great care to avoid a movement that would set the breasts careening within her bodice.

When at last I could force my eyes away, I found Dawn's face taut and drawn. Her waist, which nipped in sharply from the hips, was unusually small for a woman of her build. It was as though the breasts had seized control of her body and were taxing her other flesh to support their opulence.

"I'm pleased to be meeting you, too," Dawn said when I greeted her. "You're the first friend of Ranchek's he's let me meet."

"A long time ago I invited you to Long Beach to meet my parents," Ranchek said.

"Before we were married."

Her speaking the word aloud made him edgy; if she said it again Ranchek would probably begin to sweat.

"I didn't want to meet them that soon," Dawn said. "I'd only known you for a little while, and if I had seen how they treated you, I'd have started behaving the same way. You'd have wound up marrying a mother, like everyone else."

"What's wrong with that?" Ranchek demanded. "Why should I be the one who's cheated?"

At the Blacks, Ranchek, by now sweating profusely, had barely got through the introductions before he collapsed from gin. The rest of us ate and talked across him. When the time came to leave, Josh Black helped me fold and jam him into the back seat. Dawn drove us home, handling the car like a truck driver. She tore over the gravel roads and toward the canyon pass that led out of the Valley. In the back seat, Ranchek gabbled to himself.

"They're terrible," Dawn said when we were well away. "She lets him walk all over her."

"She loves him," I said.

Dawn made a rasping rude noise. "She's afraid of losing him. It's not the same."

We sat for a while, Dawn driving easily and humming to herself. At the mouth of the Sepulveda tunnel, she brought in her left arm from the car window and steered with both hands on the wheel. The sun had nearly set and the inside of the tunnel was hardly darker than the evening sky. Dawn switched on the headlights. As we came out the other side, she said, "You do what I do."

"What's that?"

"Hold your breath all the way through the tunnel. Did you know you did that?"

"No."

"What do you think we're afraid of?"

The question nettled me, but she was waiting for an answer. "Being trapped."

Either my ominous tone offended her or she found the sentiment unsuitable for Ranchek to overhear. She did not answer, and we rode the rest of the way without more metaphysics.

The next night, finished with an avuncular essay on teenaged waywardness, I drove to Ranchek's apartment. "Ranchek," I began, when he opened the door, "put that thing down and listen to me."

He was crouched over a barbell in the center of the room, panting loudly and wiping his hands on tennis shorts already blotched with sweat. For his daily hour of exercise, Ranchek would close his door and pull the shades; the room was dank anyway, and today it was like the boiler room in a basement

21

gym. Stepping in made me glad again that I had found a place of my own at the beach, a few miles west.

"I can hear while I'm doing this." He picked up a weight and hoisted it to the ceiling, its edge knocking a spray of white plaster down over my shoulders.

"How can you listen while you're grunting? Listen, Ranchek, I've been thinking it over since the party. You cannot go on using Dawn this way. She's a woman, Ranchek, not some convenience you maintain, like your car or this apartment. Do you hear? You must take a serious look at your life."

"But my life isn't—" He put down the weights so he could move his flattened palms slowly together, as though curtains were being drawn. Ranchek had worked his way through college as an usher in a Long Beach theater and had watched hundreds of movies dozens of times. He had told us how the end of every picture was ruined because the curtain rod across the screen was never oiled properly. Ranchek clung to that memory and he liked to end his own conversations with a dramatic line of dialogue and a pantomime of velvet drapes closing majestically.

"But my life," he repeated, making curtains of his beefy hands and drawing them nearer each other, "isn't looking seriously at me." His palms were almost pressed shut. "Squeak," he said, "squeak, squeak, squeak."

🏴   🏴   🏴

Jeanne Darling wrote an astrology column for the Hollywood newspaper and several others, and she brought her forecasts into the office twice a week, always stopping at Billy Stein's desk to flirt harmlessly with him. Billy led her back to meet me with the curiosity of a child scientist mixing random elements in a flask and hoping for noise, green smoke, a bad smell. "Meet Jeanne Darling."

"You're Cancer," the good-looking brunette told me.

"The Crab. How did you know?"

"It's my profession."

In those days Jeanne kept her face heavily made up and her hair curled too tight. A little further into the decade, women began washing their faces, hiking their skirts and combing their hair into gentle folds and falls. As a result, six years after our first meeting, though she was by then thirty-five, fashion had restored to Jeanne Darling her fresh-faced girlhood. But on the day we met she was still playing the tough moll from those Saturday matinées we both remembered. As she hopped onto my desk and crossed her legs, I felt I failed her by not wringing French street songs from my typewriter.

There was no Mister Darling, or there was, but divorced five years before and far away in Kentucky or Georgia. It must have been Kentucky—I remember Jeanne speaking of herself as a bluegrass widow. In place of a husband, Jeanne usually had in tow a man named Ray Morella who came with her as far as the newsroom door and watched suspiciously as Jeanne made her sociable way from desk to desk. He was short, hairy, dark, not ugly but not handsome. After they left, I would sometimes hear young photographers marveling that a woman as attractive as Jeanne should waste herself on such an unremarkable man. They were boys who let their lenses do their looking for them, and they hadn't noticed that as Morella watched Jeanne his pride was painful to see. I first liked her because when she returned to her lover in the doorway her smile to him was as affectionate as any she had given the strangers in the newsroom. When he offered his arm she took it, while other women, as I knew, might have refused him simply to see the stricken look on his face.

From her failed marriage Jeanne had salvaged a son, whose upbringing, she insisted, was a puzzle and a trial. Within a week of our meeting she invited me to take her to lunch, and talk about the boy from my vantage as a daily adviser to popes and presidents. By that time I realized that Jeanne's husky Southern voice carried through large spaces with considerable force, and I secured a booth in the far corner of the delicatessen. But from her first words I had to resign myself to an hour of active discomfort. "I'm afraid Sonny's growing up to be a fag."

Fellow diners looked up, angry or intrigued. I wanted to assure them, especially one pair of young men, that Jeanne was not so insensitive as she sounded, that she was shrewd and possibly kindhearted. Since I couldn't address the others, I said to her, "We're not the only people here, Jeanne."

"Was I shouting? I'm sorry, my love. I should remember how shy you Cancers are. But what can I do? I don't understand boys at all. He's six years old and he still sleeps with a doll. Can that be normal?"

"What does Ray say about it?"

"Ray is no help. He hates Sonny. But there you are: Sonny adores him just the same. Isn't that perverted? What if he turns into one of those queens who want to be peed on or something?"

"What?"

"Wait until you've been around Hollywood a while, love. You can't imagine what goes on."

"If you don't keep your voice down we're going to be turned out." The faces around us had become distinctly hostile, and between each mouthful of cole slaw one young man was casting looks of hatred, more at me for some reason than at Jeanne.

"It's not that I have anything against queers." Her voice still rang loud, but mollifying. "It's only that he would probably want to be a hairdresser or a decorator or something, and his horoscope says he's not going to be artistic at all."

"I'll call the psychology department at one of the schools and ask whether a six-year-old boy should be sleeping with a doll."

24

"Oh, would you? Tell them it's a girl doll but he calls it Freddy. That might mean something." Our pastrami sandwiches had come, and the meat and mustard were muffling her voice. "I'll bet you'd be wonderful with Sonny," she said. "But you know how masochists are. He probably wouldn't like you at all."

The Saturday morning that a man named Robert Rorke first called me, a secretary preceded him on the line to say, "Hold the wire, please, for Mr. Rorke." I knew no one by that name, but mesmerized by her crisp assurance I held the receiver to my ear a full three minutes. At last a baritone voice said hello twice, gruffly. Rorke introduced himself as the friend of a friend from college and said he had been in Los Angeles for a year, working at a large stockbrokerage on Wilshire Boulevard. He was heading for the beach and would drop by my apartment within the hour to meet me. By the time I said all right, he had already hung up.

What, I wondered, awaiting his arrival, does one say to a stockbroker? How would I keep a conversation going without looking as though I were angling for tips? But Rorke, when he got there, allayed my apprehension. In the course of the afternoon he said not a word that touched even remotely upon his work. He talked, talked and talked. But for all the canny sharp angles to his monologue, everything emerged distant and vague. He barked, wheezed and, occasionally, to simulate laughter, he coughed. Out of that continual noise came nothing one could remember later or read as a market prophecy.

Rorke was two years older than I was, but he seemed young and untried, an impression that survived the engraved business card he flung at me, the Jaguar convertible parked illegally on the street and the astonishing redhead who came

25

trailing after him. "Faye," said Rorke by way of introduction, "will have gin on the rocks."

"Would you happen to have a tangerine?" the girl asked in a sweet voice I had to strain to hear. "A twist of peel is awfully good in it."

We compromised on lemon. She accepted the glass gratefully, one more tribute to her beauty, and in fact she was truly lovely: tall, pale, with a cascade of auburn hair halfway down her back. From her blue and white sailor shirt and white slacks I gathered that Rorke had advised her of their destination. But when I asked if she cared to swim, she said no, her job prevented her from going into the sun. She danced in a Las Vegas revue and the director wanted her skin creamy.

The rest of the afternoon is dim to me now. Searching for common ground, I brought up the best book I had read lately and Rorke pronounced it godawful. I gave up then and submitted peaceably as he led me down the first of many avenues of ennui.

Every weekend afterward, either with Faye or alone, he arrived to drink bourbon and harangue me. It wasn't that the topics he chose were simply uninteresting. They seemed to have been selected with a malicious ingenuity that could provoke me to real anger. We had entered on that year's presidential campaign, and it was impressive, if infuriating, the way Rorke turned aside any mention of the current nominees to expand instead on the year Woodrow Wilson won his second term.

A less unyielding mind might have imbued even that unpromising subject with mild contemporary interest, might possibly have contrasted the religion and rhetoric of a Democrat from Princeton with those of the Harvard candidate. Or alluded to the coincidence that forty-four years earlier another Republican candidate's heavy beard had hurt him with the voters.

But Rorke was adamant, and he was skilled at keeping his discourse free of present-day references. He talked dryly about prohibition and statistically about the suffragettes. He dwelt on political bosses long forgotten and campaign slogans that, even allowing for the frenzy of a torchlight parade, must have died on the lips of any crowd.

Mulling over when he had left what made Rorke's method unique, I decided that he had transformed ordinary dullness to a form of aggressive bullying. His capacity for being boring had to be taken, finally, as a boast that while any fool might have charm, and any weakling could fascinate or beguile, only he had the stamina and resources to be dull.

When he wasn't dull, Rorke was rude. For Faye Tayne that dismal choice may have constituted his attraction. He was usually brusque with her. But when he did ask her opinion or defer to her wishes, Faye was incandescent with delight. The fact that occasionally he could be thoughtful was enough for her; that, and whatever help he might be extending to her between jobs.

My own reasons for serving as Rorke's host every weekend were obscure to me. I wanted to see him as lonely, even sensitive beneath his veneer. I liked to believe I was behaving generously to him. But his arrival also relieved my solitude on Saturdays, and I may have hoped his bad nature contrasted noticeably with my own forebearance, to the stunning Faye, to myself.

Between bookings in Las Vegas, Faye lived at a woman's residence in Hollywood. The three of us met there many nights to eat dinner surrounded by some of the prettiest girls in the city. Rorke would cause a stir in the dining room, not because he was handsome or popular but because the other girls liked Faye and hoped for her sake that the dinner, this one time, would end without his carping about the underdone meat.

Rorke was short and thickly built, and his width made him formidable. His gingery blond hair was crewcut; on the weekends he wore dirty white shoes. I never heard him say anything suggestive, but his height put his eyes just about breast level with many of the showgirls he met, and I'd see them squirming slightly as they talked to him.

His nose was flat and his ears close to his head, a fighter's face, flushed and rough, except that Rorke had never boxed and his college wrestling career had been gentlemanly and short. He must have known he looked best in dark suits, but he chose instead bright twill jackets and orange herringbone trousers that guaranteed, by the sheer contempt they revealed, to offend anyone who had to look at him.

Whenever a friend of Faye's glided by our table, Rorke, his brows puckered, would peer up and nod distrustfully. Very rarely, telling of a client's losses, Rorke might laugh, and that cheerless guffaw caused the girls at other tables to glance over and smile with relief. Faye told me later that on balance they considered her lucky to be Rorke's girl and they waited, less patiently than she, for the day he would rescue Faye from glamour and excitement by asking her to be his wife.

卐   卐   卐

When I began last year to make these notes, I had no object in mind except to obey a need I felt. I was beset then by the most unsatisfactory kind of unhappiness, a warmed-over grief with nothing fresh about it to teach me something new. I retreated to this book to work my way to a few conclusions, charting my friends' marriages as astronomers follow the stars, less to prove a pattern than to detect one. My experiment demanded candor, and I took care that the book shouldn't fall into the hands of anyone whose life I was tracing.

Whenever the Steins were expected, I carried the green pad

out to my car and locked it in the trunk, since Billy looked for excuses to ransack my closets and rummage through kitchen drawers. At that, I expected him to contrive a flat tire one day, demand the use of my tire jack, and find my secret in the trunk. On days Billy was due at the apartment I thought of wrapping the book in brown paper and mailing it to myself.

With Ranchek I took none of these precautions. He noticed very little and entertained no curiosity about my life, except for occasional references to the girl in France. Those he ventured not maliciously but rather as a doctor presses a cyst, diagnosing from the patient's wince the intensity of his pain. When Ranchek came over, I simply stuck my notes among the other books on the shelf, convinced that a man whose own library consisted of the one college text *Public Relations: Talent or Technique?* would never notice them. But one day while I was mixing his drink in the kitchen, Ranchek picked up a copy of Genêt, put it down quickly, and took up Camus. His taste, though, ran as little to rats as to roses, and by the time I got back to the living room I found him leafing avidly through what I had written. "So!" he whispered melodramatically.

I shrugged.

"This is how you repay the affection and esteem your friends have lavished on you."

"You shouldn't be reading it."

"How will you face Robert Rorke?" he asked piously. He didn't know Rorke.

"Let him write about me," I said, "I won't be angry."

Ranchek's smirk was particularly irritating, a puckering of lips that said he knew better but was too well bred to disagree. "I know why you're writing all this," he said.

By that time I had lived ten years in dread of a serious conversation with Ranchek. In a permissive age, each man must set his own limits, and for me the final capitulation, my farewell to values and standards, would come at the moment I looked into Ranchek's solemn face and said earnestly, "Tell me what you mean, George."

Instead I said, "It's a way of passing the time, Ranchek. Don't take it seriously."

"No." His look of superior wisdom was tempered now by compassion and a faint air of melancholy amusement. "No," he repeated, "you're trying to use us to justify yourself."

He was right. It was my good luck that I had been looking away, toward the ocean, and could say, "You're a master at plumbing the human psyche."

"No." Beatitude welled in his round damp face until he shone in my room like a votive candle. "We all know what you've just gone through," he said softly. "And we knew years ago, the day Ann left France and you pretended not to care but you spent the night with Rosie. We knew then. We know now. If you'd like to talk about it—" He broke off at the point where the discreet old priest always coughed and paused. If this were the movies, I should begin to weep.

"I might like to talk about it," I said, "if I had any idea what I'm supposed to say."

"Oh." Disappointed as he was, at least Ranchek had delivered his telling line. The scene was ending with him serene and me obviously shaken. "If you don't want to confide in me, of course I understand. But I should warn you"—he was the parish priest again, the full authority of St. Peter's at his back—"that it isn't going to work. No matter how this notebook ends, you'll still have to make your own decision. You'll still have to live with it. No two people"—Ranchek paused before he confirmed my worst apprehensions—"are alike."

Ranchek did me one favor that day. Once he realized that I was keeping score of a half-dozen marriages, he became determined in the name of fair play that I leave nothing out. Skipping ahead in the notebook, he remembered the direction of the Blacks' marriage and reminded me of an incident involving Josh that I should include. I was all the more willing

to retrace and insert the anecdote here because it gave me a
chance to write about whores:

A few years ago the American military bases in France
were shut down, one result of the friction between those
countries throughout the nineteen-sixties. But at the time I
was stationed there, small enclaves of American soldiers still
extended down the Atlantic coast to the Spanish border. Sixty
miles from Biarritz, our ordnance depot was a slack and dusty
base where three hundred homesick young Americans
lounged at desks in Quonset huts or passed the days at a makeshift motor pool.

During those tranquil years, so little federal money was
budgeted for the Army that the rifle range was closed,
pending repairs, and the American teacher at the dependents
school bought colored chalk out of her own salary. Our barracks were shabby; the trucks and jeeps barely ran. Only the
Enlisted Man's Club prospered, and it was kept solvent by an
expedient forbidden by the higher echelons—the Tuesday
night striptease.

These shows were hardly professional. Every Tuesday afternoon, the club manager toured brothels and small shops in
the vicinity to find women who would come to the camp and
disrobe for twenty dollars. Most of his recruits were whores
who considered the show good advertising.

Until I was shipped to France my experience with prostitution had been entirely literary. Freshmen in my college dormitory had organized expeditions to houses that seemed always to have moved the previous day, but I never went
along. Prostitution, like war, was an amusement of man to
which I would not lend my body. But when the day of decision came, claiming conscientious objection in peacetime had
seemed a showy form of righteousness, just as sitting alone in
the barracks while my friends were heading for brothels near
the gate looked like priggery or a reproach. I went with
them.

The huts, like the women, were squat and dirty. I drank raw cognac for an hour and then selected the smallest whore, as though her size would minimize my offense. We went to her room, a lean-to tacked to the back of the bar. There she did those things that had made France the envy of the civilized world. I knew the mythology well enough not to kiss her, though whether because she would object or I should, I couldn't remember. While she washed, I put money on the dresser.

It had been a degrading experience for us both. I told myself that several times as I went to join my friends at their table. A woman should not open her legs to a man she does not love; no truth ranked higher than that. But a memory intruded: the French women who came to our camp's mess hall, who stooped over boiling pans to feed us, who cleaned away our garbage. In eight hours they earned less than what I had left for Rosie. A woman should not handle the garbage of a man she doesn't love? Nonsense. One act is intimate, the other is not. But given Rosie's practiced groans, her competent quick manipulations and hasty douche, which was which?

The cognac in my glass was white—it hadn't yet colored from aging in wood—and that was another dislocation. Cognac was always golden as prostitution had to be debasing. But then what had left my brain stimulated and my body so utterly content? I did not conclude that I had been duped, either by the Friends or by society at large. I did think, in my innocence, that I was the first man to appreciate the efficacy of vice.

At the Tuesday night striptease, we never saw the local whores on stage. The sergeant was showman enough not to expect an audience to be excited by women available forty-three paces from the front gate. For talent he sometimes went as far as Bordeaux, and he strove for a genuine touch of burlesque by insisting that his girls wear breakaway net corsets. He had found only one of them in Paris, however,

midnight black, and every show ground to a halt while the
second girl on the bill recovered the corset, ran to the toilet,
stripped, slipped it on, put back her own clothes and emerged
to reverse the process.

The girls were clumsy, they moved badly and danced always to the same recording of "Night Train." And yet the
evenings were erotic. With our wives or women far away, we
lived in a fortified camp not much different from a prison.
For those who indulged in it, prostitution relieved the body
but not always the pressures of the imagination. Each Tuesday night the men brought to the club a week's glum desires.
To feed their dreams on pallid breasts and matted hair, they
packed together in cramped wooden seats around the bar, the
heat from each man working on the next until they aroused
each other; until, finally, they made each other nervous. For
an hour after each show the room was quiet and angry.

When the lights came up and the girls were back in their
clothes, the sergeant usually hurried them to a car waiting to
race them out the gate and down the narrow road to Bordeaux. But one night he was delayed and the girls were told
they would have to wait thirty minutes while a jeep was req-
uisitioned and a driver found for them. One girl stalked directly to the women's toilet and stayed there. The other, a tall
brunette, came to the bar where some of us were sitting.
Doug Goodwin and I had once spent time with her and she
greeted me gaily. "My sweet!" she cried. "Buy me a drink!"

"No." When I had last seen her I was sure she preferred
Goodwin.

"If you'll introduce me to the lovely lady," Josh Black
called down the bar, "I'd be honored to buy her a dozen." He
was drunk enough to make his matinée manner almost authentic.

"Annette," I said. "Josh."

He bowed and kissed her hand. She punished my churlish-
ness by turning a regal back to me and sliding onto a stool as

she ordered a scotch. In Bordeaux she had drunk cold tea; I wondered if she knew what scotch tasted like. But she took it neat, threw it back and ordered another. When Black asked her to dance, she accepted demurely.

He led her to a bare spot on the floor where the folding chairs had been cleared away and began bouncing her to a fast rhythm from the jukebox. Neither of them paid attention to the seventy-five men still sitting at tables around the room, men who were watching them with cold eyes. I understood the coldness. My own liking for Black cooled considerably as his hands roamed down the girl's back.

Black's manner of dancing compounded the resentment, the way he pushed his plump belly across the floor. Spending my first fourteen years in California had left me sensitive to bodies—parts, joints, movements and repose—and I retained some of that awareness through the next eight years on the East Coast, where people regard bodies as pikestaffs to hold their heads. The attention I later gave Dawn's breasts was not unusual for me, and to an argument that bodies reveal more than faces I might have agreed, unhappily.

Black's belly reminded me of his dog's smug fatness, a mass of fat seemingly unconnected to either his narrow shoulders or his puffy thighs. The other sign that he was overweight was a fold of flesh below his chin, which gave his fine profile the appearance of being carved from candlewax. As a result, Black looked like a tall, thin, even scrawny man with a false belly strapped around his waist. As he danced, the belly wriggled and squirmed, insinuating that it was irresistible. I am adorable! Black's belly cried. Love me!

Thinner, harder men saw that belly pressed against Annette and felt no love for it. The first dance they suffered silently, but at the start of a second, one man said something, loudly enough for Black to hear, softly enough to ignore. Then another boy yelled some other word. Two men rose from their table and started moving onto the dance floor. Across the room twelve or fifteen men stood up. They worked with Josh in the finance office and took any insult to him as a challenge by all mechanics to all clerks. Doug Goodwin was near the front.

Within a second, every man in the club was on his feet. Fists were swinging, and a few punches actually landed. Goodwin hit somebody's nose, bloodied his fist and got a black eye in return. The men on our post liked everything about fighting, except for the taking of blows, and they were more than willing, when the sergeant dashed in shouting that the next round was on the house, to drift back to their tables.

The uproar had left Annette alone near the side door. Doug Goodwin, his left eye swelling darkly, cleared a place for her at the bar and ordered two doubles.

I stayed another half-hour. When I got back to the barracks, I found Josh Black already in his bunk asleep. I wasn't surprised that having caused the row, he had managed to slip away untouched. But it was only after Ranchek commented on it the other day that I recalled the proprietary interest Josh had taken in Goodwin's black eye. "Doug fought my battle for me," Josh would say, throwing an arm over Goodwin's shoulder. "He's carrying my war wound."

Each Sunday morning, as dependably as Robert Rorke called on Saturdays, Billy Stein would arrive at my door in Venice Beach. He poked fun at my apartment's size, but he couldn't deny that it looked out upon miles of the Pacific while his own had an unobstructed view of a reducing salon. Billy came by because Margo taught folk dancing on Sundays at a temple not far from my place, and he would wait to drive her home.

His approach was so consistently stealthy that he must have been trying to trap me with an overnight visitor. But at that

time I seldom went out on Saturday nights. I stayed home.
When self-pity overtook me, I would shuffle through the
three letters and the wedding announcement that proved my
memory of France was no hallucination.

Failing to embarrass me, Billy then squatted on the brown
couch, consoled himself with cola and gossiped about our col-
leagues on the paper. His information exhausted one morning,
he said suddenly, "Let's walk over and see Lonnie."

"I don't know anybody named Lonnie."

My lack of interest made him more eager. He began prais-
ing Lonnie, and with each new inducement I became more
adamant about staying home. Lonnie was brilliant, it seemed
—a master chessman, math wizard, prodigy in French liter-
ature. And he sported a master's degree in Renaissance
history. Listlessly, I said, "Maybe some evening."

"Lonnie works nights. He parks cars at the Pelican. Do you
know where that is? The restaurant in Malibu?"

"To pay for his doctorate?"

"No, he's given all that up. He just parks cars."

I reached under the couch for my shoes.

As I was unknotting the laces, Margo walked slowly
through the open door. She was seven months pregnant but
she moved as though her child were already overdue. I took
her caution as proof of her concern for the baby, and it was
several months before I realized that she had found the burden so distasteful, had been so aware of her lumpish
appearance, that she resolved to do nothing that would make
her more ridiculous. Above all she would not hurry or puff or
sweat. She would move like a French Sisyphus, stoically and
with full knowledge of her absurdity.

"You're early," Billy said.

"It's no good trying to teach when you can't show them
yourself." Margo made her round face into a long one. "I quit
and turned the second class over to Pimples Shirley."

"We were headed to see someone called Lonnie."

"It can wait," Billy said.

"No, I'd like to go with you." Margo was as insistent as he was casual.

"Fine," I said. "Let's be off."

We walked out into the sunshine. As I pulled the door shut, I tested its handle. The week before, two boys had broken into the next apartment, and though I had nothing to lose but four dozen books and a worn gray suit that was too warm anyway, I had heard of thieves pawning stolen bedclothes or fixtures off the bathtub.

We went the long way, across the sand, to let Margo walk in her bare feet. We moved up Clubhouse Avenue, past the shingled rooming houses and shacks with newspaper stuffed in their cracked windows. All the buildings, like the old folk on the benches we passed, seemed to beseech repair and better treatment.

Margo trailed, swinging her sandals by their straps and muttering "Damn!" when the sidewalk burned her feet. We stopped at a brown clapboard cottage and Billy pounded loudly on the door. Lonnie didn't seem to be home.

"He probably got drunk and stayed overnight with some girl," I said.

The Steins both stared at me; Margo looked savage. "Lonnie has an ulcer and he drinks only milk." Billy spoke gently to acknowledge that I slandered out of ignorance. "And he's celibate. He hasn't touched a woman since he read the Vedas two years ago."

I was on the verge of an obvious comment on the dangers of reading and stopped only because Billy Stein, who took nothing else seriously, was unmistakably impressed by his friend's sacrifice. Even grateful for it.

꙳   ꙳   ꙳

Moving to a neighborhood as unbuttoned and beggarly as Venice did not mean I was extending the range of my friendships. Other tenants along the beach kept to themselves, and a good proportion disappeared each month to escape back rent.

This constant movement brought into my life the one tape recorder I have owned and a phonograph record that still takes up space on a closet shelf. A plump male nurse across the street with whom I had exchanged a nod of the head brought them to me one night. The record was Ravel's *Bolero*, and he was crying as he put it in my hand. "Keep this stuff for me, will you?"

"What's the trouble?"

"I'm going back." His nurse's jacket was crisp and white, his hair freshly cut. "I wrote more paper and they revoked my parole." At my blank look, he added, "Bad checks."

"Oh," I said. "I don't know how long I'll be here."

"That's all right. I haven't got anybody else to ask. Say"—it was meant to sound like an afterthought—"you couldn't give me a few dollars for the machine, could you? I'll throw in the record."

A few days after that transaction, Jeanne Darling came to Venice to swim, and she was delighted with the recorder. She took it out to the sand and propped it between us on the cotton blanket. Last year, when I moved, I came across the machine again and inside was the tape Jeanne made. Pushing the red button, closing my eyes, I could be back on the beach with her.

It was a hot September day, I remember; the sun seemed no more than five yards away. In a bathing suit, Jeanne's uncorseted figure proved to be genuinely boyish. Her legs were long and slim. The black one-piece suit revealed at the small of her back a birthmark the color and size of an oval penny.

Sunbathing was one temptation I could resist. Nothing could be more futile than the way old women and young men would lie on the sand for hours every day, getting up only to turn from back to fore. They never read or talked, and they seldom even listened to transistor radios. They simply lay like burnt offerings and let the sun work its will on them.

When I did go to the beach, I stayed precisely one hour and justified the time by bringing along a few of those liberal magazines printed on scratchy paper. But with Jeanne beside me on the blanket, I found myself admiring her dark color and wondering whether I couldn't extend my time to ninety minutes. It would mean subscribing to another fortnightly.

"This is heaven!" I hear Jeanne's sigh clearly, but a heavy surf that day is making my answers hard to decipher. "I feel as though everything I'm saying will run right down into the sand and evaporate. What will you do with this tape?" My answer is lost in the thudding sound of the ocean. "Because," she said, "I'm in the mood to talk. Feel that sun! In weather like this everything inside me opens up. I can feel my lips falling open. My mouth starts moving by itself."

"What is your mouth going to say?" I sound edgy and strained.

"I am going to speak to you this afternoon," Jeanne said in a newscaster's voice, "about the time I tried to kill myself. Show me how to play the tape back so I can hear how I sound."

The tape goes dead until the spot where she began again. "My God, I still have that ghastly accent, don't I? Men are supposed to like it but I know you really don't. It is absolutely impossible with a Southern accent to make anything you say sound intelligent. If Einstein had talked with one, he'd have been shut up in an asylum someplace.

"My suicide: It was the second month I was out here. Sonny wasn't quite a year old, so it must have been five years ago. One night I went into the bathroom and took out three bottles of pills I had accumulated and counted out twenty-four of them. Aren't you going to ask me why?"

Was I trying to provoke her for some reason, or stop her before we would both be sorry? I am sure I wasn't asleep.

"Even if you asked, I couldn't tell you." There is more piney woods to her voice than I remember. "I suppose I was lonely, but that wasn't the reason. I worked in a secretarial pool downtown and lived in two rooms in Echo Park, and I hadn't gotten over the feeling that I'd disgraced myself forever with the divorce. But none of those things was the reason. Even with everything all wrong, I was happy, most days.

"One night I came home from work and fed the baby and put him to sleep in the bedroom. Then I lay down on the living room couch. I was facing the wall with my knees pulled up when it went through my mind that if I started to scream now I wouldn't be able to stop. The baby would wake up, neighbors would come. I'd still be screaming. I thought that if I let myself start, I'd scream until my heart stopped. Have you ever felt that way?"

I have listened closely for my answer, replaying the tape five and six times with no success.

"Why that night and not some other? I don't know. I felt the scream rising in me like puke. You know? When you go running for the bathroom. I ran in there with my lips pressed shut.

"I got out all the pills from their bottles. When I swallowed the first one the screaming went away. It had been building up inside me, I could hear it. And then it left and everything was quiet. I counted out twenty-three more and swallowed them two and three at a time. That left four in the newest bottle, the one I'd just gotten for my nerves. Those I left. Each of the doctors had warned me how strong the pills were and I was sure twenty-four would be enough. But do you know what I really think? Are you listening to me?"

"I'm listening."

"I think when I left those four pills in the bottle I had already decided not to go through with it. I wanted to be able to say to the police that if it wasn't accidental, why did they think I hadn't taken them all.

"I went back to the living room and sat on the footstool. I saw the walls I had been going to paint. The slipcover was wearing out on the arm of the green chair. Everything was brilliantly clear. My nails needed a manicure. When I reached up, my hair felt stringy. So much to do. Then I yawned. I wondered if the pills had started working or if I was just tired.

"I thought about who would find me. Probably it would be the manager, an awful old woman who complained every morning about Sonny's crying. She'd find my body and call my mother. There'd be a funeral. But who would miss me? Nobody. At the church my mother might cry a little. But she didn't care. Sonny's father would be only too happy his alimony payments were over. Sonny was too young for it to matter.

"I had thought once in a while how nobody cared whether I lived or died and then it had made me sad. This time, on the footstool, I got mad. If nobody cared anyway, why kill myself? At least I should wait until by doing it I could hurt somebody. Are you smiling over there? Maybe it was funny. I ran to the phone and called the fire department and said that accidentally I had taken too many pills. The man asked me for my name and address, not a bit excited, all very routine.

"I went into the bedroom and changed into my best nightgown—pale blue with long sleeves and a jacket. Then I got into bed and waited for them to come and pump my stomach."

I hear myself say, "I think we all have those moods."

"That's what I asked you. If you had ever felt that way."

"Let's go into the water. Turn off the machine and—"

�   ✳   ✳

By the time late in the fall that Josh Black got his first acting role, the five of us from the Army weren't getting to-

41

gether very often and I wasn't sorry. Many evenings, tired from a day spent denouncing smog, I was glad to cut off a slab of cheese, peel an orange and go to bed. The Blacks, Ranchek and Doug Goodwin were at the other end of the telephone, and that single wire was all the connection I needed. I thought about getting married, but unless I was ready to risk another gray-eyed blonde, no other woman seemed worth the trouble.

Josh's play was *The Merry Wives of Windsor*, given by a community playhouse in the northwest San Fernando Valley and starring him as Master Ford. Opening night fell on a Friday, and Dawn was detained at the bank where she was chief teller, but the rest of us were there. Goodwin and I were paying for our seats. Ranchek had contrived to get Josh's second complimentary ticket.

At the box office I was scooping up my change when Ranchek sidled up to whisper, "How much are they? Five pins?"

"Behave yourself, Ranchek. This is a big night for Josh."

He ran through his repertory of contrite faces as we found our seats inside. The theater had once been a drugstore, and a pay telephone was still mounted on the back wall. Rough spots in the flooring showed where the prescription counter had stood. The room itself was low and oblong, with a raised platform surrounded on three sides by folding chairs.

"Do we applaud when Josh makes his entrance?" Ranchek asked Jenny Black.

Strain made Jenny even less spontaneous than usual. With the cast party in mind, she had chosen to wear a black velveteen dress and small hat with a narrow veil. In one hand she clutched gray gloves. "I don't think it would be professional," she said anxiously. "Josh wouldn't like it."

She sat between Ranchek and me, and Goodwin took the aisle seat to my left. I asked whether he had seen the play.

"The only Shakespeare we had in Tennessee was the one

42

where the black man smothers the white girl. If he hadn't killed himself afterward, there were a couple of boys in the audience that were ready to come on stage and do it for him."

"This one is about unfaithful wives."

Goodwin seemed hypnotized by his brown shoes, brightly shined for the first time in the three years I had known him. "That's the reason for the small turnout," he said. "There's not much women here in the Valley need to learn about that."

"Some wives are happy with their husbands."

He nodded toward Jenny Black. "She is," he agreed.

As the time drew near for the play to start, Jenny reached over to grasp my arm. "You've seen Josh before," I said, "at college."

"I never get used to it."

"He'll be fine."

"Ssssh!" Ranchek leaned past Jenny to glare at me. "Some of us here would like to get our money's worth."

In the absence of a curtain, the lights dimmed and went back up. Jenny gripped my wrist as though we were at the peak of a roller coaster. I unpried her fingers and chastely held her hand. When Josh appeared we contained our applause, and he delivered his first lines amid only rustling and coughs.

Watching him bound across the stage in blue tights, I couldn't say whether he was good or bad, but when I caught sight of Robert Rorke and Faye Tayne walking out at the first intermission, I was more dismayed than surprised. The next day I told Rorke I had seen him in the Valley.

"Faye wanted to see a girl from the club. Nothing."

"I know the fellow who played Master Ford."

Rorke's hard blue eyes lowered.

"You know that guy? Do him a favor and tell him to go back to Wisconsin."

"Indiana."

"Whatever town he's from."

☙ ☙ ☙

On the Sunday that Margo Stein went into labor, I drove to the hospital in Burbank. It was Roman Catholic and chosen, I was sure, less for its fine reputation than for the dismay it would cause Margo's mother. That lady was already in the maternity ward's lounge when I arrived, lobbying with Billy for a boy to be named after her late husband. A few minutes later, Billy's parents hurried in with names of their own to advance at the opportune moment.

The family exuded an air of being gathered for a miracle, and though I wanted to be beguiled, I was getting cranky. Dislodging Billy, I took him for a walk around the block. "Are you nervous?" I asked him when we were safely outside.

The wind tossed his long silky hair into his face, shielding his expression. "I don't think anything will go wrong," he said. "The doctor says Margo's perfect for childbirth."

"Margo agrees?"

"She will. I hope." Like every other gossip, Billy was reluctant to reveal much about himself. But this day was already so strange—Margo suffering pains he would have gladly taken on himself, their parents offering prayers from a corridor rife with crucifixes. And the sun was directly overhead when Billy had been sure Margo would give birth at midnight. For once he talked uncautiously. "I hope Margo can be happier as a mother than she's been as a wife. It's possible. I know it's going to be easier for me to be a father than a husband."

Billy was a head shorter and I crooked my neck to hear him and focused my eyes on our feet, to keep us in step. "What's the difference?"

"Oh, a husband is supposed to be romantic," Billy said lightly. "He has to keep winning his wife over and over again. Because if she gets tired of him, there's no reason for her to stay."

Skipping and hopping to match his shorter stride, I felt guilty about looking down on the top of his head.

"A father," Billy said, "gets an outlet for a kind of love that's more than sex. When he buys shoes for the baby, that's different from buying shoes for his wife. Buying for her is still part of winning her. With a baby in the house he's become the provider. He doesn't have to be a hero any more. That's too dangerous now for everybody. Now he's supposed to be steady and dependable. Overnight that's what the woman wants. If he could never say the right thing to her, now he has the baby to talk to. When his wife overhears him, she knows he's really talking to her."

We had circled the hospital's green lawn and were heading back to the maternity ward. "Trouble comes," Billy said when we were alone in the self-service elevator, "if a father who wasn't a very good husband finds out that the mother still wants to be a wife."

In the ward I withdrew to a corner and waited with the family until dinnertime. But it wasn't until midnight, after I had given up and gone home to the beach, that I got the call from Billy: Margo had given birth to a seven-pound boy, to be named Jacob for her dead father. Billy was tired, but as he relayed the news he strained again to be ironic. I caught the counterpoint beneath his bantering: Forget what I told you, forget what I said.

⊕   ⊕   ⊕

Weeks and months slipped past, until, though I still considered myself a stranger, I had spent nearly a year in Los Angeles. Twice during that time classmates from Yale looked

me up on brief trips west to let me know that I was wasting
my life. One, who had worked in the successful presidential
campaign, would soon be moving to Washington to invig-
orate our society, and it was impossible to expect him to understand the lassitude one woman had wrought in my life.

I went each day to work. The Blacks and Doug Goodwin
lived far away in the Valley, and Ranchek was the one Army
friend within the newspaper's delivery range. Though he was
too frugal to subscribe, he did steal copies regularly from the
rack outside his Chamber of Commerce office.

His irregular marriage to Dawn ground along with
Dutch-treat dinners, violets on their anniversary and then
three weeks running when he wouldn't call. At the bank
Dawn answered her telephone, "Mrs. Ranchek speaking." But
when she bought a new car she registered it in her maiden
name. I nagged at him, commiserated with her, and was
thanked tepidly in both quarters for my interest.

Then one night Ranchek arrived at Dawn's apartment with
a doom-struck face that she knew he had been practicing in
his rear-view mirror. He slouched on her shiny black couch
and worked his toes morosely into the white shag carpet. He
sighed and shook his head. Everything Dawn tried to brighten
his mood failed wretchedly. At last, resorting to one of his
own jokes, she asked, "Is there something you want to get off
my chest?" He told her.

The next day on the telephone, with less prompting he repeated the story to me. "Is it true?" I demanded when he had
finished.

"True as tongue can tell," Ranchek said with a pathetic
tremor. "I have been canned. Or sacked. Depending on
whether your frame of reference is anal or genital."

"Ranchek, your chamber has never fired anybody. You
told me yourself that the last director stayed thirty years,
even with the town losing population every census."

"Mr. Thompson did not commit my sin, the sin that has no name."

"They all have names."

"You may be right. But you'll admit the best ones are easier to do than spell." He continued dreamily, "I think I shall make up a joke about a pederast who called himself Shakespeare because he had little Latins, endless Greeks."

"Tell me why you were fired."

The cause, it developed, was not one I was ready to rally round. Ranchek had once written a parody of the chamber's monthly bulletin in which he compared his town with Dachau, to the latter's advantage. When he first composed it, Ranchek had read the whole labored effort to me, and I had advised him then that Nazi camps were among two or three things on earth that resisted humor. He was undeterred and kept the script in his desk to read to other friends until, through a series of mishaps, the parody had been sent to the printer and very nearly set in type.

"I won't say it serves you right," I told him. "But I'm not surprised that the board should ask you to resign."

"I try to take comfort in the thought that being fired for bad taste in Southern California is in itself a distinction."

"They paid severance?"

"A pittance."

"You must find a new job."

"Of course," Ranchek agreed heartily. "That's been the Ranchek tradition. Historically we have never been content to loll on the world's white sands. We have been up at dawn to serve our fellow man."

"Where are you now?"

"Up at Dawn's." He never sounded more smug than when he had bedded his legal wife.

"You had better go down today and file for unemployment insurance."

"How inspiring for all of us to observe," said Ranchek at his most unctuous, "that in scarcely a year another East Coast immigrant has become a native Californian."

All the same, he went that afternoon to the state offices. But once his eligibility had been established, his job hunting became less than desultory. First he pleaded the Christmas holidays, then the New Year's slump. By March he announced that his apartment was bankrupting him and that he was forced to move in with Dawn in Westwood. He carted along his bullfight poster, which he hung over her bed. The weights and dumbbells he stacked in her dressing alcove, and he hid his off-brand bottles of liquor at the back of her well-stocked bar.

Whatever Dawn thought of the arrangement, she treated him as before, with the same indulgence and asperity. She heaped his plate with rich food and warned him all through dinner that he was getting fat from indolence. One night while she was in the kitchen, I lowered my voice and asked, "Are you really looking for a job, George?"

Ranchek was lying on the rug, tracing patterns with a potato chip across the surface of the onion dip. "He called me George!" he shouted into the kitchen. "He must be unhappy about something."

"Of course I'm not," I said. "But you're probably getting restless not working."

"Absolutely," he replied, lying perfectly still.

On my desk I had marked a calendar with the Wednesday on which Ranchek's unemployment benefits would expire, and when that day came and went without a word from him, I called Dawn's apartment early the next morning.

"Hello," said Ranchek sleepily.

"Ranchek, with your state payments ended now, what do you propose to live on?"

He corrected me gently. "Whom."

"That's what I thought. Do you ever go out to look for work?"

48

His answer was the sigh of a man determined to rise above his grievances.

"Can't Dawn find something for you at the bank?"

"I couldn't ask my wife for a job," he protested. "That's nuptialism."

"Ranchek, how do you spend your days?"

I could picture his round face composing itself into a solemn expression. "Self-improvement," he said at last.

"You watch television all day. You're watching it now."

"No!" At least I had pricked his vanity. "Not at all! I may take an occasional nap. I may sit around in my undershirt. But I do not watch television."

"Game shows, soap operas, reruns of last year's series—you watch them all."

"I don't," he cried petulantly. "You can come over right now and feel the tube."

"It's no business of mine, Ranchek," I said. "But I can't believe that this long period of idleness is good for you. You might consider taking a job as a salesman until you find what you really want."

"What a good idea!" he said eagerly. "And you should be a career counselor. With your sympathy and tact, youngsters would flock to your cubicle. You could give them a choice of brushes or encyclopedias. You—"

"I'll call again when you're not being silly."

If you are raised, as I was, to believe that all honest work has equal value, the only man you can despise in good conscience is one who doesn't work at all. Setting off for work each morning along the seaside walk I'd see thirty-year-old surfers padding out toward the ocean's edge and ask myself how they could be content to owe their pleasures to a dole. Ranchek troubled me less because he didn't seem to be enjoying his leisure.

When Dawn's birthday came around in May, Ranchek had already been out of work several months, but he insisted on surprising her with an armload of presents. I carried over a bottle of wine and found Dawn surrounded by boxes and wrappings.

"It's been a lovely day, the best birthday I've ever had." Dawn held up two sets of babydoll lingerie, one trimmed in fox fur. The scent of gardenias, from cologne bottles and bath salts permeated the room. "Those two years that George was overseas, I hated waking up alone on my birthday."

She said nothing about her birthday last year, which Ranchek had celebrated without her in his own apartment a mile away. These days Dawn was acting as though theirs had been a normal marriage that was only disturbed now by Ranchek's being out of work. She took his behavior of the last year as the result of an emotional crisis suffered in the Army—whatever might be the peacetime equivalent of shell shock.

As I was leaving, Ranchek made a joke about Dawn's age. A woman turning thirty might be excused some skittishness, but she reproved him mildly and reminded me about the Blacks' party the following Sunday. "I'm looking forward to it," Dawn said. "We don't see enough of Josh and Jenny."

I glanced over my shoulder for any trace of sarcasm. Dawn had maneuvered herself into the crook of Ranchek's arm, and she rested there contentedly. Should any neighbors be watching, the Rancheks in their doorway were buxom bride and stalwart groom brought radiantly to life.

꒪ꛯ   ꒪ꛯ   ꒪ꛯ

I missed that party for some reason, but a few weeks later Josh Black called after dinner to ask me to drive to the Valley college where he was working nights as a watchman; he wanted my advice on an urgent matter. Doug Goodwin had driven to Venice when his noon shift ended, and we were planning to drink beer at a bar on Lincoln Boulevard.

Reluctantly Goodwin agreed to go with me instead, but on the way he warned me, "If Josh says he wants your advice, it means he's got something to brag about."

Mildly, courteously, Goodwin disliked Black, perhaps because he regarded Josh's attempts to get into the movies as presumptuous. Here he was, after all, Douglas Goodwin, better looking, better built, manlier and more deserving, and he worked in a factory. Why should Josh Black expect any more from life? Goodwin omitted from that equation any consideration of talent; he had seen the same movies we all had.

The college lay at the north end of the Valley—three low brick buildings spread across acres of red mud. In the custodian's hut where Black spent his nights, I had seen the architect's plans for the completed campus. A gymnasium, laboratories and a fine arts complex were due to rise from this wet dirt where Goodwin and I now struggled to keep our footing. It was impossible to believe that by the nineteen-seventies one of the largest colleges in the state would be operating here.

Black greeted us at the door of his shack holding an electric heater. "Let's go over to the library." He tossed Goodwin a ring of keys. "They've moved in some chairs."

The library was architecturally hard to admire. It had been finished a few weeks earlier, and the shelving was now installed—miles of empty black metal bars twisting back and forth through the vast spaces, a maze without a Minotaur. On the ground floor, pine tables and a dozen chairs had been delivered and pushed together to barricade the back door. Black connected the heater, plugged in a gooseneck lamp and invited us to prop our feet on a table.

He seemed equally pleased to see Goodwin and the case of beer I handed him. "This won't cause you trouble?" I asked.

Josh shook his head. "Nobody comes here at night. Last year some neighborhood kids threw stones at the windows in the administration building and that's when they hired a guard. Since I've been here it's been quiet."

He passed a beer to each of us. Rings on the tops of beer cans were new and their edges sharply honed. As Josh pulled up on his beer he sliced deep into his finger, and he cursed and sucked at the sliver of blood. When he could take his finger from his mouth, he said, "I've been cheating on Jenny. I feel rotten about it. I don't know what to do."

Goodwin listened gravely and scratched his head.

"Who's the girl?" With Black so eager to tell, it would have been cruel not to ask.

"Do you remember the actress who played my wife?"

Goodwin excused himself to look for a toilet and he stalled there for fifteen minutes until his beer was gone. When he came back, Black's affair had only progressed to the first kiss. "I've had plenty of other chances," he was saying, "but there was something about Darlene—"

"There was this girl back home called Darlene." Goodwin stretched out on the table like a cadaver and folded his arms across his chest. "She had real bad eyes and these big thick glasses—"

Black intercepted smoothly. "The Darlene I'm talking about has perfect vision. She's got beautiful violet eyes—well, you know that, you saw her in the show. Everything was simple while we were rehearsing and during the performances, but it's impossible to get together, and she's giving me a lot of trouble. With Jenny eight months pregnant, it would be terrible if she found out."

"Is the girl married?" Goodwin was gone again, this time to locate a draft he claimed to feel on his feet.

"Her husband is a lawyer in Studio City. Three children. I tell you, I feel rotten about this." Black stared with loathing at his cut finger.

Reading about another man's affairs can be interesting enough, but I have found that hearing the same stories in person is usually a trial. I blame the difference on the competition that springs up between any two men at the first provocation. Enduring Josh's story, I almost interrupted to tell him about a checker at the supermarket two weeks ago.

His confession, though, did explain changes in Jenny that I had set down to her pregnancy. It was the year that a political crusade was attracting attention, an amalgam of timid engineers and stentorian housewives who claimed to have uncovered subversion in high and improbable places. Drawn to this fringe, Jenny reserved Tuesday nights for meetings that would help her fathom the conspiracy.

She came home earnest and heated, primarily from having to concentrate so desperately on getting each name and affiliation exactly right. Otherwise, she lacked the temperament to be fanatical and she confided to Josh that most of the other women in her study club tended to go overboard.

Jenny soaked up their political scandals but never tried to convert Josh, who laughed at her. She was content to say that one day he would accept the truth, one day when the true facts were told. Her access to privileged information satisfied her; she was not moved to act. Now I wondered whether, by focusing on intrigue in Washington, Jenny had found it easier to ignore the affair her husband was conducting five miles from home.

Goodwin had toured the building several times before he rejoined us and I could ask him what course of action he recommended for Josh.

"Are you going to do any more plays at that theater?" Goodwin asked him.

"I doubt it. The director is a real hack. I'd like to join a little theater group in Hollywood."

"This Darlene wouldn't go with you?"

"Frankly," said Josh, "I don't think her work is of the caliber."

"Let her know you don't respect her talent," I said, "let pride do the rest."

"I can't," Black said. "I've already praised her too often."

"Before you went to bed," Goodwin said.

"Yes."

Goodwin opened three more cans of beer. Josh, hating to admit he had finished his story, started again on the delights Darlene had provided him. "You unmarried men don't know how lucky you are not being tied down."

"Yes, we do," said Goodwin.

"Still, even with the worry I'm having right now, I wouldn't give up my marriage to be single again. The best thing I ever did was marry Jenny. Have I ever told you how we met?"

Goodwin looked at his watch. Josh smiled for the pleasure he was about to impart and leaned farther back. "In college, Jenny was brilliant." Goodwin looked as dubious as when Black had claimed that his mistress had perfect vision. "She was quiet, though, and she didn't go out much. I was starring in all the plays and pretty well known around the campus. She didn't tell me until after we were engaged, but some of the girls in her sorority warned her not to go out with me because of my reputation."

Now Goodwin was doing his best to seem interested. His own education had ended in a high school diploma awarded by the Army's extension program, and I remembered from France that when any college graduate began to reminisce, Goodwin listened attentively. He didn't want to seem envious.

Once or twice I had urged him to return to school, and each time I got an evasive answer. "I'm too lazy," he would say, and it did no good to argue that he had just stood twelve hours in front of a lathe. He seemed to have made up his mind that any chance for formal education had come too late, but his diffidence may have been only the visible peak of his pride.

He couldn't return to the classroom at age twenty-five because he might fail. Or because going back he would be admitting that the hacks of long ago, the grinds who studied while he drank and wenched, had employed their time more wisely than he.

Black's tale went on rattling over our heads; his premarital seduction of Jenny proved to be identical in every respect to his conquest of Darlene. The recitation ended with a declaration of love for his wife, the woman he now realized he prized above all others. He would disencumber himself of this other woman, whom, we learned at last, he hadn't seen for three weeks. Except that I was eight beers to the good, I might have felt ill used. "It's two o'clock," I said.

Goodwin was on his feet and out the door before Black had unplugged the heater. As he locked up, Josh said, "You'll have to come back when we get some books in here."

"I kind of like it this way," Goodwin said. "It suits California."

Josh laughed. "I thought Mississippi was the only state you hillbillies looked down on."

"We don't look down on anybody," Goodwin said, but as ever he was so soft-spoken that Josh didn't realize he was being reassured.

The sun had already begun to set on the Friday afternoon that Robert Rorke arrived unannounced, looking so shaken that I had to adjust my own feelings hurriedly to accommodate his. I never found it easy to control my emotions at that hour. It was the single moment in the day that had a powerful hold over me. At noon, the sun struck the surface of the ocean hard enough to stun me with its impersonal brilliance. The night had comforts of its own. But at the balancing edge, when the sun's reflection on the water, instead of obscuring the daylight, brightened the day one final time—that hour at the beach was a sad hopeless time for me.

Whatever Rorke felt that day, though, was worse than my dejection. He was trembling badly, his body seemed shrunken, his glittering blue eyes were soft, and a face that was heavy and raw most days looked smudged in the half light. I lacked the will to smile, but my features assembled into an expression of welcome.

Rorke stumbled directly to the faded couch that faced the window. He accepted a whiskey I brought from the kitchen. "What's wrong?" I asked.

The reflection on the wall behind him was forming one block of yellow light that hung over his head like a blade. I watched it slide until it almost touched his stiff yellow hair. There was no other light in the room. Rorke's face was hidden in shadows. "I got a call from my mother today."

The edge of sunlight reached his hair, cut through the stubble and turned his scalp pink. Another inch and the light slid off his hair and down his forehead. It was moving now toward his eyebrows, and in a minute the sun would be in his eyes. I thought of pulling the shade, but I stayed in my chair when Rorke began to cry.

I didn't say anything, nor did he. Now the sun was cruel. It sent a beam of light to expose his wrinkled forehead, then went for the furrows where his brows had been before his crying pulled them down. For a few seconds more, his wet eyes would be safe in the dark.

A fraction downward and the light hit his closed lids. He squeezed his eyes tighter and released a sound he had been holding back. I listened to him groan and watched the sunlight follow the tears down his face. The light caught moisture at the corners of his mouth, examined it there, moved to his chin.

His voice was low as it spilled out. He told me that his mother had been a drunk and a whore. Her husband had left her and given their only child to his sister to raise. Years of silence, then a drunken call on his twelfth birthday. At a high school graduation, a sudden hideous appearance, the worst moment of his life.

The top of the sun's reflection had sunk to his lips. Rorke could open his eyes. Yellow light spread down his chest like a long bib tucked into his collar. Or as though he had spewed sunlight from his mouth and let it seep down his shirt.

He had heard today that his mother was dying or claimed to be. Once he had flown from college, skipped an examination, to find her in a hotel in West Virginia, not dying, just drunk and lonely. He had been angry but he couldn't match her bitterness. Why had he forced her to lie? she shouted. Why had he never come until he thought she was almost dead?

Behind me the sun must have reached the water. Its last rays sank into Rorke's lap. The window cut them oblong, and they creased over his knees and skidded toward the floor. I tried to look at the yellow patch as sunlight, but to my mind it was Rorke's contamination pouring from him. I waited for it to spatter his shoes and drench the floor.

Rorke wanted his mother to die, he said. Tonight. His father had died two years ago. Why couldn't his mother die? Not in a charity ward in Norfolk, not lingering, with Rorke at her bedside pretending that he cared. Now! Die now! He had told her that and hung up the telephone.

All his yellow wastes were spread before me on the floor. Rorke was drained. The room was dark and until he lit a match I could imagine he had disappeared. The bright yellow spot had begun to flow across the carpet. I watched it moving toward my shoes and wanted to lift my feet out of the path of his sickness.

Listen to me, I said. I don't want to hear about you and your mother or you and your father. You are not fifteen and a boy. You will soon be thirty. Your mother is nothing important, only one more woman who needs help. You must help her. That's all. You don't have to love her or judge her, hate or worship her. You help. Whether she deserves it or not, you do what you can. I don't care about your childhood. I don't want to hear what was done to you twenty years ago. I want to know what you will do now, as a man.

Or that is what I wanted to say. But the sun's pattern had stopped at the toes of my shoes, blocked by the shadow from my shoulders. In a minute I would be safe. Then, as the room grew darker, as the rectangle slid upward and disappeared within my shadow, I shoved one foot into the mess of yellow light and held it there.

Rorke's sobbing ended. I coughed up a few sensible words. I reminded him that there were doctors trained to treat these symptoms that were paining him, doctors who would listen, explain and work to heal him. He made a good salary, I said, and spoke of his stock portfolio. Shouldn't he consider the cost of treatment one more prudent investment?

※　　　　　※　　　　　※

On a Sunday morning they judged mild enough, the Steins drove to the beach with Jacob, a fat and complacent infant they toted upstairs to my apartment in a wicker basket. Margo heated his bottle in a pan and fed him competently, without cluckings or baby talk. Neither parent said much about the child, but where I took Billy's to be a proud silence, Margo's was more equivocal.

With the baby fed and washed, the four of us set off to call again on Lonnie Chapman. This time Billy's knocking roused a sturdy young man in a faded wool bathrobe. He suffered Billy to pump his hand and permitted Margo to stand on tiptoe and kiss his cheek. I was greeted with an incurious nod, but his immediate pleasure in the baby seemed genuine.

We trooped through a dark hallway, Lonnie's curly head

leading the way. The face he turned to encourage us was wide and handsome, if somewhat equine. His pale lips parted to show strong white teeth, wasted on a vegetarian, and his robe, hanging open to the waist, disclosed a thickly muscled torso equally inappropriate to a mystic.

As best we could, we guests cleared seats amid piles of dirty laundry and empty cat food cans. Lonnie sat cross-legged on his bed with the skirts of his robe tucked deliberately under his knees. Though sun was beating hard on the drawn shade, the mood in this cluttered room was something between a séance and a confessional. No one had much to say. The three men seemed content to watch Margo cradling the baby in her arms.

Near my chair a chess set had been strewn over the floor, and I asked Lonnie if he played. "No," he said calmly. "No games."

"None?"

"Not baseball, poker, Chinese checkers, soccer or solitaire," he said. "Nothing."

Had he been scrawny, his tone might have been apologetic. But Lonnie expected his bare chest to prove that he wasn't ascetic by default. Loyally Billy said, "Until he gave it up, Lonnie won chess tournaments all over the state."

"He played football in high school, but he never won any prizes for that." Whatever Margo intended him to hear in her teasing, Lonnie Chapman ignored. "No," he agreed. "I didn't."

I folded my arms and surveyed the shambles on every side. It wasn't much different from a slovenly room in a college dormitory, except for one missing element. I looked past the bricked-up fireplace and the bed with its heap of soiled sheets to the bathroom, where a hot plate rested on the toilet tank. "You have no books."

"No games," he repeated.

"You never read?"

"I read for twenty years before I woke up to what I was doing. A man who reads is building barriers against life. I'd go to a professor's house and see those walls of books from floor to ceiling, like insulation in an attic. I don't need insulating."

"You're never going to read?"

"If you say you won't do something, you're as obligated as when you say you will. While you're here today I won't read, and I doubt that I'll read after you go. I seem to have broken the habit. It took eight months. The first week I'd read anything. I read the instructions on the fuse box until I memorized them, and the chemical analysis on the cat food cans."

He spoke in a low firm voice. His manner was direct. He was not trying to convert me, nor was he apologetic. When he smiled it was in the same uninflected way, not winningly.

I appealed to the Steins to know if Lonnie was serious. "Yes," they assured me in unison. I persisted: "Billy works for a newspaper. Out of friendship, shouldn't you make an exception and read his stories?"

"It's out of friendship that I don't." He smiled candidly, and Billy Stein beamed as though a gold star had been pasted on his forehead.

"I understand that you park cars up the beach," I said. Lonnie nodded. "Isn't that boring without something to read?"

"You came out here from New York?"

"On the bus." It had become a point of pride.

"Then you remember that in the subway it's the well-dressed men and women who pull a newspaper or book out of their pockets the minute they sit down. It's the others who ride mile after mile staring straight ahead."

"Yes."

"Tell me which group has the better imagination. Which group seems less worried about being bored?"

I laughed self-consciously, because his argument could apply to the beach and the hundreds of bodies lying inert there. What revelations were being visited on them while I kept myself versed on Cuba?

An empty cat food can rested on the arm of my chair. I picked it up and turned it on my palm. "Where's your cat?"

"I don't have one." As my confusion deepened, Lonnie Chapman went on smiling in the most agreeable way.

Our visit ended. Walking back to his car, Billy Stein assured me that Lonnie had been joking. "He's got two cats, a calico and a Siamese. Besides, you should have known Lonnie wouldn't eat cat food. It's got meat."

Margo said, "Lonnie likes to shake people up."

"Not the path to sainthood," I said peevishly.

"Lonnie doesn't want to be a saint," Billy said. "He's trying to be something else."

"What?"

"That's what he's trying to find out."

Conversations of that sort quickly exhaust themselves, and I did not press Billy further. I left the Steins and walked back alone along the ocean front to my apartment. A haze had blown up from the sea, and I couldn't see across the beach to where the waves began. On the green wooden benches, old women bundled in black were talking the language of their youth. In their heavy coats and kerchiefs they seemed to find the deepening fog more congenial than the sunshine. Only one woman, her Yiddish failing her, swore ferociously that the dampness made her corns ache.

I knew many of the old women well enough to call them by name. They returned my greeting fondly; being blue-eyed and blond, I wasn't expected to be polite.

Back in my room I thought about Lonnie Chapman and the unfruitful turn his life had taken. Clearly he had no vocation for celibacy, no prospect of reaching the illumination promised in drugstore editions of Zen. I wanted to drive him out of his room, push him into the midst of the old women on their bench, force him to commiserate over their rheumatism or the price of kosher chicken. That would be kindness on his part, that would be goodness. Or so it seemed to someone learning to appreciate the voluptuous qualities of solitude.

⚓   ⚓   ⚓

For a second time I argued myself into accepting the Blacks' invitation to spend New Year's Eve with them. Then, the day after Christmas, Jeanne Darling called to say that Ray Morella would be working that night and that she couldn't bear to welcome the new year alone in her apartment. "If I stay here," she said, "Sonny will wake up at midnight and beat on a kettle with a spoon. You will save me from that, won't you, my sweet?"

I took the occasion to ask what exactly Morella did for a living. "You know!" Jeanne said. "I've told you a hundred times."

"Tell me once more."

So I learned that Morella was one of three partners in a steakhouse on the Sunset Strip, and that Jeanne had avoided talking about it because she loathed the place. I had gone once and found it, behind the rococo trimmings, a routine dive. "It's your own fault," said Jeanne when I told her I'd been there. "Nobody nice goes."

I warned her that while I'd escort her happily she might find the evening staid compared to parties in Hollywood. But she insisted that a placid evening would be healthy for her and I arranged to pick her up at nine.

The night arrived murky and cold, and Jeanne slid into the front seat and almost into my arms. Her thin wrap was no protection against the air and the heater in my old car was broken.

"Could you hear Sonny crying as we left?" she asked. "He does the same thing every night. I don't know what to do. He's flunking second grade. Are you ready for that? Second grade! When I was that age, teachers wrote home notes about whether we shared our toys."

Except that Jeanne's mail was postmarked at the Beverly Hills post office, a cachet that raised her rent 20 percent, her apartment was no different from the cell block where Ranchek had lived or the pastel barracks where he now dwelt with Dawn. Across the front of Jeanne's building two spotlights played throughout the night, one amber, one rose. "The evening I got into Los Angeles," I told Jeanne, "I saw all the lights and thought they were left from Christmas."

"Hideous," Jeanne said. "That whole building is not to be believed."

"Find a new place."

I turned west on Santa Monica Boulevard and drove slowly, looking for the entrance to the new freeway. "If you promise not to repeat it," Jeanne said, "I'll tell you some news. Ray and I may be getting married. He's promised to buy a house in the Valley."

"That's fine," I said, and then felt foolish since my enthusiasm was so much greater than hers. "I've known him a long time," she said. "It will be good for Sonny."

The freeway bypassed the twists and bends of the canyon road and skimmed instead across the hilltops. Below us the old road and its tunnel looked as primitive as a dirt trail. Even in a decrepit car straining at fifty miles an hour I was exhilarated. "It's not driving any more," I said. "It's flying."

At Sepulveda Boulevard I coasted down the off-ramp and headed north. For his own reasons the contractor of the Blacks' subdivision had named each street after a city in India; Ranchek said because of their comparable levels of literacy. We passed Bombay Avenue and Agra Lane, Jeanne humming discords she hoped would pass for a raga. Her good spirits waned when we pulled up in front of the Blacks' house and she saw the sign they had posted on the unkempt lawn: "Blacks' Hole of Calcutta."

"You forgot," Jeanne said sourly, "to tell me they were droll."

But as Jenny ushered us inside Jeanne roused herself and began dispensing the graciousness of an Atlanta matron paying a call beneath her station. She astonished Jenny, social kissing not having penetrated the Valley, with a butterfly flutter of lips near her cheek, and for Josh she exuded scented lace and lavender. "You told me he was a friend from the Army," Jeanne whispered for all to hear. "But you didn't say he had kept his military bearing." Josh bent to kiss her hand.

Once again the Blacks had limited the decorations in their living room to a few strands of pink crepe paper strung from the overhead light fixture. The same six cardboard bells, relics from last year, were dangling from the mantelpiece. "Why no fire?" I asked Josh.

"We thought it was too warm. Besides the flue plugs and the room fills with smoke."

"We don't want a fire!" Jeanne exclaimed. "How would the wolf get down the chimney?"

With a stagy laugh Josh drew her away to introduce the other guests, neighbors for the most part and repeats from last year. I looked for Darlene in a circle of faces I recognized from the play, but she didn't seem to be there. Several neighbors wore denims and neckerchiefs, and one blonde was snug in riding breeches. Jenny caught me looking at her. "Now I know I'm out west," I said.

She smiled absently and drew me into the kitchen. "We're serving rum punch in the dining room," she said. Without a hope of success, Jenny was trying to play the practiced hostess. "But if you'd rather have something stronger, you know where we keep it."

Doug Goodwin came slouching into the kitchen alone. He greeted Jenny formally and nodded thoughtfully at me. Goodwin never brought a girl to the Blacks' parties and tonight Jenny apparently felt reckless enough to ask why. "Tell me," she said, "is it her you're ashamed of? Or us?"

Goodwin could hardly tell her that the women he knew were usually married and they spent New Year's Eve with their husbands. He could only say that his current girl was indisposed and look relieved when Jeanne Darling joined us. The moment she heard Goodwin speak, I noticed, Jeanne dropped the palpitations from her drawl and she addressed him without mock flattery; apparently something in his Tennessee accent told her to save it for the Yankees. Jeanne was uncomfortable with him. When Black returned to claim the first dance of the evening, she followed him out gratefully.

Left behind in the kitchen, Goodwin started on a long story about his landlady's niece. He was nowhere near the finish when the Rancheks appeared, Ranchek steering Dawn in front of him like a minesweeper. She had lost enough weight to risk an orange knit dress, and Goodwin broke off his story to say softly, "Making love to Ranchek's wife would be like getting caught in an avalanche of ripe squash."

"Hallo!" Ranchek shouted in to us. "Is that the American Legion meeting in the kitchen?"

Dawn stamped in to confront us. "Ranchek and I are having an argument," she said. "Maybe one of you can settle it for us. I say a sense of humor is no proof of intelligence and he says it is."

"Either way," I said, "what interest could Ranchek have?"

"You see, George!" she said triumphantly. "That's what your friends think of you. But really, do you think that because he makes me laugh it means he's smart?"

"He married you," Goodwin said. "That proves it."

"No!" Dawn was impatient. "I'm serious. Did either of you see his intelligence score on the Army records?"

"They mean very little," I said. "One day Josh Black got ink and an eraser and improved his own score thirty points."

Black, escorting Jeanne back to the kitchen, overheard me. "Twenty," he said. "And to be fair I took the same amount off my weight."

Jeanne had not met the Rancheks and from Dawn's behavior or an ambiguity in the introductions concluded that they were blood relatives. "A girl never takes her younger brother seriously," she told Ranchek. "She won't believe how attractive another woman might find him."

Ranchek hooted. When her mistake was pointed out, Jeanne performed the embarrassed dimpling expected of her. Dawn took it all in good grace. "It's true," she said. "I am older than Ranchek. At least you didn't say mother."

Doug Goodwin plowed ahead to ease the strain. "What could be a real test of George's intelligence anyway?"

"You're missing the point," Josh Black objected. "All you have to prove is that Ranchek isn't funny. Then the question is mute—moot."

Black had been lingering by the punch, and I hoped he wouldn't collapse before the hour we could decently leave.

"All right, George," Jeanne coaxed. "I know it will be difficult. But say something dull."

Tonelessly Ranchek recited, "I have been out of work a very long time."

"I don't know about the rest of you"—Dawn's words popped out like buttons off a blouse—"but that's certainly starting to bore me."

Josh Black applauded vigorously. From the grin fixed to Ranchek's face it was impossible to tell his reaction. An awkwardness was again settling over us, and Dawn told Black that she liked his sign outside. "Did you know," she continued hurriedly, "that in India, on the spot where the real Black Hole used to be, there's a bank now? I read that someplace."

Josh said, "I'd like to go to India someday. The trouble is, they don't make many pictures there."

. Jenny spun into the kitchen, intent on getting her husband

66

to circulate and acquainting me with the weekend ranchers
and their wives Jeanne had already met. I submitted docilely,
for I had a plan.

One problem I faced at parties was that I drank too fast. In
my hand a drink moved involuntarily to my lips, reversing
the action of those perpetual motion gadgets in dime stores I'd
remembered as a boy, the birds with long beaks that dipped in
and out of a glass beneath them. I could watch my arm bending, my hand carrying the liquor to my mouth, with the help-
lessness of a man obeying a force stronger than his own. Up
came the glass, my lips parted, I drank. Again: the glass hadn't
got as far as to my side before it was coming back up. I took
larger sips, hoping to deaden whatever muscles were contest-
ing with me. That only oiled the mechanism and made it work
more smoothly. Up, drink, swallow, down. Up.

My alternative to getting drunk was to disappear for an
hour or two when the drinking was heaviest. From a history
of dismal evenings I had learned to seize the moment I could
slip away: Too early, with the host still sober and guests arriving, and someone would be sent to search me out in the
basement or backyard. Too late, and the implacable muscles
in my arm had begun to function. But during the instant a
party was aloft and not yet fixed in place, there was a chance.

Tonight I sensed the time and marked out the nursery as
my refuge. The Blacks had entrusted their infant daughter to
a neighbor for the night, and they were using their own bedroom for the women's coats. I headed down the hall and
ducked behind the closed door of the other room. I remembered a couch crowded next to the baby's crib and felt my
way toward it without turning on the lights. I had scarcely
stretched out and shut my eyes when the door opened again
and Jenny and Josh stepped across the threshold. In loud hiss-
ing whispers they took up an argument at the point it had outgrown the kitchen.

Jenny was angry because Josh was drinking heavily after

promising to stay sober. He resented her counting his drinks. After a few accusations back and forth, he let her know it was her attitude that had driven him to another woman.

Coldly, Jenny said, "I told you never to talk about that again. I told you what would happen if you did."

Two people quarreling by themselves puzzles me. They are alone and yet they address complaints to an imaginary jury charged with weighing their merits. They never see that their grand rhetoric is wasted, or appreciate how foolish they sound, posturing and cursing with no one but an adversary to appreciate the performance. Of course tonight the Blacks had an audience, but they couldn't know that. They fought with the same pointless fury as though they were alone.

Playing to the stalls was natural enough for Josh, but when Jenny matched his melodrama I was surprised. She sounded as though she were kneeling for a medieval oath when she repeated, "I told you never to talk about that."

Black snarled and slammed out of the room. Jenny waited a moment and slipped away after him.

Within five minutes I was asleep. But to elude a host successfully depends on a sure sense of when to awake and reappear. When the luminous dial of my watch indicated that I had enjoyed a ninety-minute respite, I straightened my jacket and shook the wrinkles from my trousers. In the bathroom, I splashed my eyes with cold water. The eyes in the mirror shone with the prospect of being turned loose near the vodka. "One drink," I said aloud. "One."

In the living room the light was dim and the dancing sedate. Dawn floated by gracefully in Ranchek's embrace and smiled at me. Jeanne Darling had pulled up a chair to the dining room table. A bottle of bourbon was half empty at her elbow. Without rancor she asked, "Where on earth have you been?"

"Someone had to go for ice."

"You simply could not believe how dull it's been. I do like your friend, though."

"Goodwin? Yes."

"No, Josh Black. He's been charming."

"Where is he now?"

"In the kitchen, I think." We were looking in that direction as Jenny burst through the kitchen door. She surveyed the room, located Doug Goodwin and marched to his side. Grabbing his elbow like a policewoman, she steered him to the center of the floor, and they danced slowly and dreamily.

I found Josh pressing his forehead against the refrigerator door. "How are you, Private Black?"

"Oh, it's you, Specialist. Where is my wife?"

"Dancing."

"With Doug?"

"Yes."

He nodded sagely. "That's fine. I always said he was the man she should have married. I knew it in France the first day they met."

"I have doubts." I looked at my watch. "Twenty more minutes and this year will be over."

"This year, next year. What's the difference?"

"You've been out here how long now?"

"Twenty-eight months. And I've been in one play with a bunch of amateurs."

"You shouldn't get discouraged."

"Why shouldn't I? A writer can go on writing. But if you're an actor and you're not acting, what are you?"

"Typical?"

"That's the trouble—the competition." Black shuddered. "It never gets better, only worse. Every month another thousand boys come out here and make the same rounds and try for the same one-line parts."

Black's special horror, he said, was making the rounds of

agents' offices. He would come home from patrolling the college, pluck stray hairs from between his eyebrows, oil his ringlets until they glistened but weren't flat with grease. He'd put on the suit he saved for those mornings—a subdued gray check—and study himself in the full-length mirror in the hall. Jenny's alterations kept his hips looking narrow and gave him the fullness he needed through the shoulders.

Josh stored his glossy photographs at the bottom of a dresser drawer, where he hoped they wouldn't curl or yellow from the light. He had posed for them in Indiana before he was drafted. Lately an agent had advised him to get more recent pictures, but he was waiting until he lost ten pounds.

In the Army we had seen those pictures with their three classic poses. Black serious, knuckles raised to his chin, partly hiding the sag of his jaw. Black smiling, an arch baring of teeth. Black dangerous, stripped to the waist, fists clenched, a menacing downturn to his mouth, his body lighted to look almost muscular. The photographs seemed professionally done, they were probably appropriate for his trade; but it was impossible to imagine a girl in St. Louis sending away for one.

The week before Christmas, in an agent's office on the Sunset Strip, Josh had hit his lowest point. A receptionist looked him over and informed him that the agent was out, his assistant was out and his secretary wouldn't be back for at least an hour. But, she concluded, "You can wait if you want to." Raising one of her plucked eyebrows, she let him know that if the decision were hers, he would never see the inside of a studio.

Perched on a stool, Josh ducked to wipe his face with a flowered cloth on the kitchen table. After interviews like that, he said, he dreaded coming home. He knew that while he was gone, Jenny had kept very busy, bathing the baby, running the vacuum cleaner.

Then as he came through the door, she would glance up and ask how it had gone. But she wouldn't let him tell her.

Seeing the answer on his face, Jenny was already consoling him. The first year she would pull him into a chair and sit in his lap, stroking his hand and kissing the cleft Josh cultivated in his chin. After the baby came, she had gone on working, mixing formula or boiling diapers but trying as hard to cheer him up.

The agent was no good anyway. Jenny could say that and forget that as she had shined Josh's shoes that morning she had mentioned reading that the man was the best agent in Hollywood. When Josh was turned down for a television role, Jenny was sure the movies were the faster way to a more enduring success. But the next week, when he lost the chance for a test in a film, she was predicting that within five years every theater in the country would be nailed shut. At night, as they watched television together, every actor who came on the screen was repulsive to Jenny. Too rough, she complained. Too loud. Prissy. Fat. All bones.

"I know what she's doing and I hate it," Josh said. "And I need it. It's not walking into an agent's office that scares me now. It's not being turned down. That's only the beginning. The worst part is coming home to tell Jenny. What if this time she isn't quite as indignant as she was a month ago? What if she says that maybe—just maybe—I wasn't exactly right for that particular part?"

He laughed drunkenly. "Now she's the one who has to give the performance. She does the acting that keeps us both going."

I had been taught that the only failure was the man who gave up, but Josh looked so wretched that I asked if he didn't think of quitting.

"I think of it all the time. I think of nothing else. But Jenny married me because I was an actor. We weren't even twenty then, either one of us. It's not that I made her promises. We never had to talk about success. Nineteen years old. Of course it was going to happen for me. Now I'm supposed to tell her that she's married to a twenty-six-year-old janitor? That she's stuck in a broken-down rented house with a kid we couldn't afford? She married an actor. I'll be an actor for her."

"Jenny probably wants what's best for you."

"She found out about Darlene."

"How?"

"I told her." Something in my expression annoyed him. "If you're failing," he said brutally, as though the way to hurt me was to call himself a failure, "you take any chance you get to brag. Darlene was the first success I'd had in six years. Did you see the review of our show in that weekly shopper? 'Joshua Black was adequate as Master Ford.' Adequate. From a throwaway paper dumped on the front yard every Thursday. The night the review came out I saw a copy at the college and I left work early to get ours off the lawn before Jenny could see it.

"But she had called the newspaper to find out when their review was running and she waited up all night for it. The minute I got in the door she started: 'What does some old maid on a shopping rag know about the theater?' She wanted to call the trade papers in Hollywood and demand that they send their own critics out to see me.

"Her eyes were angry but the rims were red. She had been crying. I listened to her and I knew that she didn't care how I was feeling. She was taking that review as an affront to her. I, me, my talent, had become we, our marriage, her talent. I was sick of it. I told her the reviewer was right—I had been giving my best performance offstage. There wasn't much passion left when the curtain went up."

He drank pale liquid from a cup, and as he took another sip his hand shook. "I need coffee," I said. "I'll make some for both of us."

Black shrugged. I searched the cupboards until I found a coffee can and the percolator. The instant I plugged in the cord, lights went out in the living room and a shout went up.

I thought I had blown a fuse, but it was only the first minute of a new year. With the lights past the doorway dark, the fluorescent tube over our heads penetrated like an X ray.

Coffee was perking and I had laid out cream and sugar for Josh when Ranchek came lurching through the door. "Branch water!" he bawled. "Or give me a limb and I'll milk it myself."

"What's happening out there?"

"Everyone is kissing everyone," he said joyfully. "It's like the end of the war."

"Who is Jenny with?" Josh asked.

"Douglas MacArthur Goodwin. If I were you, Private Black, I'd be apprehensive. Thank God he hasn't spotted my wife, the lovely but self-effacing Dawn Ranchek. What chance would I have against our nation's most decorated hero?"

"Goodwin is not decorated." One way to deflect Ranchek was to take him literally. "He didn't even get the Good Conduct Medal."

"You should see his face," Ranchek persisted. "The lipstick looks like war paint."

"We'll drink our coffee," I said to Black, "and join them."

"I'm happy here," Josh said petulantly and sank farther on his stool.

"I'm happy here!" Ranchek took up the refrain. "How refreshing in times like ours to hear those words! You will remember that it was a philosopher in ancient Greece who said he would rather be a man happy than a pig unhappy. And who can seriously dispute his choice?"

Ranchek's education at the hands of the Long Beach school authorities had been precarious, but I had fallen prey too often to his silly jokes to risk correcting him. In the Army he had once referred to the Lewis and Clerk Expedition, and when I raised the obvious objection he informed me loftily that he tried to avoid Britishisms.

"What did the Greeks say about work, Ranchek?" I asked.

"Moderation in all things."

Black said, "Don't let Brad bully you, George. You and I will form a federation of men who don't work. You can be president."

"Honorary president," Ranchek stipulated judiciously.

A pretty dark-eyed woman had come into the kitchen. "I've always wanted to know what men talked about when they were alone."

"In the Army," Black answered, "Ranchek here used to tell us about his first prostitute and the terrible feelings of disgust afterward. His, I mean. We never heard her side of it."

Ranchek glared at him. "If you will permit me to correct a few details," he said witheringly. "The woman of whom you speak was indeed a professional. She went under the name of Rita, went under rather regularly, I might add. My parents engaged her on the streets of Long Beach as the entertainment for my twelfth birthday party.

"Other children's families had outdone themselves that year with clowns, magicians, acrobats, ponies, even an excursion to hear a porpoise blow Happy Birthday on waterproof bagpipes. By the time my day rolled around, every diversion had been exhausted. Save one."

"He's getting ready," I warned the woman, "to be silly." Ranchek told variations on this story whenever we let him, and tonight Black was sure to press for the unexpurgated version.

"That's terrible!" the woman said when Ranchek finally finished. "How can you talk like that about your mother?"

Ranchek grew so red and flustered I thought he might genuinely regret exposing a stranger to his nonsense. "What can I do to make amends?" he bleated. "Perhaps if I told about the time my father was arrested in Griffith Park—"

The woman took herself away. Bleary and pale, Josh said, "I guess you'd better shut up, Ranchek."

"We should be getting back to the party," I said. "Especially our host."

"Jenny's out there," Black said. "She knows what to do."

"I'll say she does!" Ranchek shouted, and they laughed immoderately.

I went to assure Jeanne that we could soon be leaving, but in the dim light I saw her talking placidly to Dawn Ranchek and I looked instead for Goodwin and Jenny Black. They were still dancing, with Jenny pressed against him in an unconvincing show of sensuality. Goodwin, looking over her head, made no attempt to pull himself away. As Ranchek had reported, his face was covered with daubs and smears from muzzy pink to smacking red. I tapped his shoulder and handed him my handkerchief. "It's the white flag of surrender," I said. "You've won. Wipe your face."

Obediently he surrendered Jenny to me and mopped at his cheeks, chin and down his neck to the breastbone. Jenny and I had danced two steps when Goodwin was back behind me. "We were talking about something," he said mildly, "that I'd like to finish up."

I looked to Jenny. She nodded apologetically and I took my arm from around her waist and went to join Jeanne at the dining room table. "There you are!" Jeanne's voice was huskier than usual. "Dawn's been giving me advice about married life. And how I need it! It's been nine years since I fibbed a little and wore a white dress down the aisle. Do you think that's where the expression 'white lie' comes from? The only advice we got then was from our school nurse. 'Let him get it all out of his system on the honeymoon,' she told us. 'It will save you a lot of nuisance later.' "

"That's not Dawn's advice?"

"Oh, I was just telling Jeanne that I thought being married was worth any sacrifice you have to make." She had probably drunk even less than I had, and she was steady on her feet, a monument to good sense in an orange knit dress, as she

75

warned Jeanne against nagging a man. "All night I've been sorry about what I said to Ranchek in the kitchen," Dawn said. "About his not working. I didn't mean it. I'd like him to find a job because it would be better for him. But I'm willing to pay the bills until he finds what he wants."

"Do you like it?"

"Paying for everything?" Dawn saw my point. "No, I don't like it. But I don't mind. I only worry that it's going to start to bother George."

"Look! Look!" Jeanne was pointing excitedly. "There goes your friend with Jenny Black. Into the bedroom."

"They're old friends," I said. "Whenever he has a problem he talks it over with Jenny." Jeanne looked skeptical, but Dawn was easily convinced; Ranchek told me men at the bank often came to her for advice. I said, "I left my drink in there while I was making a phone call. I'll get it before Doug gets talking."

In the bedroom I flicked the switch and laboriously took no notice of Jenny slipping from Goodwin's arms. No desire, as I understand the word, animated either of their faces. Jenny looked more relieved than anything else. Goodwin's expression was blank. "Doug," I said, "I'm starting to feel the drinks. Would you mind taking Jeanne home? Then if it's all right with Jenny I can spend the night here on the couch."

He nodded slowly and Jenny dashed away for bedclothes and blankets. "I don't want to break up the party," I said. "But Jeanne promised her baby-sitter she'd get home early."

Goodwin understood that impassiveness was one source of his good looks. He nodded again. As Jenny was making up the couch, I went to tell Jeanne about the arrangements. "It can't be the liquor," she said. "There hasn't been enough of it."

With a minimum of conversation Goodwin gathered Jeanne into her wrap and the two of them disappeared out the front door. In the kitchen, Josh and Ranchek were still laugh-

76

ing, and I interrupted them. "You have an overnight guest on your hands."

"Who's that?"

As I told him my story I could watch Josh's mind at work. "Jeanne lives a long way from Doug," he said. "It would be a whole lot easier for Ranchek to take her home."

"I'm sorry I didn't think of that," I said. "They've already left."

❦   ❦   ❦

The next morning I got up as the sun was rising and crept from the couch to the hall. The door to the back bedroom was closed, and Josh was snoring in a chair in the living room. Another day I would have stayed to put things right—scrape the dishes, empty the garbage, tear down the streamers, crumple the paper hats. Cleaning up was the best part of a party. That morning I only moved Josh's black shoes from in front of the door where he had kicked them. I slipped the latch quietly and made for my car, feeling as relieved as a housebreaker.

Southwesterly winds had rendered the morning spotless. There wasn't a trace of grime or yellow haze, and though I had left the Blacks in a welter of waste paper, the wider world had been polished overnight and set straight. In the clear light, braced by a fresh breeze off the ocean, I was tempted to forget last night and depend on things to fall into shape, as the whole outdoors had whistled itself clean.

Shortly past noon I was still resolved to do that, and I called Goodwin's rooming house only to thank him for seeing Jeanne home. A fellow boarder pounded on his door and got Goodwin to the hall telephone. He sounded sleepy. My thanks he accepted laconically.

"Did you like Jeanne when you got to know her?"

"Not much."

"She's getting married in a few months. You'll like her better then."

"Not everybody is as suspicious as you are," Goodwin said cheerfully. "Josh called early this morning and asked me to come to dinner Thursday night."

"You're going?"

"Never pass up a free meal. That's been my motto since—"

"Since puberty."

Goodwin laughed and said the hall floor was cold on his bare feet.

✠   ✠   ✠

Surveying the bar, Black made an elegant moue. "Why did you want to meet me here? I haven't been down on Main Street since the night we picked you up at the bus station."

"I was looking for a report at City Hall," I said, "and since you were going to be in town anyway—"

"That window hasn't been washed in ten years."

"Take a chair. I'll get our drinks."

It was half past seven on a week night, but the bar was already packed with pale men from downtown Los Angeles. Most wore stained rayon shirts or T-shirts with the sleeves cut off, revealing flaccid white flesh that may once have been brown muscle before alcohol and drugs went to work. In the corner two homely boys in Marine uniforms were drinking ginger ale. No talent scout, I was sure, had ever looked Josh over more professionally than the pack of men I was pushing past to get to the bar.

Our drinks were served in glasses crusted white, and the gin had been watered until drops of vermouth floated on top like oil slick. Their pimientos had been sucked from the olives, and they too rose disemboweled to the surface. "Drink up," I said. "You've had a hard week." I didn't know what I meant, and

Josh didn't ask. When he tossed off the drink I returned to the counter for two more.

The first round had been a fluke; the bartender had seen us come in and hurried over to serve me. Otherwise I had the usual difficulty in flagging waiters or barmen, and I pushed our glasses forward with a five-dollar bill, resigned to a long wait.

But a fat blond boy in dungarees watched me standing ignored for several minutes and he called, "Hey, Johnny! How about some service?"

Murmuring apologies, the young Spanish bartender hove to my place wiping his hands on his apron. When he stepped away for the martini shaker, the boy on the stool peered at me more closely. "You two vice?"

"What makes you ask?"

"The suits."

"We're not with the vice squad," I said.

"If you need somebody to show you around," the boy said, "I could do it." Something was tattooed across his fingers. Love, probably, and Hate, finer distinctions being limited by the number of knuckles.

"Thanks. We can't stay that long."

"Buy me a beer?"

I pushed the silver from my change over to him and returned to the table. Black was more relaxed. He had slung one arm over a third chair and his tie was loose. "You know what kind of a place this is?" he asked me.

"Does it bother you?"

"When I was in the Village before I was drafted, some of us in acting class used to stop at a bar like this next to the studio."

He finished his drink, and I found my spot at the bar next to the fat boy. It was worth a beer to have him roust the bartender. As he gave the call, I put coins by his glass. "Thanks," he said. "Your buddy's a lawyer, isn't he?"

"Why do you ask?"

"He's like a lawyer I know. Whatever he says, I can hear all the way over here."

I repeated his remark to Black, who raised his glass jovially and toasted the fat boy. "Careful," I said. "You'll have him at our table."

"Those people don't bother me," Josh said.

During the course of our fifth drink, a husky sailor in winter blues came in and sat at the bar directly in front of our table. His entrance caused a subterranean stir; heads turned and the men against the wall, though none moved, seemed to draw closer. The sailor himself was tall and black-haired, with a cap cocked at an angle that did not suggest innocence.

"You're no longer the prime attraction." It was sheer charity on my part, since, as he must have noticed, Josh's looks hadn't been agitating the other patrons. Taken with his arch manner, his softness might attract women, but men, or at least this sampling, were more aroused by the sailor's bluntness and swagger.

"I understand why they want him," Josh said. He was drunk. The first five martinis had missed him completely; the sixth found its target. "Every man wants to look like that. Every man wants to be more aggressive than he really is. There's nothing abnormal about admiring that."

"Men want to acquire manliness secondhand?"

"You mean does every man want to sleep with that sailor?" Josh asked indignantly. "Of course not."

"Would you?"

"Oh." With drunken care: "I have thought about it. I am not ashamed to say I have thought about something like that."

"Why haven't you then?"

"Nobody's asked me." He tried to say it brightly but his sophistication failed. "No, I'll tell you. I've thought about how it might feel to have a man like that put his arms around me. If he did it, maybe I'd feel protected instead of being the one who has to do the protecting. That's the part that gets me down, even with a woman like Jenny. All the time I'm the one who has to be strong. When she's strong, I don't like it. Then I've got to be even stronger to stop her from taking over. Don't let's get started on that again. It's just that sometimes it would be nice to lie back and let somebody hold me and reassure me. But it couldn't be a woman."

"Are you sexually attracted?"

"No," he said quickly. "Yes, in a way I am. Lying there together I'd like to touch the back of his neck. That's all. Touching it would make me feel safe. Believe me," he said fervently, "I don't always feel that way. It's something I've felt a few times, when there was more bearing down on me than I could take."

"Do you feel that way tonight?"

Josh looked at me suspiciously. "What would you think if I said yes? Would you think less of me?"

"Do you care?"

"No." He drained every drop of the weak gin. "I don't care. It's nothing to be ashamed of. Everybody has to let down once in a while."

It had become clear to the sailor that Black was talking about him, and he swung around on his stool to face us. I went up, said a few words and led him back to our table.

"Josh," I said, "this is Bill."

He was about thirty, with a strong body and a broad tanned neck. His uniform fitted tightly enough to outline his money belt, a smaller bulge than the fleshy roll hanging over the top of Black's trousers. Installed in the third chair, Bill did not volunteer much about himself. I asked routine questions which he answered with one word or two. Stationed? San Diego. Born? Texas. Navy? Fourteen years. Likes California? So-so. Married? Once. Divorced? Yes. Children? One boy. How old? Ten. Where? Fort Worth.

Black was finishing another drink and sponging up this

trickle of information with glassy admiration. When I leaned back depleted, the sailor thought to ask us what we did. Black told him about acting class in New York and about parts he had played in college.

Something in Josh's grandiose monologue touched the sailor's heart. He leaned across the table and talked intently about his own dream. He had always wanted to be an actor himself. People had told him he wasn't bad-looking. Here he paused and I let Black administer the ritual compliment. He was sure he had talent. But—

If his story was different from Robert Rorke's, it was only that his father had been the one who drank and ran away. Bill married young, a faithless wife, and enlisted in the Navy to support a child he wasn't sure was his. Listening to him, I wondered how the idea had taken hold that there were many ways to be unhappy.

As Josh and I were tapering off on the gin, Bill had emptied four bottles of beer. I brought him another in time to hear him telling Josh, "I've never done one thing in my life I wanted. My whole life has been a waste."

The time had come. To Josh I said, "I have to drive home now, but there's no reason for you to leave."

Black looked less flushed than he had been twenty minutes ago; his voice was steadier. He was sobering up. "No," he said, "I'm ready to go." Bill the sailor was slumped in his chair, lost in the great injustice.

"You're sure?"

"I'm sure."

He had stood up and was waiting impatiently while I went through my pockets for the car keys. "Let's go then," he said.

"In a minute." I had stayed behind with the thought of introducing the blond boy to Bill the sailor. But suddenly my sympathy was gone. I had succeeded in shaming Josh into saving his marriage, something that had seemed immensely important a few hours ago. At least now he wouldn't ask his wife to do for him what he refused to do for himself. He had made a decision. But why concern myself with these other men, who radiated lust without either courage or initiative? I walked out to where Josh was waiting on the sidewalk. He had made a choice. Let the rest of them rot in their studied, indifferent poses.

⚓   ⚓   ⚓

When Thursday night came, Josh greeted Goodwin cordially. He poured him a bourbon but took nothing for himself. They made polite conversation in the living room as Jenny fixed dinner and later while she saw to the washing up. Goodwin told me afterward the evening had been amiable, relaxed and too long by half.

It wasn't until I was writing these notes that I told Goodwin about the night on Main Street. With the passage of six years, his reaction could be eminently sensible. "What were you worried about?" he asked mockingly. "Nothing was ever going to happen with me and Jenny. I never go to bed with a woman when it's going to please her husband more than her."

⚓   ⚓   ⚓

Four days before the taping, Faye Tayne was replaced as the lead dancer of a television variety show. Robert Rorke professed to hate show business, and when I met them for dinner at a Malibu roadhouse, he was not treating Faye to the sympathy she expected. "You don't care. It's my life and you don't even care." Faye's teeth bowed slightly, a condition that made her smile full and glittering but also, since her lower lip couldn't cover the enamel, made pouting hard for her.

"You know these people," Rorke said. "They want one thing and when they don't get it, you're out. I don't know why you're surprised."

Faye was near tears, and yet I couldn't believe in her disappointment. "I eat nothing but lettuce and tomato," she complained. "Every day I get headaches from being hungry. And where is it getting me?"

"Give it up," Rorke said. "Get a job."

"Look at those crumbs." Faye pointed to flecks of brown crust spilling off Rorke's bread plate and then to the clean linen around me. "Everybody doesn't eat like a pig."

"Sorry," Rorke said brusquely.

"Did you see the fellow who parked your car?" I asked them. "He's a friend of mine."

I went on to tell them what I knew about Lonnie Chapman. Faye was impressed that he practiced celibacy. "He doesn't have anything to do with women?"

I waited for Rorke to question Lonnie's manhood, but he was absorbed in breaking a bread roll precisely over his plate.

"I really respect that kind of man," Faye said when I assured her that it took honest effort to keep Lonnie chaste.

"I'll tell him a beautiful girl admires his sacrifice."

"I do. Really. But when we leave and I'm getting into Robert's car, I know I'll pull my skirt a little higher."

"All women are whores," Rorke said idly.

"You've got butter on your chin."

"What's admirable about chastity?" By worrying an abstraction, I hoped to get us through dessert without more bickering.

"You have to be a woman to understand," Faye said. "From the time we're little girls we know that men want our bodies. When we find a man who doesn't, we wonder if he isn't the one who might really understand us."

I waited for Rorke to take coarse exception to what she was saying, but he sat spooning soup, feigning nonchalance, listening intently, encouraging Faye with his silence but very impatient, I felt, for her to stop. And Faye, speaking more earnestly than I had ever heard her, groped for each word, going slowly because she was trying her argument to herself before she risked it aloud. She was being totally sincere, and again what she said carried no conviction.

The sun was down on the parking lot when we came out, and the sky was churning with dark clouds. As we approached the stool in the driveway an unfamiliar boy in a red windbreaker jumped up for our tickets. "Where's Lonnie?" I asked. "Taking a break," he said, running for Rorke's new Porsche.

"What if your friend had been here?" Faye asked me. "Would you have tipped him?"

"That may be why he's gone. To spare me that dilemma."

"No man is that sensitive." As she said it, Faye must have known she would stir Rorke from his docile silence. Immediately he said, "Whoever's getting the car, I wish he'd snap it up. I've got to dump Faye at the club and get back to the office."

"Do you work at night often?" I put the question to Rorke, but Faye answered first. "Yes, he does," she said.

⚑　　　　⚑　　　　⚑

A friend at the Santa Monica Chamber of Commerce gave Ranchek three tickets to the Academy Awards ceremony that spring, and he invited me to share the bounty. Any fascination I'd had with Hollywood had cleared up with the end of my adolescence, but the event was being staged less than a mile from my apartment. I agreed to meet the Rancheks at the civic auditorium twenty minutes before starting time.

Ordinarily I wouldn't have taken that risk with Ranchek, who was inveterately late. I once waited on a corner in Beverly Hills for seventy-five minutes only to have him come huffing up, face screwed into insincere lines of worry, and moan, "My calendar stopped." During the years he had worked at the chamber office, he had been on time three mornings, and I was sure he had missed several jobs by coming late to the interviews. But Dawn was buying a gown especially for the occasion, and I trusted her to deliver him on time.

At the auditorium four hundred people were packed into bleachers flanking a dusty red carpet. Another crowd lined the drive that led into the parking lot. I stood outside, time running short and the Rancheks not arrived. From strategic points on the lawn huge searchlights were swinging to and fro. Each cast a beam that poured back into it, like milk raining in a bucket. Under the lights near the entrance actors were bounding from their cars, and whenever a celebrity was spied, the younger girls gave a dutiful squeal.

Not every guest could be famous, and the bleachers had suffered enough dashed hopes that when Ranchek and Dawn drove up in her blue sedan no one groaned at their effrontery. As an attendant took over the wheel, Ranchek extended a courtly arm and propelled his wife onto the red carpet. Around me knowing expressions said: *Somebody's nephew.*

Midway to the door, Ranchek stretched above the crowd and handed me a big pasteboard ticket. Rustlings of envy followed me through the guards and into the lobby where the Rancheks were waiting. Dawn had woven false tresses into her own long hair and piled the chestnut mass atop her head. The silk panels of her dress touched the floor, and her thighs rubbing together when she walked made the whisking sound of corduroy knickers. Ranchek's faddish outfit included a paisley bow tie and cummerbund.

"I didn't know you owned a dinner jacket, Ranchek."

He preened, an act I had never actually seen before. Swelling his chest, turning to half-profile, he sent his huge hands in delicate fluting motions down the length of his satin lapels. "Dawn bought it for me."

"I asked him to pick out something conservative that would

86

be in style a long time," she said, "and that's what he came home with. Still, he does look handsome, doesn't he?"

"As ever," I said. The truth was that Ranchek was getting paunchy where muscular men do, low on his chest rather than through the hips, and above his cummerbund bulged one round ball of hard fat. I remember wondering how this new lump fitted among Dawn's many curves. He had washed his dark hair and fluffed it to a semblance of its former thickness. Even with his unseasonable sun tan, though, he looked tired and worn and ten years older than twenty-five.

Our seats were in the third row from the back and far to the left, which guaranteed that unless an actress swung completely around to stare in our direction, we had no chance of seeing her face. All the same, both Dawn and Ranchek were agog, he looking somewhat sheepish, as they tried to identify their favorites from a distinctive hair style or jug ears.

"Remember this night, Ranchek," I said, "to tell your grandchildren."

"I never expected to partake in a spectacle known the world over," he agreed. "Little did I dream, ushering those many years ago at the Fox Long Beach, that one day I would be here, rubbing elbows with the great and near-great." He lunged, but Dawn got her elbow away in time.

"Don't you think he should have been an actor?" she asked me. "He'd be much better than Josh Black."

"No," said Ranchek sadly. "I do not have the inspiration. Mine would have been plodding performances that would lift me no higher than the level of—" He named two reigning geniuses of the British stage. "Gladly would I have suffered for art. Willingly would I have given up all I have, or ever hope to have, for one spark of the divine fire that lifts a man above the ruck and lets him commune, however briefly, with the mountain gods. But"—his voice sank—"it was not to be. I must go on, uninspired, unapplauded—"

"Unemployed," I added.

Tartly Dawn said, "Just one night don't bring that up, all right?"

"All right."

Two minutes before air time the television lights went on, and the auditorium pulsed with a new effulgence, as though lightning had struck and lingered. Even back where we were, people were sitting straighter and whispering more excitedly. Nothing in the next two hours could match the drama of that first minute.

On the way out, the public relations director at one of the studios, a man who stopped regularly at the newspaper office, hailed me. The three of us walked with him to the parking lot. When I introduced Ranchek he remembered the name. "Didn't you get my letter?" he asked. "Some time ago? We had an opening I wanted to talk over with you."

"No." Ranchek's broad face looked perplexed. "It must have gone to my old address."

"Let's have lunch one day anyway. You never know."

"Fine, fine," said Ranchek.

No single event made Ray Morella and me the unlikely friends we had become. When Jeanne Darling first coerced him into driving her to my apartment, he resented coming but worried that if he refused she would come alone. He was convinced all other men found Jeanne irresistible, and had I told him I could admire Jeanne's looks without being driven mad by them, he would either have thought I was lying or, if he believed me, he would have tried to knock me down.

In Jeanne's company neither Ray nor I had much chance to talk, but lounging together, listening to her, we grew closer. Ray's greeting became less grudging. Within a year he was punching my shoulder whenever we met.

Their wedding had been put off twice, once when Jeanne developed an ear infection, again when she pleaded general fatigue. For so spirited a woman, Jeanne suffered from an imposing collection of aches and complaints. She often had cotton wadded in an ear or a woolen scarf wafting medicinal odors knotted around her neck. Weeks at a time she coughed or wheezed in a way that would have discouraged a less dedicated talker.

If Jeanne's presence kept Morella necessarily quiet, his clothes in the Hollywood mode were far from subdued. Ray's were the first boots I ever saw on unabashedly urban feet. When everyone else was content with two-piece suits he was favoring vests of yellow silk. Later, fashion endorsed bright colors and he reverted to black and midnight blue. He cultivated sideburns below his earlobes, and he raised a mustache, both of which, I would have bet money, were twenty years out of date—and unlikely to be revived.

Despite the care he devoted to his appearance, Ray honored the gulf between our tastes and never poked fun at my shapeless gray suits and plain black shoes. He would not have considered asking my advice about a race at Santa Anita, but neither was he offended when Jeanne and I fretted over the state of the world without asking his opinion.

Sometimes Morella ran into me along Vine Street on my lunch hour with one or another pretty girl, and he liked the idea that I was his successor in a pursuit he had put behind him. One night while Jeanne dallied in the ladies' room of his restaurant he told me furtively about the time a starlet got drunk at the front bar and he had boffed her—or bounced, or bashed her, whatever slang was current that year—first in the wine cellar and again, twenty minutes later, in the business office. As Jeanne came toward us, he cut his story short. "She's so jealous, it's murder," he assured me. I took Jeanne's displays of jealousy as one of her small kindnesses.

Once or twice Jeanne had hinted that dubious money was

invested in Ray's restaurant and that one partner maintained his Chicago connections from more than nostalgia. It was widely believed in Los Angeles, though never proved, that businesses along the Strip were apt to be tainted. But when a question invites a lie, the fault lies with the question, and I never asked Morella directly. When Jeanne urged him to sell his third interest, I assumed she was worried about his reputation, possibly even his safety, although she may have been reacting only against the food, which was bad, or the garish decor.

Since I had been exposed only to Morella's affability, his dislike for Jeanne's son was hard to take seriously. One day at the office I broached the subject by remarking that the boy seemed polite and smart. "Smart?" Ray demanded. "You think that little weasel is smart?"

He pulled a chair to my desk and began to blacken the boy's character with adjectives that were strange to apply to a child of eight. His chief complaint seemed to be that Jeanne coddled him. "She doesn't have a son," he said. "She's got a toy. She spoils him rotten."

"Not exactly his fault."

"He lets her!" When I laughed, Morella was forced to join in. "You know what I mean. He sits back and takes it for granted that she's going to fuss over him and buy him everything he wants. He never considers her feelings."

Morella had his nails manicured each Friday, and they glistened when he drummed on the corner of my desk. "I'm jealous," he said. "Isn't that something? Jealous of a kid."

He was enjoying his confession, and I kept retyping an article so that the clatter of keys would frustrate Billy Stein as he tried to overhear from across the room. "You know why I'm jealous? I look at him and I picture his father, doing it with Jeanne—going in, and this kid coming out, and there he is like a—you know—and getting bigger all the time." Morella's innocent vulgarity failed him and he broke off and gestured helplessly with his shapely nails. "You don't know what I'm talking about."

"You have the theory backward. He's supposed to envy you."

"He doesn't envy nothing!" Morella was aroused again. "No matter what I say I can't get rid of him. He's around all the time. I'm never really bad to him because, you know, he's a kid. But wouldn't you think even a kid should understand when he's not wanted? Sometimes I want to be alone with Jeanne and there he is with an airplane model, dripping glue all over my shoes."

"He'll be easy to cope with once you're married."

"We're only getting married because of him," Ray said. "From the time I met Jeanne I've asked her to marry me, and she's held out and wouldn't do it. Now she's going along because she thinks it will be good for the kid."

"Why were you in such a hurry?"

"Have you got any idea how many other men were after her? She doesn't go with anybody else now, but when I met her she was getting a half-dozen proposals a day. All I could do was hang on and keep telling her how much I loved her. You'd have thought she'd get bored hearing it."

"If a woman isn't bored the first time," I said, "the repetition doesn't seem to bother her."

"Anyway, it worked," he said.

"So there's only one rival left."

"Who?" Before he could think to look fierce Ray looked frightened. "Who do you mean?"

"Sonny."

"Oh." He sighed. "I can handle the kid. I thought you meant she was already seeing somebody else."

"A man can't be cuckolded until he's married." If my reassurance left Ray dubious, I knew for a fact what rot I was talking.

🜋   🜋   🜋

91

My enthusiasm for the hunt was gradually reviving, and I appreciated the accessibility of girls around the beach, good-hearted girls who came home for the night and left with a kiss in the morning. But to scout a different girl each night took effort and time, and after a while I began to narrow the number.

"Some Saturday I wouldn't mind going to the movies." Fran was plucking a white thread from among my hairs. "But you never like anything that's playing."

"We'll see whatever you want."

"I wouldn't force you against your will," she said. "I'll find somebody else to take me. Brad?"

"Here, Fran."

"Would you rather marry a girl because you had the same taste in movies or in bed?"

"I go to the movies twice a year."

"I know. I'd like to go every night. Brad?"

"Still here, Fran."

"Nothing. I like to close my eyes and hear you answer me."

Georgia was another girl who kept her eyes closed against the early sun. "What am I thinking?" she answered me. "I'm pretending we're both seventy and we've been together fifty years. But I can't do it." Georgia was selfish only when she slept; in the morning the sheets and green blanket were always on the floor at her side of the bed. This day she was wrapped in my mattress cover. "I'd be seventy-six," I said.

Georgia's mournful face appealed to me. She came when I called, and when I didn't, she never asked why. Speaking of her that way, she sounds like a fantasy, except that she was too stolid—overweight by at least fifteen pounds.

"When you were six years old, I didn't exist," she said.

"That's right."

"At forty-five, you'll probably be lying in bed like this with a girl who isn't even born yet. Maybe this morning her

92

mother and father haven't even met, but twenty years from now you'll be sleeping with her."

"Maybe so." I stuck the idea away and lost track of the girl, but I go back sometimes to our conversation and then I praise Georgia for her generous imagination.

🏁   🏁   🏁

I was surprised that Lonnie Chapman should begin stopping at my apartment on the way home from his night shift at the parking lot. Without a car, hitchhiking down the coast could take an hour or more, and if my light was off he didn't stop. When he saw through the window that anyone was there, even Billy Stein, he ducked back down the stairs. He liked talking to only one person at a time.

My hours at the paper were flexible enough that if Lonnie wanted to stay until three in the morning I could let him. The range of topics on which he talked cleverly might be wearing, but he listened as aggressively as he spoke and he never repeated himself.

On nights I had brought a woman to the apartment, I could hear Lonnie climbing the stairs to the point where he could see if my lights were off. Retreating, he would be even more stealthy. The next night he'd say nothing about having come and gone, and I never mentioned hearing him.

In deference to his ulcer, I stocked buttermilk along with the beer for Doug Goodwin and the cola for Billy Stein. As he drank, Lonnie's glass left a trace of white mustache on his upper lip, while my teeth turned temporarily black from the red wine I drank. He would have preferred I not drink at all, since with every glass I was a little less respectful of his ingenious moral constructions.

I could seldom trick Lonnie into commenting on the day's events, but on the night of the President's murder he made a concession. "The worst part of a day like this," he said, "is the urge to make a judgment. I didn't want to kill today and I didn't. But as I heard the news I felt like saying that no one should kill. It was a hard feeling to resist."

"I understand," I said sympathetically. "Relax on one commandment and you'll be back to honoring your father and your mother."

"Start making rules and you're lost."

"Any man who wants to kill the President should do it?"

"I'm not interested in saying whether he should or shouldn't. Today I didn't want to kill anyone. That's as much as I want to say."

It continued to confuse me that for all his resolute tolerance, Lonnie's sympathy was strained by the frailties of his friends. One night I heard an engine roaring and sputtering directly below my window, then a clamor and my name shouted up. Billy Stein, in goggles and a white crash helmet, was dismounting from a powerful motorcycle. Lonnie in his red nylon windbreaker had just climbed off the back.

Across the street three tough youngsters were peering out from behind the dirty glass in a deserted storefront where they had been camping. Lost in admiration for Billy's machine with its immense capacity for making noise, one boy cast his first shy smile at me.

Billy was patting the flank proudly. "What do you think?"

"He's wanted one since junior high school," Lonnie said. "His folks got him a cello instead."

"I used to wear my leather jacket to orchestra practice." Now Billy was stroking the seat. He straightened the mirrors and wiped imaginary dust off the reflectors. "This means Margo can have the car for shopping."

"It's a present for your wife?"

"She hasn't seen it. I got it after work and drove right to Ventura to open it up. On the way back I stopped for Lonnie."

"My neighbors are paying you their greatest compliment," I said. "They're trying to figure out how to steal it."

"You should get yourself one," Billy said. He jumped on its starter and raced like a trick cyclist around a small space between the parked cars. "You handle it well," I said when he skidded to a stop at the toe of my shoe.

"I've got to go." Waving a jaunty goodbye, Billy tore up the alley toward a cold dinner and his wife. Lonnie and I sat on the curb. "In another three years," Lonnie predicted, "Billy will be taking flying lessons. He'll have a quarter interest in an airplane and on weekends he'll fly down to someplace in Baja. People think that men who do things like that are bored, but it's their wives who are bored, wouldn't you say?"

"I don't speculate on the sex life of my friends."

"They speculate on yours."

I didn't have an answer then, but a week or so later, Ranchek blundered along and administered Lonnie's comeuppance. Ranchek seldom met my more recent friends; I had decided after one evening with Robert Rorke and Doug Goodwin that friends are best kept on short tether. One night, though, Ranchek showed up while Lonnie was midway through his second glass of milk, and I had to introduce them.

"Sitting around splitting heresies?" Ranchek had been experimenting with tequila and Mexican beer. As he lurched around the room, belligerently convivial, fetid billows of that mixture hung over him. Convinced that they were safe in their separate orbits, I had told Ranchek about Lonnie's sacrifices, and he took them up now with bearish good will.

"I have perfected a drink made with cherry brandy and bitters," he said. "You toss one down every time you don't go to bed with a woman. A celibation, I call it."

"When a man gives up women," I said, "other men should encourage him. One less competitor. But instead it's insults, isn't it? Or jokes?"

Lonnie shrugged and Ranchek had fallen back into a contented musing. "My faith taught me," he said seriously, "that men may sin in thought as well as deed. But I see tonight that it never specified in whose thought the sin had to take place. If I imagine someone else committing a crime, my thought can equal his deed." He looked hard into Lonnie's face. "I am going to picture you performing obscene acts with Rosie of the Third Place," he said. "She was a prostitute near our camp." Ranchek turned to me. "You must remember Rosie?"

"Barely."

"All right then." Ranchek closed his eyes. "There's Rosie walking into the bedroom behind the bar. It's the old shed that used to be a chicken coop, and the wallpaper doesn't cover the cracks in the wood. It's May, but a chill wind penetrates the slats and gives Rosie gooseflesh as she takes off her dress—the purple silk one with no back."

Ranchek collapsed against the couch and let his head loll with passion against the wall. His hair oil will leave a grease spot, I thought, unless his balding patch has enlarged since last I looked. But even tonsured, Ranchek will sweat himself into the plaster.

"Now you're approaching her." His eyes were still closed. With my own weak imagination, I couldn't understand how other people summoned up sharp pictures and arranged them to their taste. Not even four years had passed, but I had only fleeting impressions now of a face I had expected to remember.

Since Lonnie was smiling faintly, I let Ranchek go on. "She's stepped out of her—"

"Ranchek," I said, "a detailed narration isn't necessary."

He was feigning a trance or a religious vision and didn't permit himself to hear. "Now!" he exclaimed. "Oh, my God, no!" Ranchek began to writhe with embarrassment. "You can't do that to her. She's too small, too frail. No, stop it! Fight, Rosie! That's right! Kick him! Harder! Oh, sweet Mother of God, this is awful!"

Ranchek flayed out with both arms. After a moment, eyes

96

still shut, he drew himself up, calmed his heaving chest and said softly, "There's only one way to end this carnage." He turned his face from Lonnie and whispered in the direction of the door, "I'm sorry to ask this of you, but he's become a raging beast. Yes, yes, you'd better unhook it. That's right. I knew you could get his attention."

"Now, slowly, slowly. That's better. Get out of here, Rosie, while you have a chance. Good girl! All right, Dawn, the more you cooperate, the sooner this ordeal will be over for all of us. That's right. A little more movement there. And there."

I shut my own eyes while Ranchek murmured encouragements to Dawn. A disheveled girl ran through my mind weeping and clutching a purple dress. She vanished, leaving behind the vague sense that I should be in the bathroom laying out clean towels.

"Ah," Ranchek sighed slowly. "Finished, are you? What? What did you have the gall to ask me? No, it would certainly not be all right. No, once is more than enough for your kind." He popped open his eyes and regarded Lonnie sternly. "I sincerely hope that you have learned your lesson."

Lonnie had no idea that Dawn was Ranchek's wife; he nodded calmly. I was less relaxed, and it was to cover my unease that I said, "Well, Ranchek, did she enjoy it?"

"Oh, you know women," he answered languorously. "With them it never lives up to expectation."

　　　　　※　　　　　※　　　　　※

In the fall of that year, Josh Black's service to the Valley college was rewarded with a promotion. Buildings, completed on schedule, had been flung across the grounds, and the library already overflowed with books. To protect these new investments, the trustees established a full-time security force with Black as captain and a squad of students under his command.

"If you work days," I said when he called to tell me, "how will you make the rounds in Hollywood?"

"I'll get Sunday and Monday off. If something really good came up, I could always get away for a few hours."

"I hope the money is better." In the Army we had known from the insignia on each arm who drew ninety-six dollars a month or one hundred and twenty. One mark of the passing years was an increasing reluctance to discuss money. That first civilian year everyone volunteered from habit how much he made and spent, but gradually our candor disappeared until I had no accurate idea of what Doug Goodwin earned or Black was paid.

"Yes, more money. You single men don't know how much a wife, two children and a dog can eat." Jenny had given birth that year to the second child they had been dreading, but, in a complete reversal, the infant boy had become the center of Black's life. He took to saying that he had never felt himself fully a man until he sired a son.

"What does Jenny say about the new hours?"

"That I'll have more time at night for little-theater work."

"True enough."

"I'll be wearing a uniform again." Black wanted to sound blasé, but he had rejoiced in his Army khakis, the only one among us who kept them mended and meticulously pressed.

"Olive drab?"

"Blue, with gray shoulder patches."

"What about a weapon?"

Black laughed richly. "I don't know how things were in the Ivy League," he said, "but in California very few of your desperate criminals enroll in college."

☙ ☙ ☙

The first time Doug Goodwin disappeared, I had been in Los Angeles about ten months. One day I called his

boardinghouse and the manager said that the previous Friday
night Goodwin had paid his bill, packed his clothes in the
trunk of his car and driven off without a word. I assumed that
somewhere in the Valley a girl was pregnant and Goodwin
would lie low until she found a doctor or a husband.

It had happened in France when a secretary at the camp, a
Parisian girl with finely molded breasts, had come to Goodwin with her bad news. He had whistled through his teeth the
rest of the day and applied the next morning for a two-week
leave to Munich. The day the girl found out he was gone she
boarded the overnight bus to Paris and returned to her family.
I could never speak of her after that to Goodwin; he managed
to imply that I disapproved of his conduct, which was true,
and that of all sins, censoriousness was worst.

But in this instance my suspicions misled me. Within a week
he sent a post card from a rural route in Tennessee to say that
he had felt the itch to return to his family's farm. Since his
father was ailing, he thought he might stay on a few weeks.
Lester, the shop foreman who had driven out with him,
would be heading back in a day or two because he had a wife
and child waiting in Glendale.

Over the years that pattern repeated itself a half-dozen
times as Goodwin threw over his job, his room, and his current woman to drive two nights and a day to Tennessee. I
tried to predict when his flight was due, but I found no sure
signs. Twice he went in the spring, and I decided he was
drawn by the fragrance of loam, or whatever dirt the farms
in those hills squat upon. The next time he left in December.
My second guess was that he quit whenever he stood at the
brink of a promotion, but my indirect questions didn't turn up
any evidence.

On each trip Goodwin took with him a different young
man, a co-worker from the factory, men three to five years
younger than he, often married, with wives who might hate
Goodwin but shared their husband's fascination with him.

He made an unlikely piper; at least I detected little joy or music to him. But he did offer his low-keyed resentment, and a fatalism that might have scared the boys away if it hadn't been offset by his rueful smile. In Goodwin's company, young men of few adventures could believe that their own world was mean, not so much evil as inadequate. They came to think that by fleeing now, jumping into a car at midnight with a case of beer open on the back seat, a man in this mediocre age could still set sail for lands where life would be less commonplace. Goodwin never represented Tennessee as such a land. His unspoken promise lay in the long urgent drive. Somewhere over those miles of flat road a sign would appear, an answer would reveal itself. But he said only that he was about ready to take a ride back home.

One morning he rapped on my door at three o'clock and invited me to join him on the trip, and I understood the full power of Goodwin's appeal. "Come on along," Goodwin said. "It will do you good. You've been working too hard."

A clean-cut boy was already in the car—Gordy from the plant—enough like Goodwin to be his brother. He waited nervously, afraid to be going, terrified to say no.

I rubbed my eyes to assure myself that in another minute I would be safe in my bed. No. I shook my head. No, I would not be driving across the country, not this night, never this way, in the middle of the night, with thirty dollars in my pocket. I shut the door, angry with Goodwin for my feeling that I had failed a test.

꿈　　　　꿈　　　　꿈

When Robert Rorke brought Faye to the beach on a Saturday, she kept on her dark glasses, and I peered at her face when I had the chance. There were traces of dark flesh on her right cheekbone. "You've got a black eye." I hadn't seen one since Goodwin's fight in the Army, very few before that, and none on a woman.

"A bedlamp fell on me."

I accepted her story because I had never really believed that men hit women. In books and movies they might, but only when they were the weaklings of the story; I could imagine Josh Black hitting any woman, except Jenny. In paperbacks the photographers left around the newsroom, quarrelsome men like Rorke struck only nymphomaniacs and spies.

By the next week the swelling was down and the discolored skin hardly showed beneath Faye's makeup. I was tempted to ask again what had happened, to see if she remembered to tell the same story. But since she had been considerate enough to lie, I said, "Faye, you look better than ever."

Ranchek called in January every year on the day I had arrived in Los Angeles. Some years my only reminder that time had passed came when I picked up the telephone and heard Ranchek's muffled voice: "This is Señora la Reina de Los Angeles calling. At the sound of the tone, you have been sheltered in my bosom four years. Bong."

Bong. The rest of the day it rang ominously in my head. On a sheet of rag paper, feeling uncomfortably like Robert Rorke, I added up the number of words I had written over those years: nine hundred and sixty thousand, which divided out to three cents per word. I counted the women: fewer, more expensive.

In those four years Josh and Jenny Black had produced two children, the Steins one son. Over those fifteen hundred nights Ranchek and Robert Rorke had been true to one woman and Lonnie Chapman to the vows he had embraced instead. Only Goodwin and I drifted from woman to woman.

I called my body to account. But with its arguments necessarily filtering through my mind, I found myself, like every censor, cutting out the best of them. Until the body protested: Let me defend myself but not with your words. With my sense of touch, with impulses that jump from my fingertips to spark and die in the air, or ignite the flesh.

Remember my abrasions, my balance when I have held back but can no longer, when something slips but is not gone, when every nerve joins the clenching back and pushing forward, when my legs are heavy, my neck sore, but their aching is submerged for the instant I am living in my slippage. Talk of that time when your control is gone and nothing, no effort of will, no fears or prior promise, can stop my rushing jet of life.

Even as I record this protest, the body scorns it. Words again? Where are the sensations? On paper I am losing a debate I never lose in bed. You pretend to be fair but the words insist on putting a question: For what? That question is never heard on those nights you abdicate to me. For what? It is your revenge, that question. For what? Ask me the next time I bring you to my threshold. Ask, if you can, at the instant I am opening the door for which you have no other key. You will have your answer then. For what? For this.

Seeing the Rancheks at least once a week, I missed any subtle changes in their life together. By my reckoning, Dawn was still unnaturally considerate of Ranchek. When she was sharp with him, her reproaches were mild compared with what he deserved.

Ranchek exhausted every implausible excuse, but at last he went off to lunch with the publicity director we had met months before. Impatient for the outcome, Dawn left work early the day of the interview, and she was already at the apartment when I arrived. Ranchek had locked himself in the shower, she said, and nothing he shouted through the door made sense.

"What's your guess?" I asked. Dawn linked her thumbs and held up eight crossed fingers. "A job is open at the studio," I said. "An editor at the paper knows the man who quit."

As Dawn was pouring a beer for me, Ranchek staggered from the bathroom. In his white terry cloth robe, he looked like a polar bear. "Hello," he said hollowly. "How are you today?"

"Never mind me. Has the long drought ended?"

Ranchek began making parched noises. In dismay I appealed to Dawn. "Tell us," she said firmly.

"First of all," I asked, "were you on time?"

"Give or take a few minutes. Mr. Carter apologized for going ahead and ordering his lunch without me." When Ranchek forced his brown eyes wide, the ingenuousness was meant to suggest total recall.

"What did you wear?" Dawn asked. "Your new gray suit?"

"Not entirely," said Ranchek. "Just before I left, I got toothpaste on the jacket. So I wore the gray pants with my blue blazer."

"That blazer you had in the Army, Ranchek? You could hardly get into that coat four years ago. It must fit like a tattoo."

"Those restaurants are dark," Dawn said. "It wouldn't matter."

"Did you have a drink?"

"Mr. Carter was just finishing his second gimlet. He told me to go ahead but I said no."

"You told him you didn't believe in drinking at lunch."

Ranchek looked balefully at me. "Of course I didn't."

"Let him go on," Dawn said.

"How did he broach the subject?"

"He said he understood from my résumé that I had majored in public relations in college. He wanted to know why I left my job with the chamber. I said I wanted to diversify."

"That's good," Dawn said. "They never check references. Even at the bank we don't always do it if we need a girl fast enough. We let the bonding company worry about her."

"At least, Ranchek, you won't have to be bonded for public relations."

"I would be happier in a society that required the same safeguards for its promises as for its property."

Dawn said, "Did he talk to you about money?"

"Not directly," Ranchek answered. "In ordering lunch, I joked that I knew from the trade papers what a bad first quarter the studio had had, so I wouldn't order steak."

"He laughed?"

"Chuckled, more, I would say. It was a pleasantry I might have foregone if I had known he had ordered the filet mignon."

"Yes," I said. "Did you at any time during the interview spill your water glass into his lap? Criticize the amount he left as a tip? Back into his car on your way off the lot?"

"No," said Ranchek, pretending to think. "No. No."

"Did he say he would call you?"

"If anything turns up."

"I'll bet you've got the job," Dawn said. "I'll bet you'll be hearing from him next week that they want you to start the first of the month."

"That would be nice," Ranchek said.

※　　　　　　※　　　　　　※

To call on their son, Lonnie Chapman's parents breached the several barriers that separate Brentwood from Venice Beach, and their two-hour visit left him shaken. He hurried around the corner as soon as they left. "My God, they're sly," he said. "I can't let my guard down for a minute."

"Tears? Threats?"

"Smiles. Praise. Encouragement." Staring past me with a look of hatred, he burned like a bush, with his own fuel and tinder. "My mother," he said, "told me all the bad news about my cousins. Which one is getting divorced, which one lost his money on a car franchise. As though their bad luck should make me happy."

"It did."

"Of course it did. And she could tell. She wanted to see if I was getting anywhere with what I'm trying to do, and she saw that I wasn't. She left happy. Then my father delivered his money-isn't-everything speech, and by the time he finished, we were all agreeing that there isn't anything else in life. They know exactly how to get me."

"They've come before."

Describing Lonnie I reach instinctively for easy zoological similes though they give a distorted picture. Stalking the four corners of my room now, he was mostly but not entirely feral, as though the grizzled head of a piano virtuoso had been grafted onto a wolf.

"I listened to myself today," he said. "My father was saying something that was supposed to be encouraging, but it wasn't what he said. I heard his voice. It sounded just like mine. I looked at him, where he's gone bald in front—here." Lonnie pulled at his own thick hair, "And it's the same place I can see my own hair coming out. I can go through the next twenty years trying to live so my life means something to me, and one drop of his bitter white juice cancels out everything I do and makes me one more bald, greedy old man. That's the most I can ever be. Before I was even there to argue, he had it all arranged. He could be generous today because he knows that I'm knocked up. I'm pregnant. With his seed. He can sit back and watch himself growing inside me."

Have I remarked that humor wasn't Lonnie's primary endowment? The lack is harder to detect in an intelligent man because the world's incongruities keep him smiling. But I had learned that Lonnie did not take well to joking and, tempted though I was, I made no comment on this hysterical pregnancy of his.

I was reminded of an afternoon when Ranchek had been on the verge of a similar tirade. The subject of friendship had come up, and I was saying that we exercise as little choice in our friends as our families. We take up with the man at the next desk or the family that moves next door, and since we show so little enterprise, the people we collect testify less to our taste than our indolence. "Our friends," I remember saying, "are not necessarily those people we like best."

Ranchek had been listening without enthusiasm. "Dawn says friends are just substitutes for a husband or a wife. Dawn says that they're only important until a person gets married. Dawn says no married man needs a friend."

Dawn had said none of those things. Ranchek liked to quote her as saying things that were patently untrue until his listener would exclaim, "What nonsense!" That allowed Ranchek to sigh deeply and murmur, "I know and you know, but try telling Dawn."

On this particular day Ranchek had continued blithely. "It used to confuse me that a boy's best friend could be both his dog and his mother." He paused. "Until I saw that if the mother is a bitch—"

"Under the law, Ranchek, your mother deserves equal time."

"She had twenty-one years." He sounded embittered, and I had to make a hasty calculation. After the years of backtracking and sidestepping, did I want to encourage Ranchek to unburden himself? Was I obliged to hear him out? I was still debating when I felt myself grin unpleasantly. "Squeak, Ranchek," I heard myself saying, "squeak, squeak, squeak."

"If you pull the curtains that fast," he admonished me, "they flap together at the middle of the screen and raise dust."

That afternoon there would be no squeaking away from Lonnie's disclosures. He described his father's success in the television repair business, a rather average case history that he repeated unmercifully, making me glad my own parents were safe in their graves. Whatever my future troubles, I was without living relatives to blame for them. My only family now would be wife and children. With that thought my self-congratulation ended. To myself I said: I should have had the wife I wanted.

Lonnie had disposed of his father and passed to the Steins. "You haven't seen Margo in some time," he said.

"She's invited me. I've been busy."

"Do you expect to see her soon?"

Why let him hand me orders so hygienically? "Would you like me to?"

Lonnie had not permitted himself to sprawl on the couch as he usually did. Perhaps, for some increment to the spirit, he had resolved to sit forever straight. "I saw Margo a few days ago," he said. "There's something she's been wanting to say to you. If she can't, she'll probably tell me."

"Ask me to see Margo," I said.

"I won't ask you to do anything. If you want to, you will."

"No games, you said. But you're trying to push me forward like a pawn."

"Knight." Lonnie's hard teeth were even whiter than his nocturnal skin. "A year ago I would have said bishop."

🃏   🃏   🃏

So it happened that on a vivid Saturday morning in January I passed through the gates of an amusement park with a plump brunette at my side and a small boy toddling ahead of us. Billy Stein had arranged these passes for his family, but when he was sent to Sacramento on short notice, he asked me to spare Jacob disappointment by taking him and his mother to Anaheim.

In the middle distance the spires and turrets of a miniature castle rose up gray and gold. To our right the approximation of a Swiss mountain loomed over us, tunneled, like the cheese, with dark round holes. To get our bearings we strolled around a Western town complete with horse-drawn streetcars and soda parlors where the saloons should have been. Jacob gripped his mother's hand and inspected the mock village disapprovingly. "I've never been here," I told Margo. "I hope Jacob likes it."

"Forget Jacob." It was the first thing she'd said since I picked them up at their new house in the Valley. Saying it, she gave the boy a tug to keep up.

Gusts of winter wind were rounding out the cuffs of my trousers and pressing Margo's peasant skirt against her thighs. Above us banners and tridents flapped and wound down their poles and then stuck straight out again, like tongues. In the sunshine my sweater felt warm. When we stepped into a shadow cold breezes were lurking there to frisk us.

I had been warned about the long lines for each ride, but we were early and had our free choice. Jacob spotted the jungle boats and pulled us toward them. We boarded the lead boat and established ourselves alone at the rear. We had barely set off down the siltless brown waters before Margo said, "I'm twenty-one."

"I remember your birthday." The boy was on my lap, toying with the boat's artificial rudder.

"The first time I came to this place I was fifteen." Margo's voice for a second was eager and girlish. "Our whole class drove on buses the week after it opened. If anybody had told me that day I'd be back six years later, married and with a three-year-old kid, I would have laughed in his face."

At the front of the boat, the guide pretended to steer a wheel, though we were coasting smoothly on steel tracks beneath the water. Through his microphone he promised us a voyage across the great rivers of the world. Margo raised her voice to talk over him. "At fifteen I was sure everything was going to change by the time I was eighteen—the day I was legally a woman. Everything I didn't know at fifteen I'd have learned by that birthday."

She had begun without a preamble and I was apprehensive. "The things I didn't like about myself, that worried me," she said, "they would have disappeared. The way I wanted to bite the twats off all the sweet blond girls in my class. The way I wanted to make them scream with pain, those prissy mouths with just the right amount of lipstick. Those feelings would be gone when I was eighteen. Without any effort from me. On that day I'd grow up and be a woman. It had to happen because I knew nobody else felt the way I did. No woman could possibly feel that mean and bitter. Being angry all the time at fifteen didn't count because it had to end."

We had rolled into a cove with a herd of make-believe elephants that splashed and trumpeted as our boat circled them. Jacob had slipped away from me while Margo was talking and sat across the boat, his eyes half-closed like a narcotized commuter. "He's too young to enjoy this," I said, though his face looked shriveled and old.

Margo ignored us both. "That same year," she said, "when I was fifteen, I had a dream about my father. Except, the way dreams are, he wasn't really my father, he was my uncle or a stranger. But I knew him. I had made him cry and I was crying with him and drying his face on my blouse. For a long time afterward I thought about that dream.

"I made up a story about it. Lying in bed before I went to sleep I'd imagine calling him from a telephone booth. I'd disguise my voice and tell him how I had seen him on the street and wanted to get to know him better. I'd ask him to come to a motel I had picked out on Sunset Boulevard. I'd be there already with the lights off. He'd come and screw me and go away without knowing who it was.

"You were never fifteen, were you?" Margo didn't pause

long enough for me to take offense. "It's a funny age. I knew he'd like doing it with me. But I knew if he found out who I was, he wouldn't. So that proved to me that some kind of regulator was going to be put into me when I grew up. I might want the same things, but the reasons for not doing them would stop me. I'd be in charge of myself. I'd have control."

We were passing under a waterfall when the boat began to spin in the rapids. "Pull the rudder! Pull!" the guide shouted at us from the bow. I knew it was a prop connected to nothing and our dangers had been programmed by computer, but I pulled the rudder and the boat righted itself. We headed for calm water.

"The next year my father died." Margo, determined to finish, hadn't even noticed our predicament. "It was too early for me to lose him. I hadn't broken away enough before he was gone and I was left standing there. Then Billy came along and took me out a few times. I married him."

Margo reached out for Jacob and set him down hard on his cushion. "There I was. Eighteen, married, pregnant. You can't be more of a woman than that. But nothing had changed. I still had the same ugly feelings. I walked down the street wanting to hit old women in the face or pull a man's hair and kick him in the balls. I said to myself that I wouldn't feel that way when the baby was born, but I did. Then I said I couldn't still feel that way when I was twenty-one. But I do."

She had gathered Jacob in her arms and I helped her off the boat. We left the jungle and walked to a drawbridge that led to a land of fairy tales. As we crossed the moat, the whirling colors on the other side forced even Jacob to open his jaded eyes. Mammoth pink teacups, each big enough to hold four children, were spinning around and up and down as a calliope piped a wild tune. "Heads down in your cup!" a male voice called to the riders. "Keep your head down in your cup!"

A huge snout careened toward us, a dog, capering on two

human legs and pushing his yellow muzzle through the crowd of children. By that time I knew Jacob wouldn't cry, but I reassured him anyway. "That's Pluto," I said. "Lord of the Underworld."

Jacob watched the animal skeptically, and when Margo released her hold, he darted to another boat, in the shape of a giant swan. We went after him for another trip around the world, this time gliding into a dark tunnel. Margo tried to talk, but she was defeated by shrill noises from every side. Hundreds of dolls had been wired to sing about the smallness of the world, and at each bend on the waterway their racket grew louder, the metallic voices more piercing.

Luminous figures popped up from ambush and squealed good will toward men. Painted Dutch faces wailed of mutual understanding while Hawaiian dolls in straw skirts swayed to an ultrasonic screech. Tolerance! The dolls screamed for it. Brotherly love! A nightmare, a cacophony, and a fair approximation of the world it was celebrating. I understood why the electorate has never entrusted nuclear weapons to a sensitive man.

As the last shattering platitude faded behind us, we jumped from the swan and made for an overhead cable car that ran the length of the park. We were in a basket high off the ground when Margo took up her refrain as though she had never been interrupted. "It must have been easier when girls weren't supposed to know anything," she said. "If my grandmother could have arranged a husband for me, Billy would have been the man she'd pick. Then if I had been disappointed, I could have blamed her. But were girls disappointed then? They didn't know any better. Nobody promised them an orgasm every night."

"I'm Billy's friend." Waiting for a chance to say it, I had felt virtuous; saying it, silly.

"I'm not talking about Billy," she said. "I'm talking about everybody." The wind ruffled her short bangs and gave me indecent glimpses of her white forehead. "What if I had been taught that no woman enjoys sex? I'd have got married thinking it was repulsive. Girls like that were relieved when their husbands left them alone. They didn't walk down the street wondering how that man would be, or how she could get him into bed."

"They had other problems."

"I'm twenty-one," she said. "Do you know how many men have asked me out in my life? Three. Do you know how many have kissed me, not counting my uncle or those kissing games when I was a girl? Two. One man has fucked me, and I had to marry him to get that."

Clamped to her knees, Jacob was staring ahead of us to the huge plaster mountain. The cable for our basket stretched through its topmost opening, and as we passed inside, the air was cold. In the gloom I caught glints from the double track of the toboggan ride. A carload of children whizzed past below us and vanished through a jagged hole near the mountain's base. Their screaming died away slowly.

"One man," Margo repeated. "That would make my mother proud. The only man who ever touched me was your father. She's never said it, but that's the way she thinks. To me, it means that only one man ever wanted to touch her. That's the difference. Women her age could think every man on earth wanted to screw them. How can I believe that? Look at my husband's friends, too pure to fuck a friend's wife —one of them sworn off women altogether. But that makes Lonnie easier to be around. I don't hate him the way I hate the rest of them—coming over to eat and talk and never grabbing my ass in the kitchen."

"Do his friends appeal to you?"

In her round white face the eyes were dense as coal. "No," she said. "But who else? I hear about women going down for the milkman. I get our milk at the supermarket. When we moved last year, a man was coming to put in the phone, and before he got there I spent an hour fixing myself up. At nine o'clock in the morning I was putting on eye shadow. Then he came and he was ugly."

"Does that matter?" I didn't really want to ask. I wanted her to be quiet. I wanted her to be happy, but if that was impossible I wanted her to be still.

"Some days it wouldn't matter who the man was. If I could lie in a dark room, the way I pictured it with my father, and the door opened and I couldn't see who it was and he fucked me and left while the lights were still off, then I wouldn't care who it was. Those are the nights I'm burning up. You can say that sounds stupid but it's what happens to me. I get a burning between my legs, or more like a twitching. Even if Billy is there, when he's finished I can still feel it. Those are the nights I'd like to have thirty men lined up outside the door. I wouldn't care what they looked like if they could make the burning stop."

We had reached the platform at the other end of the cable. A pretty blonde in a red vest unlatched the door to our car. "Hello," she said, "are you having a nice time today?"

"What the fuck do you care?" Margo said. The girl ran to the next car.

During the elevator ride to the ground, Margo was silent. Jacob hadn't seemed to listen to his mother, and I wondered if he had heard it all before, when Margo gossiped with girl friends in her apartment building. But now Margo had moved to a house, and she hated other women, and she had no friends.

We walked to the rocket to the moon, our ersatz family drawing smiles from the other tourists, particularly the older women. I'm not married, I wanted to tell them. And if I were, my wife would be blond and slim and poised and elegant, and our child wouldn't scowl. If I were married, my marriage would be perfect.

Inside the rocket we were seated around a circular screen

113

sunk in the floor. As I fidgeted in the half-light, waiting for the cone to fill with other passengers, Margo said, "A few months ago, the man at the gas station asked me where I lived, something like that. He could have been making conversation, I couldn't be sure. I got nervous in case he didn't mean anything and thought I was taking it wrong. So I was nasty to him.

"Then at home that night I was angry for not at least finding out his name. Billy was working late and I called the station. All I could do was describe the man and say I thought he had short-changed me. Whoever I talked to said he didn't know the man's phone number or even how to spell his last name. I was sure he was lying and he knew what I wanted. The next morning they'd all be talking about the sex-starved cunt who called at ten o'clock in a sweat to get laid. I didn't go back to that place. It's never happened anyplace else."

"Margo, why are you telling me?"

She looked away, her voice was vindictive. "It's good for you," she said.

Our seats quaked to simulate blast-off, and Jacob leaned forward to watch the window on the capsule floor. The Earth, streaked and pitted, took shape below us and shrank slowly to the size of a fist. Then amid jolting and the dimming of lights, a guide informed us that the capsule had reversed itself and the cold surface rushing at us from the screen was the moon.

"Think about the good things in your life," I whispered, hoping that if I made that point now she would be more cheerful for the ride home.

"Dancing was good," she answered hoarsely. But when I encouraged her to say more, she stared at her feet. On the screen, our descent had begun and the Earth reappeared.

I tried one final time as we walked from the rocket to an enclosure of miniature cars. "If you miss dancing you should go back to it."

"Look at me!" Margo said impatiently. "I weigh twelve pounds more than before the baby, and I was too fat then. I could know exactly how to do a step, feel it with my whole body, see myself doing it better than any of the other girls. From the second I pictured it until the second I took the first step I was perfect. Then everything was wrong and I was the fat girl again, making a fool of herself."

"Sometimes you must have done it right."

She handed Jacob her purse to hold. Folding her arms across the top of the fence she leaned gracefully into the wire mesh. She may have struck the pose to reassure herself. For the first time I could imagine her at a ballet bar.

"When I did it right, it was the best time of my life."

Margo's face, after all, was a girl's face and her body, plump as it was, made a beguiling outline as she hung on the fence. "It didn't matter then that my father was dead or that no boy asked me out or that I had married the first boy who did. If I had one good pass, nothing in the world mattered except my body. Not me or what I felt, only my body and the beautiful forms it was making."

She fell back from the fence and we retraced our steps to the Western town. "I can feel it when someone else gets it right," Margo said. "The ballet, when it came last spring, Billy was working late and I went by myself on opening night. After it was over, I left the theater thinking that if life could always be the way it was that night I'd never have to dance. Or do anything. I could sit and watch forever and be happy."

"Start dancing again."

"Sure," Margo said.

In silence we steered Jacob to a merry-go-round. He allowed himself to be hoisted atop a wood stallion and cantered around the hall. Duty done, we found my car in the acres of others and got on a northbound lane of the Santa Ana Freeway for the drive back to Los Angeles. Margo wanted to hear a song that was popular that year and she punched relentlessly at the dial of the car radio until, as we entered the four-level interchange, she caught its last eight bars.

⚜ ⚜ ⚜

I had impressed on Ranchek how disturbed I would be if my other friends heard I was writing about their marriages. The more I cautioned him the more impatient he became to betray my secret. He concocted an excuse to call Jeanne Darling, whom he hardly knew, and give her a lurid account of what I was writing. She sped over the same rainy evening.

"Why didn't you tell me?" She pecked my cheek as she threw down her wet raincoat.

"It's something I'm compiling for myself," I said. "It wasn't worth mentioning."

"George Ranchek says you've got my pills and the stomach pump in it."

"I guess I might. I'm not showing it to anyone." Jeanne was tugging at the spiral notebook in my hand. When I surrendered it, she flipped unerringly to the first page on which she figured. "You've used my name!" she cried.

"If I ever type it, even for myself, I'll change the names. I'll call you"—I paused as though trying and rejecting several possibilities—"Jeanne Darling."

"Not bad."

Throughout the sixties Jeanne had worn contact lenses, though she lost them every few months or washed them down the bathroom drain. When the insurance company canceled her policy, she switched to huge round glasses with plain hairpin frames and lenses tinted gold.

Climbing into the one chair with upholstered arms Jeanne tugged inefficiently at her short skirt and opened my notebook in her lap. This new beach cottage had a bedroom and I went there, lay on one of the twin beds and took up Gide's

Symphony Pastoral from the nightstand. In the other room Jeanne was turning my pages briskly. Once she made a noise, but whether she laughed or cleared her throat I couldn't say.

An hour and twenty minutes passed before she threw open the bedroom door and came to stand over me. "Just what do you think you're doing?" she demanded. I waited, eyes on the page, for her to pat my cheek and show she wasn't serious. "I mean it," she said. "What's your excuse?"

She had pulled off the golden glasses. Without them her face was pale. At the worst I had expected a quibble or two. I couldn't remember anything that would account for this cold anger.

I said, "I'd like to know what's left of a marriage when you take the husband and wife out of it."

"You'll have to explain that to me. I'm only a dumb Southern broad, as you seem to enjoy pointing out."

"I can see the man," I said, "and the woman. But I don't know what they make together. A spider weaves a web. What does a marriage look like?"

"All right." I may have pacified her. "Keep looking. But you've got to be fair. You've got to give us a chance."

She had banged down next to me on the bed and I expected the nearness of our bodies to temper her anger. But she stayed rigid, and the distance between us was greater than when she had bent over my face. "Look at the two of us!" she said. "You're lying there and I'm sitting here. Do you understand that?"

"Yes."

"Touch me." She pushed her arm at me aggressively and I saw how thin it was and how pale were its fine hairs. "Go ahead! Touch my arm." This agitation was more than wounded vanity. She herself seemed alarmed by the force of her feelings. I encircled her wrist with my thumb and forefinger. "Now do you see? I'm as real as you are. Do you see it?"

"I never doubted it."

117

"I'm not a device," she said. "Or something to drag in every few pages. I'm not part of any pattern. If you find a pattern it will have to be in spite of me, not because you've pruned me down to make me fit. Look here." She thrust the notebook in front of me. "You have me worrying about Sonny all the time. How much of my thoughts do you think he's occupied over those nine years?"

"I don't know."

"I don't know either." She smiled grudgingly, but the shadow from my bedlamp made her teeth gray. In fact nothing about her tonight was vivid. Her face was chalky after her burst of anger, and without the tinted lenses her eyes were close to having no color. This woman beside me was not the heedless bright girl in my notebook, and I wondered whether her bloodlessness wasn't a trick to punish me for the way I had touched her up in my notes.

Jeanne said, "You've shrunk us until you've got us dancing on your hand. But without you we're still whole. When you're not with us we're alive. I am. I don't want to be a few curious moments in your life."

"What, then?"

"I want you to describe more. Look at my face. What do you see?"

"The peak of your hair is slightly right of center. The roots are lighter, closer to brown, than the blackness of the hair itself. Your eyebrows are plucked, the left one arches higher. Your nose widens after the bridge but before the nostrils. I can remember when the skin over your jaw was so tight there was an indentation on the underside of your chin. Now the line is less firm and that hollow is gone. Your upper lip is thin but you extend its curve with lipstick. You have a slight depression on the right cheekbone, about the size and shape of a fingernail paring. You fill it in with face powder."

"My right ear sticks out more than the left one, but my hair hides that. Otherwise you got everything. All you forgot to say is that I'm a very attractive woman."

"Of course."

"I'm not some dizzy Hollywood character. I'm serious. What happens to me is serious."

"Yes."

"You're only writing what I say. That doesn't show who I am. What I think and feel, that's what you claim you're interested in, and you don't have any of it."

"I apologize."

"I'm the one who should apologize." Her shrillness had upset her and I could feel her relaxing. "Coming here and carrying on like this. But you say you're trying to learn something, and I think that over the last few years I've found out a few things that could help you. Ignore what I've learned and I end up one more silly dame. And that's a lie."

Jeanne went across the room to the second bed, pulled the pillow from beneath its yellow spread and lay back with her arms around it. "Why don't you keep the beds pushed together? Oh, I see. All right, we'll start. On the night I married Ray, tell me the feelings I had."

"I can't do that."

"I'll help but you've got to try."

"It was a hot day here," I began dubiously. "In May. It must have been even hotter on the desert, so when you left Las Vegas after the ceremony, you may have wished you had stayed in a hotel there. But Ray had business here in town, I'd imagine, and that's why you left the wedding chapel and flew right back. When you landed here, you must have been tired."

"Exhausted!" Jeanne said. "But that's the single solitary thing you got right. Now think, love. Think about it. It is always the woman who decides where they're going to spend the wedding night. Always. The man may never listen to her again for the rest of their lives, but that night he wants to please her. I was the one who insisted on coming home. Ray wanted to stay in a hotel. But I was already worried about how being married might change him. Remember, we had been together such a long, long time.

"I was terrified that he'd come out of the bathroom, crawl into bed, say good night and go to sleep. I wanted him back in my bedroom, where we had gone the first time. My bedroom, my apartment, so he couldn't feel like a husband. The most depressing sight in the world, do you know what it is? A man's back, when he's in bed with you."

"You spent your wedding day worrying about that?"

"You can smile," she said, "but I really was worried. It was no secret to Ray that I wasn't faint with first love. But I had always liked him, and what I liked best was the way he treated me in bed. He had always been—what's a delicate way to put it?—harsh with me. He told me how much he loved me, but he never treated me tenderly or gently, the way most men did.

"Oh, damn!" she said. "I can watch your mind work. Now I'll be your main exhibit in some hall of freaks. Ray didn't twist my arm or put out cigarettes on my shoulder. I'd walk out on a man like that. I only mean that it's flattering after so many years that a man still comes to you because you excite him, not to do you a favor or punch you like a time clock.

"So naturally I was worried that being married might change him and, really, our going to bed had been the best part of living with him. He used me. I liked it. I even liked it that he hated Sonny. I told everybody I was getting married for my boy's sake, but I would never marry a man because he'd make a good father.

"We took Sonny with us that day, you know, and at the chapel I saw Ray rumpling his hair, and I thought, Oh, God, what if he starts smoothing my hair now or petting at me? Now that I'm his wife, what if he starts being kind to me? I'll come right back to Nevada, undo in Reno this mistake I'm making in Vegas."

"You got married thinking about getting divorced?"

Jeanne treated me to a long examination that meant nothing; without her glasses she couldn't see as far as my face. "Every woman thinks of divorce that day. Even when she's ecstatically happy. She may not think of the exact place, like Reno, but the idea of divorce is hovering there at the back of her mind, the way suicide does. They comfort a woman, the way having her own secret bank account does. Divorce, suicide—with those weapons to defend herself, no man can destroy her."

"Jeanne, you see my problem. I can't guess what you're thinking. And if I could, the words I write will still be mine, not yours."

"Words," she said. "Words don't matter. Only writers think they do. When you start writing about me again, let me know so I can help you. After all, dear, if you're writing about marriage, you're writing almost entirely about women. Isn't that true?"

"What about the other wives?"

"I can help you with Billy's wife. Margo has never told you about San Francisco, has she?" I must have looked blank. "I knew she hadn't. She's sorry enough about what she's already said to you. But I know the story and I'll give you the details. She won't mind. It's been long enough. The others? You can't make mistakes with a girl like Dawn, or that dancer. Jenny Black? No matter what you do, she's impossible. Nobody understands women like that, even other women. You can write whatever you want. Nobody can prove you're wrong."

"You make it sound futile."

Jeanne swung one shapely leg over the side of the bed, then the other. Getting up she stretched halfway into an exercise and then realized it might make her look ungainly and dropped her arms. We went back to the living room where her coat was spread to dry.

"Not futile," she said. "But you're only going to end up with some very rough guesses. You must see that, don't you, dear? There's no such thing as an honest book."

🏴   🏴   🏴

Hearing Jeanne's voice on the phone the next morning annoyed me. I thought after a conversation as long as ours I deserved a respite. "I've been wondering, dear," she said, her voice higher pitched than usual, "what it is you plan to write about Ron Cooper."

"What happened, I suppose."

"But you didn't mention him in what you wrote about the Army. Couldn't you leave him out?"

"I don't see how."

"Oh, well, no." She was midway between tears and a large whooping laugh. "But I thought that since it's all over now, you might want to forget him."

"Jeanne, nobody else is going to see my notebook. Whatever I write about Ron won't matter."

"You say that, and I'm sure you mean it now. But you've already thought about changing our names. That means you're thinking about finding a publisher."

"I promise that if I do, I'll make Ron white."

It was the right tack with Jeanne. "You can't think that's what's bothering me? Brad, can you? Hell, I don't care about that. That part's fine. Oh, hell, leave him in, then. But you should go back and tell about being in the Army together. After all that's why I got to know him. You should prepare the way."

Jeanne's objection was fair but her solution wasn't practicable. From the day we parted in France until I saw him three years later in Los Angeles, Ron Cooper had changed so completely, or my feelings about him had, that introducing him at the beginning of my notebook would have been to describe a stranger.

It is true that if he hadn't been on leave in England, Ronald would have been invited to my going-away party in Biarritz. He would have made a fourth that night in our crowded bed. In many ways he was our black albatross, but we wore him gladly on our necks. Ronald was twenty then, a brown boy with reddish hair that, thanks to dutiful applications of grease, hardly curled on his head. His high-pitched, giggling voice could be appealing, once in a while.

Ronald arrived at the post months before most of us, and he took every new arrival into his custody for a day or two, teaching him the petty tricks and monopolizing his time at the movies and snack bar. After he had sniffed over a newcomer to his satisfaction, Ronald surrendered him to the wider barracks life and the man found other friends to drink and gamble with. After those first days Ronald would still be a benign presence, a brown smiling wraith, but distant and reserved.

His duty on post was the operating of a small gymnasium, and he treated his preserve like a fiefdom. When Ranchek wanted to press weights or Doug Goodwin decided to box the leather bladder, they could have the gym to themselves at night. But they—and a very few others—were the only ones Ronald liked and favored with his key.

Other boys, Southern whites with oiled pompadours, would hear him say that he was too tired to open the gym right then. No, he couldn't give them the key because that was against regulations. Yes, that was final, and he didn't much care whether they liked it or not. Goodwin was plainly flattered to be exempt from Ronald's Southern embargo, and though he never sought Ronald's company, he was wary and polite with him.

By choice Ronald slept at the far end of our barracks, near the fire door. Three other Negroes had taken bunks nearby, but Ronald did not encourage familiarity from them and, so far as I remember, none ever got the benefit of his orientation course. A Negro had as little chance of penetrating the gym during Ronald's off-hours as a cracker did.

Beneath his show of insouciance, Ronald Cooper was the most nervous man I have ever met. He spun through the barracks crackling with tense laughter, ridiculing the other men's taste in shirts, cameras, shoes, sport jackets. But he was aware to a precise point which men he could taunt and how cuttingly. "Well, well, well," he would cluck, "look at those purple socks. You see a color like that on my street, it's on a Cadillac. We got courage in our bad taste, babe."

Since he picked only appropriate victims and dropped his teasing before any show of resentment, no one fought with Ronald or even grumbled behind his back. For me he was a strain because he could never let himself relax. On those rare times when he tried to sit still I could feel him fidget, and in his hurry to speak whatever was crowding his mind, he usually called me "Josh" or "Doug" and then a minute later hailed someone with my name. Even in surroundings as cramped and drab as our post, images and sensations overwhelmed Ronald until everything poured out, jumbled and backward, in one anxious stream.

Each morning Ronald sketched for an hour with ink or charcoal, but he wouldn't let us see the sketch books and he kept them buried at the back of his wall locker. He said that when his three-year enlistment was up, he wanted to go to art school and work someday as a designer.

Once, when the men were trading stories about their home towns, Ronald told George Ranchek that five years ago, at the age of fifteen, he had visited an aunt in Los Angeles. He remembered the street address but Ranchek didn't know the neighborhood. They did share, though, a nostalgia for the California climate—much better, Ronald said, than back in

Newark, where his mother taught school and made a home for his two younger sisters.

When his latest woman, a red-haired divorcee, found she was pregnant, Doug Goodwin arranged to meet me at the bank to draw out money for her abortion. Dawn Ranchek was handling our transaction, and she also gave Goodwin an address in Tijuana where several girls from the bank had gone and survived.

"I appreciate the loan, Brad," Goodwin said when Dawn went away to a cash drawer for the money. He meant that he was glad I wasn't being critical, but I was in as little mood for a lecture that morning as he was. In the last year or two, I had stopped considering abortion one of life's tragedies, and I was happy that Goodwin's woman could rid herself of a burden she didn't choose to bear.

What remained of my original distaste was a bafflement as to why women found themselves so regularly in that condition. To me they behaved much like Ranchek, who was a heavy smoker, yet climbed all the way to my apartment, sat himself down and announced that he was out of cigarettes. If I smoked, I would never run short, just as my car never stalled from an empty gas tank. With the precautions available to them, what excuse for these women flocking to Tijuana?

"You understand the directions?" Dawn asked as she was counting out the ten twenty-dollar bills.

"Through the center of town," Goodwin repeated. "One block past the stadium. Number six-six."

"There are two doctors," Dawn said, "both called Lopez. One is American, and if she goes on Sunday she has a better chance of getting him."

Goodwin had switched again to the night shift at a plant

that built Army helicopters, and he was looking gaunt and tired. With war flourishing again in Asia, he was guaranteed eight hours of overtime each week, enough to pay me back within three months.

As we left the bank, he said, "This is the fourth time I've been through this."

Have I written that Goodwin's attitude toward sex had never convinced me? He let all of us know about each conquest but took pains to be so offhand that he hardly seemed to be talking about women; I had heard men more excited about their golf scores. In the least offensive ways, with perhaps a little more insistence as we got older, Goodwin reminded us that he was irresistible, going about it as though he expected credit less for his virility than for his modesty.

Now I hadn't ventured a reproachful word and he was trying to pry one out of me. But I was mulling over an editorial argument against farm subsidies and I couldn't care that morning what Goodwin planted or plowed under. I said, "Every girl I know takes the pill these days."

He nodded. "When Betty Jean gets over this, I better be sure she gets some of those." But I knew he wouldn't, not as long as there are trapeze artists who disdain a net.

☙ ☙ ☙

For some time I had been running my own steeplechase, and in September Faye Tayne won it: she got a job before George Ranchek did. Faye was hired with two other girls to sing and dance in a small Gay Nineties revue three blocks east of Ray Morella's restaurant on the Strip. Opening night I was committed elsewhere, but I agreed to come the following Saturday and Faye promised to invite the perfect girl for me.

I was no longer as bedazzled as when I first supped with Faye and Rorke at her club, for I had come to realize that Faye's introductions, well meant as they were, seldom profited me. She had an excellent eye and procured the rarest women, but in her keenness to have my qualities appreciated, she reduced them to a state of terror.

She impressed on her friends the brilliance of my past and my prospects, skipping over how little pay and what scant prestige I enjoyed at the moment. Before I arrived, she primed the girls with news of the day and her briefing sessions might be followed by a question period. One girl named Lois became so exhausted that she had a headache by the time I rang the doorbell. Another, Sarah, simply froze. She said nothing through the evening and then, with a desperate denunciation of capital punishment, lunged for the sanctuary of her residence club.

The girl this night, Linda, was another in that series. When I joined her and Rorke at a front table, she inveighed briefly against school segregation and then joined Rorke in his silence. With the full social weight fallen on me, I dredged up a piece of stock market gossip from the paper's financial editor.

"You've got it wrong," Rorke said irritably. "It's an over-the-counter stock. The airline deal has nothing to do with it."

I accepted his revisions and asked how Faye had been doing. "Great," Rorke said listlessly.

"How did she get the job?"

"She auditioned for it." Something about his tone suggested that Faye's casting had taken place in private and after hours. Linda sensed what he was implying. "No, it wasn't anything like that," she protested. "Faye came here at ten o'clock in the morning with thirty other girls and she was the very first one they hired. At the club we even tease her because the owner hasn't asked her out. It's all business." Rorke ignored her.

By eleven o'clock when Faye and her partners burst on stage, all the tables were filled and a dozen men had paid the cover charge to stand at the back bar. No whistling or applause greeted the girls, but they were making more than enough din on the red player piano they pushed ahead of them.

In a low-necked striped dress Faye looked more voluptuous than usual; the corset with its bustle had also supplied her a bust authentic to the Gay Nineties. But I didn't see much of Faye's performance. At the moment she appeared I caught a glimpse of Rorke as he inspected the faces of the other men in the audience, and from that point I watched him watching them.

When Faye did a modest grind, a young man grinned at her from the next table. She caught his eye and winked. He blushed. Rorke wheeled around in his chair to inspect the fellow. When he realized I had noticed he cocked a contemptuous thumb toward him. "Yokel."

The girls converted me with their pianola to the brassy songs of the nineties, all two-four sexuality and ostrich plumes and rosy red flesh. "Red-hot mama," the slender girls sang, mere pilot lights to the great baking ovens of the past. "Red-hot mama, you're the one I need."

With their last song the other two girls peeled down their garters and tossed them into the crowd. Faye only dropped hers demurely on our table, and Rorke slid it into his jacket pocket. "Hers cost two bucks," he said, "so she uses it over again. The others can buy garters for thirty-five cents. But she's the star. She's got to have black lace."

Applause was tepid as they ran into the wings. Only the blushing boy and I gave a couple of twacks. Rorke didn't take his hand off his drink. Faye slipped into a full-length red robe before she peeped shyly through the curtain and ventured out. The robe was slit up the thigh and her leg flashing into sight was more provocative than anything in her act. "I was awful tonight."

"It's not your singing they come for," Rorke said.

"Don't pay attention to Robert," Faye told us cheerfully. "He's had another bad day. I don't know why he even works at such a boring job. You wouldn't, would you, Bradley?"

I was accustomed to being the soft cushion off which she

could bank shots and clip Rorke, but tonight, to keep the game honest, I said, "I don't have Bob's head for figures."

The second show was shorter than the first. When it ended we crowded into Rorke's sports car for the ride back to the girls' club. As the night wore on, Faye had become more captious, but Rorke was brushing away her jeering like flies off his face, and their bickering allowed Linda and me to get acquainted.

"You promised," Faye was saying in the front, "but I should know by now that your promises aren't—"

He hit her. He had been muttering, "Oh, Faye," or "I'm sorry," and then without a change in his voice he said, "Shut up," and punched her hard in the face. We were stopped at an intersection, and Faye screamed and pushed the car door open. She threw herself into the street just as the light changed. The car to our right didn't move, nor did we. Between the two automobiles Faye lay full length on the pavement, shrieking.

"If you don't do something," I told Rorke, "we'll have the police here."

He looked baffled. Leaning across the empty bucket seat, he called to Faye. "Get back in."

"No!" she screamed. "Go away! Leave me alone!"

I pushed the seat forward and climbed out. "Are you hurt?"

"Yes! Look at my eye! It's going to get black again." She was sobbing, but she raised her hand and let me draw her to her feet. "Oh, God," she moaned, "look at my stockings."

"Get into the car." The man to our right was still not moving. Drivers behind us were honking steadily and I expected to hear a police siren next. "No," Faye said, "I'm not going to let him hit me. I'll walk home."

"I'll go with you," I said and Rorke nodded. He drove off with the other girl in the back seat.

At the curb a dozen teenagers and a few old men had collected. To escape them we cut down the first side street off Sunset. The moon was high and mockingly romantic, its light filtering through the trees and dappling the sidewalk.

"Has he hit you before?"

Faye had stopped crying but she choked and gulped on her tears. "Twice."

"Why?"

She shrugged and her breasts jiggled beneath her sweater. She was out of breath and walked slowly, hesitating in the dark patches beneath the boughs. The scent of flowers was stronger than usual and sweeter.

"Why do you put up with it?"

"I thought we were getting married."

"So he can beat you at home?"

"He promised to stop."

We were passing the front window of a house without blinds. In the small living room a man sat reading a newspaper while a woman with a cat in her lap watched television. That could be me, I thought. Why isn't that me? I led Faye along to a house with its drapes drawn.

"The world is full of men."

"I tell myself that. But if a day goes by and Robert doesn't call, I get frightened and call his office, and that makes it worse. He hates that."

"Because he's busy?"

"He hates it when I start to depend on him. Two times since I left Las Vegas I haven't had the rent money and I've had to take it from Robert. He gave it as soon as I asked but he hated my asking."

"And he's hit you twice?"

She laughed, happy peals of laughter on the dark street. "I wish it was that simple. It goes back to when Robert saw me the first time in Las Vegas. The director had us looking haughty and cold, and Robert fell in love with that look. Now to go to bed with me he has to think of the men who got excited over me looking cold."

"You don't know that."

"I do. But you can see how that ruins everything? He says he wants me to get out of show business, but he doesn't. Not at all. Other men have to pay money to see me. That's terribly important."

She stopped by a grassy bank. "Can we?" We hunched down in the dark. The grass was already damp with dew, and I pulled up my legs and tried to rock on my heels. Faye fell back and stretched her arms and legs, like a child making angels in the snow. Once I had lain like that with a girl in the tall prickly grass near a road in France. Afterward, the girl had combed nettles from her hair and promised all the things I wanted to believe on our last day together.

"I was a pretty girl," Faye said.

"I'm sure."

She sat up to kick off her shoes and roll down her torn stockings. She stuffed them into her tiny green velvet bag and lay back on the grass. "Being pretty should have made everything easier. But it didn't."

"Your tragedy was not being plain?"

She bounced up and hugged my forearm. "Bradley, I love you. Of course that's not what I mean."

"Do you like to have Rorke hit you?"

"I don't want him to. But if he won't come to bed, I want to make him want to hit me. Not do it, just want to."

"Feeling that way you'd still marry him?"

"Opening night when he came to pick me up his coat had a little bulge in the right-hand pocket, and I was sure it was a ring box. When the second show was over, he would come backstage and propose. But I got my hand inside the pocket, pretending to look for a handkerchief, and it was a wadded-up tax form. I went to my dressing room and cried."

"Ten years ago," I said, "I was sure people wanted what was best for them. Even when I got over that, I thought they wanted what they said they did."

"I have four hundred dollars' worth of work to have done on my teeth." She was hugging my arm for warmth. "People think it's a joke: a woman gets married and has her gall bladder taken out on the honeymoon. But I can't afford the dentist's bill unless Robert marries me."

"Have you told him?"

Her lips made a rubbery sound. "Robert doesn't even want to hear that I shave my legs and under my arms. If he found out that my eyeteeth are bad, he'd see himself climbing into bed with one big rotten mouth. Then he'd stay up every night poking around in his briefcase. Somehow the nights I stay over at his apartment are always the nights he's got work to do until three in the morning."

Faye stopped talking and put her face up to mine, close enough to be indistinct, and any woman I wanted to pretend she was. I pushed up from the ground and pulled her back to the sidewalk. She was strolling more languidly than before and holding tight to my arm. When she hummed a ribald song from her act, I whistled with her. In a length of moonlight she turned to me. "How is my eye?"

"Like a roulette wheel," I said, "half red, half black."

"Will you take a chance on me?"

"I'm no gambler."

I had been selfish. Faye had seen the darkened car edging along the curb before I did, and she intended the sight of our kiss to rouse her lover to propose.

When Rorke's car came in range of us, the headlights flickered like heat lightning and went out again. He seemed to be alone. "He's come to apologize," I said.

Now Faye was tugging on me to walk faster. "What does he expect?" she said. "Curb service? If he's going to talk to me, he can come over here."

Rorke pulled past us and parked up the street. Climbing out he approached gingerly. "Are you all right?" he called.

"My eye hurts."

"I'll take you home."

"I'd better go to the club." They paid no attention to me, but leaving would have forced myself on them. I stayed in a shadow.

"Come with me tonight," Rorke said.

Faye sighed and nodded. She went to his car, murmuring a low thanks in my direction. Rorke with an air of largesse promised to call me early in the week.

⚜   ⚜   ⚜

"At least," I taxed Lonnie Chapman one night as he sat on a bluff overlooking the ocean, "you must oppose the war?"

My girl that evening had suffered from my affliction: she drank too much too quickly. After I had driven her back to the Palisades it was only ten o'clock, and I headed up the beach to see Lonnie. I was determined to poke and bait him until I punctured his calm.

Beneath us, algae had dyed the waves a faint and luminous red, and the breeze off the sea was pungent with dead fish. Lonnie was finishing his thirty-minute break, spooning damp cereal from a plastic cup. "No," he said, "I don't oppose it."

"Everyone is against the war."

"I'm not."

"You support the war?"

"No."

"You accept the war." I knew he'd agree to that and he did, nodding indifferently. "Accepting," I said, "is the same as supporting."

"I know the difference."

Lonnie may have thought he was being honest, but badgering him that night I detected a slight shift in his position, and

133

the expanded war was the most logical explanation for it. Even in peacetime, withdrawing from normal life had been difficult for Lonnie, and though the futility of this particular war might have reinforced him in his quietus it didn't seem to have happened that way.

No matter how he shut his ears, Lonnie couldn't shut out the hundred new voices proclaiming a morality more vigorous than his own. Youngsters were scuffling for peace on the sidewalks while Lonnie kept at home, living peaceably. Their passion had to make Lonnie question the value of his own sacrifices, forcing him to ask whether his courage might not be something closer to laziness, or cowardice. War had made the nation martial, none more so than the enemies of war, and I was convinced that Lonnie longed to enlist in their cause.

When the telephone rang, I had finished a cup of black coffee and was ransacking my desk for an editorial I kept in reserve for those mornings I had a hangover.

"Bradley Fell," I said into the mouthpiece.

"Did you just try to call me at my office?" Ranchek asked.

"A job? You finally got a job? I can't believe it, Ranchek. I thought you were part of the hard-core unemployed."

"The phrase 'hard-core pornography' makes a certain lewd sense," Ranchek said pedantically. "But with the unemployable, it is their softness and vulnerability that should be emphasized."

"Dawn must be delighted."

"She has never shared your fixation with money and status," he said. "She does take pleasure, I believe I am correct in saying, that my long exile from the workaday world has ended so felicitously."

"What will you be doing?"

"I am managing a successful campaign for the Los Angeles City Council."

"You don't know anything about politics," I said. "Who would hire you?"

"Fred Blanco!" he cried. "Remember that name!"

"Blanco's name is Richard."

"That's why you will never be a political strategist," Ranchek said. "You immerse yourself in detail. Fred or Richard, Blanco's our man!"

"The registration is against him."

"But the citizenry is for him," Ranchek hissed. "The citizens will rise above petty partisanship and sweep Dick Blanco into City Hall."

"I remember him from the mayor's race four years ago. He's a fool."

Ranchek shouted, "Citizens, the charge has been made that Dick Blanco is a boob!" With one hand over the receiver, Ranchek made a noise that was supposed to conjure up a clamoring legion. "I'm not standing in front of you today to deny that charge or any other." He paused to produce a swelling cry of approval. "I will only say that if being a boob is being patriotic, hard-working, decent and devout, then Dick Blanco is the most boobish man ever to run for the council of his city. May I present to you the archetypical boob! The quintessential boob! The boob's boob! Richard Blanco!" The roar was deafening, and Ranchek gave his candidate a thirty-second ovation, raising the decibels by permitting phlegm to collect deep in his throat.

When I hurried to their apartment that night with a bottle of champagne, Dawn was drying the last of the dishes. Saturated from an earlier celebration, Ranchek was supine by the phonograph.

I turned on the kitchen tap, a trick from espionage movies, and whispered to Dawn, "Why do you think he took this job?"

"It's safe now," she said.

"What?"

She spun off the faucet and disengaged the wrinkled bib of her apron. "He thinks it's safe." We took our glasses of champagne into the living room. Ranchek looked up from the rug.

"I'm sorry I didn't help with the dishes," he said. "I feel a little sick. Can gin get rancid?"

"It wouldn't have hurt you to wait until I got home."

"You're so right," he said mooningly. "Do you forgive me?"

"Oh, yes." But Dawn's saying it was not enough for Ranchek. His eyes brimmed with reproach until she sighed and made a lattice of her fingers. She held them before her face, peered out at him and pronounced a penance. Ranchek began his blasphemous version of the Hail Mary, and while he carried on that familiar charade, Dawn sipped from her glass and tried to talk across his mutter.

Even when her own spirit flagged, she performed with Ranchek because he had convinced her there was no more reliable way of proving her love. Dawn could pay his rent, cook his food and clothe him. She could blaze a trail across the apartment with five-dollar bills for his cigarettes and afternoon movies. And still he had her believing none of that counted unless she let herself be coerced into playing his games.

※ ※ ※

For reasons that did neither of them credit, politics suited Ranchek. His blatant hypocrisies seemed less grotesque in the political world than the real one, and reporters from the newspaper who interviewed him came away saying how shrewd he was. Blanco was running in the Larchmont district, close to the center of Los Angeles, an area where fine old houses were being pulled down to make way for apartments with brilliants embedded in their façades. Negroes and whites shared the district in precarious balance, but luckily for Blanco, with skin as white as his name, there wasn't a serious Negro candidate in the race.

I could not bring myself to attend one of the dozens of coffee parties where Ranchek treated lady voters to his winsome smile. But one day he called to demand that I join him on a picket line, and enough real excitement penetrated his show of excitement to catch my interest.

The session was to be held in front of a new building not far off Wilshire Boulevard where, though half its units were empty, a young Negro couple had been denied an apartment. By the time I had parked a safe distance from any rock throwing, Ranchek was already pacing the sidewalk along with the young couple and Richard Blanco, a bald timid man hardly five feet tall. Ranchek loomed over them all, beaming and maneuvering his candidate into focus for a youth with a cheap camera. Five weedy boys and an unclean girl looked on with their picket signs at parade rest.

"I can't write about this," I warned Ranchek. "It's too obviously a stunt. But I wanted to see what you were up to."

"I'm ordering five thousand flyers with those pictures. We'll pass them out all over the south end of the district."

"Did Blanco take part in any demonstrations before he became a candidate?"

"I am not an historian," Ranchek said witheringly. "The fact is that Dick Blanco is here today to protest a grievous injustice to two fine Americans."

The other pickets, Ranchek explained, were members of a civil rights organization at the nearby state college. "You should have more Negroes picketing," I said. "And more older people."

"Ron Cooper is coming over. You remember him?"

"I didn't know he was out here."

"Didn't I tell you? Ron's been here a couple of months."

"How is he?"

"Still colored," Ranchek said. "But in every other respect, I'd say he's changed more than any of us."

He excused himself to get the pickets marching again, Blanco in the lead. The boy photographer was told to crouch low to make the candidate as imposing as possible. The messages on the signs were straightforward, without puns or bad jokes, so I assumed Ranchek hadn't helped prepare them.

As the pickets walked in their small circle no one came along the street and no face peered out from the few windows in the building with curtains. The yard had not been seeded, and except for two shrubs and a lorn sapling planted in a clump there was only an expanse of gray dirt. I couldn't imagine anyone applying to live here or, less, being turned down.

"Couldn't these people file a complaint?" The California Assembly had passed a law that fitted the case.

"You will perhaps tell me how to get a dramatic photograph at an office in the state building? Do you suggest my candidate brandish his pen like a sword? Sit cross-legged on the counter with his pants leg hiked above the garter line?"

"What's the good in having the law if you don't use it?"

"About three thousand votes," Ranchek answered smoothly.

The aimless milling on the sidewalk had gone on another ten minutes when a husky tall Negro in a three-button business suit stepped briskly up the block and returned Ranchek's wave with a snappy salute.

The word "dapper" has become patronizing, and that's too bad, for Ron Cooper was something other than neat or well groomed. Not fashionable, in the way Ray Morella was, nor outrageous, like Robert Rorke. Ron had taken a suit of the kind I wore and set out to prove what could be done when its conservative cut fit perfectly and its fabric hung free of wilts and wrinkles. He must have calculated the knot to his tie with calipers, and his plain white cuffs nipping out at his wrists were tight as tourniquets. Ron still plastered his reddish hair flat on his skull, which made the circumference of his head look a little small for his new shoulders and weight. But his smile was broader than ever, and his nerves seemed to have solidified. At least he called me by my right name.

"Brad, Brad," he said warmly. "I've been calling your apartment for six weeks. You must have some life going." He had introduced himself to the couple and immediately wrapped one arm around the woman's waist and the other over her husband's shoulder.

"Very quiet," I said.

"Look at you! Come on, tell your buddy—you been hitting the peroxide? You never came up blond like that in the Army."

"I spend too much time in the sun. I hate the color. It makes me look like a surfer."

"Nothing wrong with that," he said. "My friends here looked a little more like you, we wouldn't be having this trouble."

"I know." I felt myself blush. "It's a crime."

"But we're going to change it, ain't we? Us crimefighters." Laughing with him, the couple let themselves be drawn away. Ranchek sidled up to me. "We can't have merriment on the sidewalk," he fretted. "It will confirm all the manager's fears."

"That they'll move in and laugh?"

"Laugh, dance, say hello to the other tenants at the mailbox, hug their children without pulling the shades—all the animal traits."

"What does Ron do now?"

"Do? Do?" Ranchek was free at last to show his scorn for that question. "He's not going to ask you for a loan, if that's what you're worried about. He's not on welfare. He's not stealing tax dollars from your pocket."

"You're telling me what he's not doing. What does he do?"

Ranchek sighed, a slow puncture. "He paints."

"Does he sell anything?"

"Sell, sell," he snarled. "I think he sells. He's working part time with this Negro group but that's as a volunteer, I think."

Ron had bounced back to us, moving with his added thirty pounds as effortlessly as when he had been skinny. Despite the heat, his skin was dry as felt. Ranchek, who sweated in the shade on cold days, mopped himself with a polka-dot handkerchief, and on my own forehead I felt a sheen collecting.

"Hey, George," Ron said, "we've got to get more pickets out here. Do you want me to bring a carload tomorrow?"

Even Ranchek couldn't admit that once he had the photographs in hand, the crusade was over and none too soon. Already Blanco, slogging forward on the picket line, was dissolving in his own yellow juices.

"All right," Ranchek said, "maybe one more day, as a symbol—"

"We don't want a symbol, George." For a minute I heard Ron's teasing twenty-year-old voice. "We want success. How about it, Brad? Is there anybody you can haul out here?"

"I'll see."

"You call the police, George, and tell them what we're going to do." Ron cracked his knuckles. He had grown into hands that had hung from his sleeves, when he was thin, like bowling balls. "We'll march a line to Adams Boulevard and back. I'll call the television stations."

Ranchek looked concerned that his gimmick was outgrowing him. He asked me, "Who will you get?"

"I'll call the Blacks and Goodwin. And Jeanne Darling. She's said she wanted to do something."

The next day two hundred marchers, candidate Blanco in the lead with a weary shuffle, picketed for the benefit of three television cameras. Shortly before four P.M. the apartment manager pulled up in a car with a jolly round man who owned the building and his nervous young lawyer. The lawyer changed from sunglasses to stately horn-rims for the reading of his statement. Freely translated, it said: You caught us; we admit it; now turn off those lights.

The Negro couple was offered a choice of three vacant apartments and after consulting with Ron Cooper took the one that was neither most nor least expensive. Ron was only mildly exhilarated by the outcome; he did not confuse one skirmish with the war. Ranchek was bemused, Blanco bone-tired. Both the Blacks and Goodwin had sent their regrets, but Jeanne Darling was there, and when the last hand had been shaken, she went with Ron and eight of his friends to an ice cream shop on Wilshire Boulevard to toast their success with strawberry milk shakes.

⚑   ⚑   ⚑

I was still suspicious of riches, even comfort, but I had to admit that prosperity became Jeanne and Ray Morella. They didn't try to look as though their new Spanish house in Toluca Lake was their natural habitat, and long after they moved in, they went on behaving like poachers on the expensive estate. Their only ambitious entertaining came whenever editors and publishers of Jeanne's column were in town on convention, and I was inveigled to one reception with that potent appeal: You must come so at least we'll have one person there we like.

Stepping cautiously down the polished stairs into Jeanne's living room I was engulfed by hearty tanned sportsmen, the publishers, and the edgy whey-faced men who edited their newspapers for them. Jeanne had invited several young women to flesh out the decor, but none could compete for attention with the hostess. Jeanne had fitted one of her husband's yellow satin shirts and fringed its bottom with rows of red beads. Except for white plastic boots that went nearly to the hip, she wore nothing else.

141

Ray Morella was mingling with his wife's guests. When he saw me he left his circle and pulled me first into the kitchen and then out the back door. "I've done all I can," he said. "Nobody notices me anyway. They still call her Miss Darling."

"She's a career woman."

We crossed the trimmed and lacquered backyard to a quadruple garage built to resemble the Alamo. I knew what awaited me. Ray spent several evenings each week now in the garage, sitting behind the wheel of his Thunderbird, traveling great distances without starting the engine.

He unlocked the glove compartment and fished out two thin cigarettes. "Good stuff," he said. "It's from a singer who stops by the club." He lit his own and took a greedy puff. "And I can still make money on martinis," he marveled.

"Someday you'll have these in the vending machine."

"I hope by that time I won't be stuck with the place. What I'd like is to sell my share and do something else."

"What?"

He swore at himself. "That's it. What do I know? I thought about a discotheque, but that would mean the same headaches. Licenses. Help. Long hours. I want to stay home and enjoy life."

"You've got thirty years until Social Security."

"I don't know whether it's because of this town or because I got married," he said sheepishly. "I never felt like this in Chicago. All I think about is retiring. I want to stay home. Get to bed early. When I was a kid, twenty-three, a restaurant was all right. It was my own corner for hanging out. Now I go down at three o'clock every afternoon, hating to leave here, and when I get inside there's already twenty people lined up at the bar wanting to buy me drinks. I look at them and think, I'm here to make money. What the hell are you doing here?"

I said, "A friend of mine from the Army spends his time in beer bars in the Valley. He says at least it's better than watching television. Television is like waking up knowing you had the same dream as thirty million other people. A psychic orgy."

"Talk about orgies," Ray said nostalgically. "Did I ever tell you—" It was a story about a weekend when he was in the Navy and his ship docked at Marseilles. When he finished he said, "Don't mention any of that in front of Jeanne. She'd go crazy if she knew."

"She thinks you were a virgin until you met her?"

"It's funny about Jeanne," he said. "We can have a real good time together, and I know it's been even better for her than for me. Then afterward she starts asking me if I gave that good a time to all the others. She's lying there waiting for me to answer and getting herself mad. I'd like to ask her what difference it would make, how that would change what she just had. But if I said that she'd never forget it. So I say no, it wasn't that way with anybody else. That's what she wants to hear. She knows about the others but they don't count. If I told her the truth, she'd think what she had felt was a trick I had practiced. That I was making a fool out of her. That she was being manipulated."

"It's true."

He bent toward me confidentially, in the manner of short men. "Sure it's true. You always take care of them while you pretend you're worrying about yourself. But women won't take charity. They need it but they won't take it."

He waited for me to cite an experience of mine to prove him right, but even for Ray I couldn't do that. Instead I asked, "How are you getting along with the boy?"

He exhaled sweet smoke. "Those years before we were married, you know? All he kept saying to me was, 'I want you to be my father, why can't you be my father?' Now the minute I try to teach him anything, he says, 'You're not my father.'"

"He's jealous."

"Now he's jealous and I'm not. I can even feel sorry for the kid."

"He's ten?"

"Something like that. Anyhow he's doing better at school. He's studying hard, and I know he only does it to spite me but I don't care. He asked Jeanne if I had been any good in school and when she said no, the next term he went to the top of his class. Now every time he brings home his report card he gets another chance to sneer at me. His age, I was boosting from the five-and-ten, and he's getting perfect marks, and what I did then I was doing for the reason he's studying hard now. But it makes Jeanne happy. And he isn't coming home with a pocketful of electrical sockets. That's what I lifted once—twenty-six of them."

He lit another narrow brown roll for me as Jeanne slipped through the side door and stepped around coils of hose and the power mower. She rapped on the window next to me. "Quick," she gasped. "A drag. Speaking of which—" She gestured in the direction of her departed guests.

"Good for business." I pulled forward and she slipped into the back seat and rested her elbows on our shoulders.

"One man owns a television station in Phoenix and he asked me to tape a thirty-second horoscope every day."

"Will you?"

Ray in the driver's seat was turning the wheel idly and re-lighting Jeanne's cigarette each time it went out. "Depends on the money," Jeanne said. "Ten years ago I would have felt foolish. But I don't worry about making an ass of myself any-more. I'm not sure I'm glad about being less self-conscious. Is it part of getting older?"

"The best part," I said.

"No, it was better to stammer and blush and be absolutely positive every man was looking up my skirt. But that was a long time ago. I can remember the exact day when I realized they weren't thinking about me every minute of the day and night. God, it was a terrible shock. Do you want to know how it happened?"

"How?"

"It was the first week I was married. To Sonny's father. I got married absurdly young, not fifteen, which is what I tell people, but young. And I was a marvelous housekeeper. That part you're going to have to take on faith. But I flew around our little apartment—we were living in Atlanta then—whisking away every speck of dust.

"Flitting around with a dustcloth, all I kept thinking was that there at his office was my husband thinking about me. I knew he could watch me as I dusted. Later when I made a pie, I was sure he was picturing me getting out the flour and pitting cherries. I was glad I made such a delightful picture and he was seeing it all."

"I can see it," I said. "You look splendid."

"Thank you, my dear. But you know how it is with foolish thoughts. I didn't know what I was thinking, and yet I truly believed that he could see me all day long and admire me while I did my housework. That night he came home from his office—he had some boring job with the power company—and he ate the pie. He liked it. He asked for another piece. He thanked me for making his favorite kind. He said he loved me. He kissed me and patted my fanny.

"But he hadn't seen me baking that pie. To him it was just there on the table. He knew I had made it, but he hadn't been thinking about me every minute I was making it. He hadn't actually seen me. He hadn't even tried. After that it was very quiet in the apartment and I started getting restless."

"And made pie less often."

"More often."

"Are you listening?" I nudged Ray. "When she starts making your favorite dessert every night, that's the time to worry."

"Worry," he repeated. "Hell, I worry now."

The second cigarette was almost gone and my lips were burning with each puff. My fingertips could hardly hold the remnant of brown paper. But I inhaled again, respecting the tradition that the tip was too precious to stub away. When I had nothing at my mouth but a red ember, I spit it into the ashtray.

"Better be careful at the carwash," I told Morella.

"Are you kidding? That's where I go for the hard stuff."

"He's kidding," Jeanne said seriously. "Ray has sworn to me that he'll never use anything stronger than this." She passed her own cigarette for me to share, and we sat a few more minutes, saying less and less, until I bade them good night and made my first contented movements home.

After years of scrupulously not contending, of reading mysteries concealed indifferently in his top desk drawer and never volunteering for assignments, Billy Stein either reformed or relapsed, depending on the value one places on hard work. Reticent as ever about his own life, he wouldn't tell me the reason, but he loitered less at the coffee wagon and was seldom found in the back shop joking with the printers. He banished the mysteries from his desk and, to make time pass, wrote more of the routine stories that the other reporters shunned. His industry was rewarded. He was given better assignments, which forced him to refine his style. Within six months he had won a minor prize and was taken to court for libel. Editors at the leading paper in the city heard about one distinction or the other and when they hired Billy away, he took me with him.

"You can't want to stay here," he said when he proposed that we both move on. "It's got no circulation."

"I've been happy."

"You're not ambitious," he said, doubtfully.

"I used to think I was."

"I've already got it fixed for you downtown."

"All right." He was anxious to help me, and I had to admit I couldn't bring to my fifth celebration of the vernal equinox the fervor I had mustered for the first four. "But no editorials. I've added to the noise long enough. Make me an editor and I promise to cut every story fifty percent."

"Not mine, though. Agreed?"

"You're ambitious."

"It's nice for people to know my name," he said. "Margo likes it when the woman at the bakery says she's read one of my stories."

Whatever her motive, whoever her target, Margo called me one afternoon to invite me to dinner with Lonnie Chapman and a female friend from Margo's school days. The girl, Rose Weiner, had lately come back from graduate studies in London, and in a season when the least intellectual women were wearing patterned hose, she proved to be an authentic bluestocking.

More accurately, she wore no stockings at all. Her hard freckled calves slimmed down to delicate ankles and then to broad feet scrubbed a raw white and exposed in open sandals. Her round face might have been described as apple-cheeked except that it lacked all trace of color, natural or induced. Those full cheeks were firm, though, and her hair, however frizzled, was under control. She jabbed at me with her sharp eyes and did not return my smile. In all, Rose impressed me as being designed and crafted for only the loftiest purpose, something to do, probably, with improving the breed.

Her manner with Margo wasn't that of an ordinary school chum. They seemed more like uncordial cousins forced together to please their families. Margo's one concession to the evening had been to fuss more over the table than if only Lonnie or I had been expected. She had pulled out the middle leaf and laid floral place mats around the dull oak top. The silver looked heavier than usual, wedding sterling. A bottle of burgundy stood uncorked in the geometric center of the table.

On my Army leaves, I had gone several times to London, or to that swath from Russell Square down to Charing Cross Road, the Strand and Piccadilly. But when I questioned Rose about her ten months she replied antagonistically. She may have thought I was trying to forge a false bond that would exclude Lonnie and the Steins, or more likely, England had been a disappointment for her. I could picture a girl like Rose, head bowed all day in the British Museum reading room, trudging home to a damp room with never enough sixpences to keep the gas heater going. I saw toothy tall boys being intimidated by her compactness or risking a tepid pleasantry, as I had, only to be impaled on those eyes.

Apart from one glass of wine that Rose accepted and left untouched by her plate, I finished the burgundy alone. With each glass I felt more like background noise, one of those piano records played to cover lulls at a cocktail party. By dessert, no one else was saying a word. Margo quit yawning long enough to clear the table. Billy Stein and Lonnie were remote and faintly sad.

Mostly, though, I remember my own voice, never rising or falling, less a brook than the ceaseless rush of a traffic stream. I talked on and on, with no one cutting in or trying to talk across me.

I was drunk and knew why. Rose Weiner, this girl for whom I felt no spark of desire, had doubled my lack of interest and taken the bid away from me. I was spoiled by women who kept watch across a table and played to my hand. Why should this prickly girl be different from the long-legged complaisant blondes? In the midst of that resentment I had one of my rare flashes of intuition. Rose could ignore me because she had already decided to marry Lonnie Chapman.

I worked out a dozen reasons why she should settle for Lonnie rather than me. But I was disturbed. Did even an impoverished and celibate vegetarian look like a better marriage prospect than I? Shameful to become one of those professional bachelors, those men who buy toothbrushes in two-dozen lots and dispense them over a month's time to women who, unless they are giddily romantic, don't confuse foresight with thoughtfulness.

Three nights after our dinner, Lonnie took Rose to the movies. He fetched and returned her on the municipal bus, though I volunteered my car and Billy Stein offered his motorcycle for the occasion.

On election day I ate an early supper and drove to the union hall where Ranchek had booked his candidate's victory celebration. The hall was harshly lit and smelled of varnish. At the front, two dozen older men and their wives were scrutinizing a green blackboard for early returns that Ranchek filled in from a portable television set. Dawn beckoned to me from the front row.

According to the figures Blanco was eighteen votes ahead of his opponent, a local florist who was indisputably the greater of two evils. Ranchek deserted his post long enough to sprint to a table at the rear and dash back with three cups of whiskey. "It's a walkaway," he assured us. "Our opponent's mother lives in one of the precincts that went for us."

Hearing him so confident inflamed my doubts. "Where is Blanco?"

"His Honor is taping a victory statement at City Hall. He'll be here within the hour, standing ready to greet his campaign workers at the precise instant they become his constituents."

"Will you be his deputy?"

Ranchek hung his head modestly. "Please," he said, "it's not the moment for mundanity. Tonight we celebrate democracy in the air."

"I made him get it in writing." Dawn was laconic. "Before he took over the campaign, Blanco gave him an undated letter asking him to join the staff."

Ranchek nodded. "Simply my attempt to relieve the candidate's mind, to spare him that frightening realization when the crown descends that he is alone in the corridors of power."

"George is going to make a lot of money." Dawn mentioned a fair-sized sum. "In fact, I may quit the bank and stay home." She intended no such thing, and I wondered why she wanted to agitate Ranchek on his night of triumph. He merely fluttered his fingers toward her. "An idle wife is the devil's playground. Besides, I am considering the possibility of donating my salary to charity." The late President had made that gesture, and apparently Ranchek hoped to blur any distinction in the public mind between the position of Chief Executive of the United States and deputy to a Los Angeles city councilman-elect.

Slowly the hall was filling with hangers-on from the neighborhood, old men in cardigan sweaters and wives with tight knots of gray hair bobbing on their heads. Ranchek at his most unctuous greeted them by name and cupped the old ladies by the elbow. "Well," I said to Dawn, "I guess he's good at it."

"He studied public relations, remember."

"Maybe Ranchek will run for office himself one day."

"You know better than that," Dawn said sharply.

When less than one-third of the vote had been counted, the computer at a television station declared Blanco victorious, and a windless shout went up from the old men around the room. Enough cheap whiskey had been sloshed at the back of the hall so that several veteran campaigners were already outside on the street singing.

"Congratulations," I said to Ranchek.

"It must be true." He was wiping his forehead with an enormous pocket handkerchief. At the rate his black hair was falling out he would soon need a towel or a bedsheet.

Since Blanco still had not arrived, Ranchek suggested we look for him at a lodge where Negroes in the district were holding a party of their own. "You should have had only one celebration," I said.

Ranchek nodded. "It wasn't up to me."

As Dawn drove us south on Crenshaw Boulevard, the look and feeling of the night changed with every block. The store fronts were chipped and faded, and the palms along the boulevard became sparse before they disappeared entirely. At a dark green building on a side street Ranchek told Dawn to stop.

It was that year of good feeling when integration seemed inevitable, and we could enter the lodge without trepidation. A rock band was playing joyously and two young Negroes were dancing on a stage. Black light from the ceiling caught the boy's white trousers; with each twist he sent out ghostly flares. The girl was less accomplished and working hard to keep up. When she fell to the sidelines, the boy beckoned for everyone on the dance floor to join him, and we were pleasantly jostled by grinding thighs and hips. Ranchek pushed up on his toes to look for the candidate, but Blanco was nowhere to be found. "I hope he hasn't been assassinated," he said. "We're all in danger now. It's something one must learn to live with."

We were nearly out the door when I saw a white girl in one corner who looked very much like Jeanne Darling, perhaps younger, but with the same cupid's bow and pert nose. I felt sure it couldn't be Jeanne, but I was wrong. Ron Cooper had invited her, and to attend she had thought it was worth telling her husband a small lie.

❦   ❦   ❦

When I understood that Jeanne Darling was having an affair with Ron Cooper I was more than casually interested. My own life filled most of my thoughts, but I had curiosity left for this particular romance. Jeanne and I were in a men's store in Beverly Hills buying a birthday present for Ray, when I tried to reassure her by saying something worldly.

"My dear!" Jeanne was exasperated. "You take it for granted I've slept with him. I haven't, love. You know I wouldn't lie about it."

"It's no business of mine."

"True." She held up a lacy white shirt from Argentina with a single button just above the navel. "What do you think?"

"Vulgar."

"Good." She beckoned to a clerk and had it charged to her account. "Now we have to go down the street to the bookstore."

"Bookstore?"

"Yes, sweet. Do you still think you're the only one in Los Angeles who reads? I go to bookstores quite often. Today I want to get an art book for Ray. I'll pause while you say 'Art book?' in that same insulting way."

"I didn't know Ray was interested in art."

"Mad for it," Jeanne said. "My husband is a man of diverse interests and one of his current passions is Giotto."

"They're both Italians," I said lamely.

"It's more than national pride, dear. He really has very good taste, Ray does. I'm terribly fond of him."

"Then why—"

"Ron? Because it's marvelous to have secrets. To say I'm going out to visit my mother and then drive downtown to meet Ron and his friends at that café on South Broadway. It makes me feel single."

"What does it make Ron feel?"

"I don't worry about that, dear. For some reason he enjoys being with me. To be honest, I'd like it better if he'd at least try to kiss me. But he hasn't. With another man I might think he was queer, but I know, even with that falsetto his friends all use and the way they call each other 'baby' every third word that it's not that. It's more as though he's testing me. Every time he asks me out I've cleared another hurdle."

In the bookstore Jeanne handed the salesman a slip with the name and Swiss publisher of the volume she wanted. From his hauteur, he assumed that a decorator had prescribed it for her coffee table. When he had gone to the storeroom Jeanne said, "It is the disappointment of my life that the clerks in bookstores and flower shops aren't nicer."

"Every doctor isn't consumptive."

"Oh, Brad," she said irrelevantly, "someday I want to sit down with you and hear what Ron was like in the Army."

"We can do it now."

"No, dear, I'm not really interested enough yet. I'll let you know when the time comes."

It came three weeks later when Jeanne called on the pretext of inviting me to dinner. As she was about to hang up, she said, "Oh, by the way, dear, you know what they say about Negro men?"

I braced myself and waited.

"It's not always true."

Growing activity on his campus caused Josh Black to work a double shift on those days his student deputies failed to show up. Josh didn't mind the long hours since the work hardly taxed him and the extra money helped clothe his boy, who was starting to outgrow his sister's infant dresses.

Josh's uniforms had become a darker shade of blue each year until now he was distinguishable from a policeman only by the patches on his shoulder. Jenny had tailored the shirts to minimize his paunch, but she hadn't fitted the trousers and they bunched on his hips and stuck out, pockets and seams, like handles on a jug.

Josh had been forced into eyeglasses during the last year, and a case with its pocket clip was bulging on the side of his chest where other men carry cigarettes. As I inspected the new uniform he drew a deep breath and pounded his chest, taking care not to crack the glasses in his pocket. "Firm," he said. "Tough. It's a healthy life. I've never felt better, even after basic training."

"You don't have much time for acting."

"No." His nostrils puckered, a reflex he identified with deep thought. "In the next month or two I think I can get some time off. That's when they'll be auditioning for the new television series."

"You must miss acting."

Now it was his brow that wrinkled. "There are two ways of seeing life, aren't there?"

"At least."

"Either a man decides early what he wants to do and goes ahead and does it. They call him single-minded and dedicated. Or a man realizes when he gets to be my age—thirty, next month—that the first goal was impossible, not even anything he still wants for himself. He gives up, and they call him mature and realistic. He's become adult."

He had defined his dilemma so favorably that I didn't raise the other possibilities. "You're choosing to be adult?"

"I still think about being an actor—the money, most of all, and having everybody back home see my name on the screen. But who really cares about them after all these years? I like this job. I like young people"—from Josh the phrase sounded odd—"Jenny and I have enough to eat and a roof over our

heads. You may think it's not much of a job for a college graduate." Looking into his eyes, I gave my head a discernible
shake. "But once I started to dream about being an actor, no
other work was worth doing. I didn't envy anyone—a doctor,
a judge. Now that my feelings have changed about acting,
one job is as good as another. I'm exactly as happy being a
guard here as I'd be as the college president."

⚜   ⚜   ⚜

I didn't go with Faye and Robert Rorke on their honeymoon, though Rorke suggested that I bring a girl and come
along to Mazatlán. The wedding itself was a quick trip to the
courthouse for a ceremony in the chambers of a municipal
judge. Two girls from Faye's residence club comprised, with
me, the entire guest list. Groom and bride were both dispir-
ited and approached the bench as though for sentencing.

To make Faye unattractive would have required surgery,
but her pale green dress left her complexion sallow where
brides traditionally bloom; any roses in her cheeks that day
were yellow ones. Rorke, in a foppish blue suit and a tie of
unharmonious stripes, had chosen colors that were exactly
wrong with hers. Such was the prevailing mood that no one
could have sworn his selection was unintentional.

Once the binding words were said, Faye distributed small
pecks democratically to her girl friends, to me, and to her
husband. Since it was my car that would be driving them to
the airport, I hadn't let the girls festoon its tail pipe with cans
and old shoes. Loreen, the smaller, blander of the girls, had
brought a tiny packet of rice, which she emptied over the
newlyweds on the courthouse steps.

At the international terminal we walked down a long echo-
ing corridor to the boarding gate, and as the Rorkes marched
ahead, I called to Faye that she should have been married
here. She looked back with a frown and didn't answer.

We learned at the gate that the plane had been delayed. None of us could think of any more festive way to pass the time than to sit on hard foam cushions and watch the red second hand revolve around the wall clock. I proposed a round of wedding drinks in the bar, but Faye, very nervous now, said they'd be sure to miss the announcement and the flight would leave without them.

When their plane did come creaking up to the gate, I was almost asleep and Rorke had fished out a newsmagazine from the black leather briefcase at his feet. As they finally took their leave, I said, "Have a good time." Stimulated by the whine of the jet engines, the starlets were shrieking, "Goodbye! Goodbye!" Faye was almost into the cabin when the bolder girl called, "Don't bother to send post cards!" I remembered that advice ten days later when Faye's post cards arrived at my door, followed, within a few days, by the bride herself.

꙲   ꙲   ꙲

It had begun, Faye said, on the flight down. The stewardess, a Mexican girl with soft, self-lubricating skin greeted them with "Buenas tardes." Unlike Ranchek, who fancied himself master of Spanish and peer with French, Rorke took a sulky pride in being ignorant of all foreign language. Since his aversion was well advertised, Faye was surprised to hear him trying a few guidebook banalities on the stewardess, who flashed her moist smile and winked at Faye.

Maybe, Rorke suggested, when they got to Mazatlán he could arrange lessons with her in the Español. "Oh, sí señor," said the girl with another wink at Faye.

She moved on down the cabin and Rorke said, "That's some woman!"

"Sí," said Faye, who was determined to give her honeymoon a chance. For the next two hours, at least until the plane landed, she was going to be a happily married woman.

Once they were on the ground, she and Rorke might quarrel, and he might hit her. But she wasn't going to be struck on an airplane.

Faye had always been afraid of flying, for the same reason she hated getting into elevators—it had nothing to do with heights. On stage, no matter how badly she performed, she knew she could escape. By law the stage door was kept open and the main exits couldn't be locked. So if they laughed, if they began to rock with laughter, if they looked at each other, tears of laughter in their eyes, and laughed in one long enormous bray, all of them together, finding solidarity and kinship in laughing at her, Faye could run off the stage and away from the sound of their laughter. Someday it would happen. Every time the curtains parted, her intuition told her this was the night they would laugh.

Such an irrational worry, and how she clung to it. Because each night when they began to applaud, she ran off stage tingling more delightedly than if she hadn't been tormenting herself all day. She loved the scare, but only because she knew she couldn't be trapped inside her nightmare. She could shake free.

But not if it happened while she was in an elevator. Or aboard an airplane. There she was a captive, and they could laugh and jeer and, just when she thought they were finished, erupt again. In a plane it could go on for hours, and for that reason no one on the flight must notice her. Her skin should look muddy, her ankles swollen, her hair a dull brown. Above all, Rorke must not slap her.

Driving into Mazatlán from the airport Faye agreed with their driver that the weather was lovely, though to her the air seemed flat and stale. The beach was one narrow arc of damp sand beneath the white outline of cramped unkempt hotels curving with the coast. Faye thought of a broken eggshell with a yolk that had run out rotten.

They were led to a room that opened onto a balcony, as

Rorke's cable had demanded. But it faced squarely on the hotel next door and only by sitting one behind the other, as in an opera box or a fighter plane, could they both see the ocean at the same time.

Faye learned the first day that Rorke didn't intend to make use of the balcony now that he had it. After dinner he hung behind in the hotel bar while Faye went upstairs to their room. "I'll be up in a minute," he said. She took from her suitcase the nightgown she had bought fourteen months ago, the day an instinct told her Rorke was getting ready to ask her to elope to Las Vegas.

Faye's own taste ran to frills, lace, black pants with risqué designs, but Rorke got nasty whenever he caught a glimpse, and her choice for her wedding night had been this plain white shift.

She tied her hair in a bow that came easily undone and slipped under the covers. She turned the sheets back neatly so that her husband couldn't imagine himself plunging into a contaminated pool. Carefully reconstructing their worst nights had persuaded Faye that of all the objects in the room, she should be the only one to look used.

When he didn't come up within fifteen minutes she turned off the lamp next to the bed and waited for him with her face lifted toward the door, letting the hall light reflect only her eyes. He would come upon her as a seductive cat curled on his bed. He liked cats. He even threatened, when they were settled, to buy a lion cub. Think jungle thoughts, Faye told herself. Of watering holes and salt licks and powerful hunting guns.

When she awoke it was morning. Rorke's side of the bed had been slept in but he wasn't there. Faye took twice her usual time to dress, and she was never hasty over her makeup or her hair. She was out the door on her way to breakfast when she heard a man laughing in the hall. She came back, rang the maid and took her roll and coffee on the balcony.

It was past ten when she got to the beach and found Rorke on a blanket with two American girls. He was radiating for them the gruff charm that Faye could scarcely remember from her first month with him. As she drew near, he got to his feet with obvious reluctance. Faye felt like a governess come to spoil his fun.

He seated her at the far edge of the girls' blanket. Faye hunched forward there, arms around her knees, hair falling over her bare shoulders, pulling at her knees, hugging them closer, trying to hide inside herself. The four of them were alone on this pocket of sand, and with no one admiring her, Faye suddenly felt ashamed of her looks. They were turning her into an awful joke.

Neither of these other girls was at all pretty, but they were laughing and teasing Rorke, pulling at the heavy reddish hairs on his leg, as though they were everything healthy and desirable and it was Faye who was the freak. Had they been beautiful, fairer than she, Faye might have been hurt or angry, but she couldn't help but admit that Rorke was justified in ignoring her. These girls were plain, worse than plain—pitted, squat, loud, cheap, stupid. Faye pulled at her knees until her breasts ached.

At lunch, Rorke was attentive to her. He ordered for them both and reached across the table to light her cigarette. He did not comment that after ten months she was smoking again.

In their room that afternoon he fell instantly asleep; at least he shut his eyes and breathed evenly. Then during the cocktail hour he went straight to the bar where one of the homely girls was waiting and matched her rum for rum while Faye took her dinner alone in the room. By ten o'clock she was asleep; the next night, by nine thirty.

The fourth day the girls went back to their jobs in Tucson, and Faye was still awake when Rorke turned the key and came into the room. He lifted his briefcase off the closet shelf and opened it on the table where Faye had been writing post cards. "If I turn the shade like this, the light won't keep you awake, will it?"

The question caught Faye off guard, and she slid down obediently between the sheets and closed her eyes. "No, that's fine," she said. Rorke dragged in one of the wooden chairs from the balcony and placed it so that Faye saw only his broad back and the heavy neck, red from his mornings on the sand. His pencil slid and skipped on the heavy scratch paper.

"I should have asked him to come to bed," Faye told me. "He would have made an excuse, but I should have done it. I couldn't stand him saying no, so I didn't say anything. It was my fault."

"I don't see how."

Faye had flown back in the same green traveling dress she wore at the wedding. At night, in the soft lights of my room, the color did less injury to her complexion. I would have hugged her to me except that a beautiful girl never arouses an emotion as simple as sympathy.

"Where is Rorke tonight?"

"I left him at his office. He thinks I went right out to the house he rented in the Valley. But I don't want to go there." She stopped and listened. "Is there someone in the bathroom, Bradley? Is that why the door is closed?"

"Don't worry."

"Why didn't you tell me? I could have come back in the morning."

"Never mind. What are you going to do?"

"What should I do?"

In those days, when I thought of marriage, it wasn't of my father's steady abuse or my mother's sly revenges, nothing I had seen for myself, only the promise of two people blending and aging into one golden self. Every marriage might not suc-ceed, but all divorce was failure. Wanting for Faye only the best and most blissful life, I sent her back to Rorke. "Be patient," I said.

"He did buy a bed before we left." She tried to smile. "That's a good sign."

⚑   ⚑   ⚑

A little later Rorke called from his office. "You haven't seen Faye, have you? I tried the house but she's not there."

"She left ten minutes ago. I think she wanted to walk on the beach before she drove to the Valley."

"She didn't get much sun in Mazatlán." If Rorke was embarrassed, his habitual arrogance was seeing him safely past it. "She picked up a bug the first night we were there and hardly got out of bed at all."

"Disappointing."

"You've got to get down there," he said. "That place is swarming with women and you can have anybody you want. Plenty of tourists, lots of local stuff. For a single man, it would be a paradise."

"It sounds good."

"I'm telling you," Rorke said, "except for Faye getting sick, it was the best two weeks of my life."

⚑   ⚑   ⚑

Two months after the election, three weeks from the first morning he went to work at City Hall, Ranchek moved out of Dawn's apartment and into his own one-bedroom apartment in the Hollywood Hills. Immediately on telling me that news, he added, "I didn't leave Dawn. She threw me out. Ask her. You will find that she confirms my version in every essential detail. Now if you have no further questions, I will be available to photographers on the south portico."

"It's pretty shabby, Ranchek."

"In that case we can make it the north portico."

When I called Dawn at the bank, she invited herself to dinner if I'd let her supply the food. She arrived juggling a pan of lasagna, a wooden bowl heaped with lettuce, tomatoes, cucumbers, and under an elbow a straw-ribbed bottle of chianti. "I know you don't cook," she said, bumping me away from the stove. "But I'd rather be here tonight than at my apartment. At least until George gets that damned bullfight poster out of the bedroom."

"Yours will be the first divorce with a court fight over which party has to take the community property." Using legal language to her was a mistake; it made her wistful. For several minutes she gave her full attention to the pan of cheese and ground meat.

Dawn had come from the bank, stopping only for lasagna from her freezer but not changing her dress. I thought of the times I had seen her behind a desk as she processed papers or talked on the telephone and realized I was never dumfounded then by the size of her breasts. Certainly tonight, beneath a plain jumper and starched white blouse, they looked large but not grossly out of proportion to Dawn's sturdy build. Her brown hair shone from the light above the sink, and the traces of age were faint on the back of her neck.

Holding my fingers back from that luminous hair, I thought how completely Ranchek had forced me to see Dawn through his eyes—as caricature, a funny-paper figure with monstrous bosoms, a walking bust to be leaned upon, wept over and fondled, but never as a woman with ordinary needs, other organs.

If that was true, he had been just as skilled in portraying me, even to myself, as his cranky old uncle, a ludicrous moralizer whose handling took all his boyish guile. Admittedly I had carried more fixed opinions to Southern California than I seemed to need, but at my worst I had never been so unbending as Ranchek liked to pretend.

I pulled Dawn away from the sink and told her what had been done to us. She was unamazed. "Let me tell you why I made Ranchek leave," she said.

The night before, he had returned from City Hall a little past six, brooding and silent in the noisy ways he had perfected. He coughed, sighed, mopped his forehead. He sweated so heavily that Dawn heard beads of sweat hit the table. A groan escaped him. When she didn't look up, he forced another, longer and lower pitched.

Dawn, curled up in her stocking feet, was midway through the crossword puzzle she had saved from the morning paper. She knew that soon she would have to ask Ranchek what was troubling him. It was likely to be his stomach.

Ranchek still suffered from the cramps and nausea that first led him to develop his body. Years with the weights had succeeded in building a physique, but Dawn considered the end result no better than remodeling an old house without providing for its plumbing. At the time they met, Ranchek's stomach made fearsome noises, of which he was proudly apologetic.

During the many months he had been out of work, Ranchek's stomach had not troubled him. Whenever he stuffed his tacos with red pepper, Dawn inquired after his digestion, but Ranchek replied softly, gallantly, that he felt fine. Dawn knew that he was, in fact, suffering no distress, though the way he lifted his chin when he answered was supposed to persuade her that he was miserable.

Across the room tonight, Ranchek went on thrashing his legs and squirming in his chair as though gripped by an awful fever. Still he said nothing. He was waiting for her to look up, ask solicitously what was the matter, wrench the nature of this newest ailment from him. Dawn sucked on her eraser and tried to guess at the Khmer word for princess.

She wanted to forget that in the bedroom closet were hanging five new suits, cut to Ranchek's improbable measurements by a fashionable tailor in Hollywood. When Ranchek siphoned from their joint account for this wardrobe, Dawn had questioned the expense, but he pointed out, only a little hurt, that he would need new suits for his job; good clothes in the long run were a better bargain than shoddy. Dawn had inherited her mother's feel for cloth, and any good material she detected in those suits was in their embossed labels.

The sighing across the room had become heart-rending. At least, Dawn consoled herself as she tried to ignore it, no new yellow sports car was nesting tonight in her carport. The magnitude of that expense had led Ranchek to broach it delicately. He needed a car, he said one night, and waited a full twenty-four hours before he added that because of his size, an economy model was out of the question. On the third day, though, he volunteered that his bulk could adjust itself to a foreign sports model, one that looked to Dawn no bigger than the cheap cars but was four times the price.

Dawn examined the brochure he tendered and found, to her relief, that the car was ugly. With its low sloping hood and indented headlights, it looked like a sly insect, no forthright bug, something with an insidious chirp and high-octane poison in its feelers. Even if the car had been indescribably beautiful she had prepared a persuasive argument against it: How wise would it be, speaking politically, for a city employee to show up at civic meetings in a notoriously expensive car, one moreover, built abroad?

"You can use mine," Dawn told Ranchek when he looked so crestfallen. "For its age, it's in better shape than I am. I'll take the bus." Ranchek's face let her know he considered hers a minor hardship compared with the sacrifice he was making.

But Dawn left him no choice, and within a day or two he brightened up and thanked her. Then, on his first trip downtown, the car blew a tire on the freeway. In the course of that inaugural week it stalled on the ramp and blocked all traffic in and out of City Hall garage. It also began to burn twice as much oil as gas. Ranchek reported each new disaster in a neutral voice. Not a word that he said, nothing in his tone, held Dawn responsible.

All the same she felt guilty. For about ten minutes. Then she got angrier than she had ever been in her life. Every trivial injustice through the years came rushing back to her, incidents so minor she was amazed at the power of her memory. And when that catalogue was exhausted, the real hurts, the ones she thought she had buried, confronted her again: That when she lost her baby Ranchek had not wired or called from France. That he conveyed afterward his suspicion that there had never been a fetus, nothing in her womb but a trap that snapped tight on him in Tijuana.

For a long time, Dawn thought, he has been trying to provoke me until I would criticize or discipline him, or put myself somehow in the wrong. He's worked at making me remind him that he was out of a job and I was paying his bills. I never did complain, or only once; or only twice. I haven't accused him of being lazy or thrown up to him his lack of effort. We survived that whole hard time without a quarrel because I kept telling myself that it would end, he would get a job. And because I was so determined that money, which had never mattered to me, shouldn't come between me and the one thing in my life I wanted.

I paid his bills, all, the foolish and indulgent ones along with the dentist bill and his ticket for jaywalking. At Christmas I took a loan, something I had never done, to let him buy the presents he wanted to give me. I never let him say: Oh, I'm a burden to you. Oh, you wish I were working. Oh, you deserve better than me.

Because I knew that when he said those things he would be saying goodbye. Something in my eyes, a word of mine, would be his excuse. Yes, of course, he'd say, I have been a burden. And he'd leave. Or so I thought.

Let him get work, I told myself, and my unnatural caution, this constant restraint, can end and I'll speak honestly again.

Ranchek will pay back the loans. He'll pay his half of our expenses, or more. When he does something foolish, I'll be able to show my irritation without his stricken look to say, Oh, yes, kick me while I'm down.

But I had it wrong, didn't I? I couldn't have understood him less. Me, who glances up at a man from my desk and knows his character, or at least his credit rating. This man I've lived with and never seen the most obvious thing about him: He wouldn't have left me if I had yelled or cursed or damned his ridiculous extravagance. He would have hung his head until my cursing stopped, until he could raise his face to forgive me. That's what he would have done. Without fail. No matter how many times I shouted or threw dishes across the room, he would forgive. Until I came to see myself as every female ogre, every grasping insensitive woman, every monster who's ever fed on a delicate soul and sucked it dry. Until I became his mother.

I won't do that for Ranchek. I am even stronger and more capable now than on that first day I met him. At the bank, the clerks and tellers call me sharp-tongued and too severe. But if I can do accurately, faster, what some men can't do at all, why spare their feelings? Why worry and scheme so that some man, who is hardly a man at all, will assure me I haven't lost my femininity? If I am too good a woman, let them all be better men.

Sex. The night he moved back I warned myself how careful I must be now, how, paying the bills, it would be easy to dominate him and make him indifferent to me, or render him impotent. I made a hundred good resolutions that night, and none of them had anything to do with George Ranchek. Just last night he was strong with me, stronger than on the night we conceived the baby. My dead son. I saw him, though he will always be a lie to Ranchek. Even last night I was too blind to see that George had come to bed to punish me. I took my punishment for pleasure.

Here's your money, that's what he was saying. Take it. Here's twenty dollars for my new shirt. Here. Count it. Eighteen, nineteen, twenty. Here's another six bucks for the steaks tonight. Here's fifteen for two bottles of whiskey, and get ready for it—here's my share of the rent. Are you counting? Here's the last penny I owe you. Take it.

Am I making too much of this? If it's what he needs from me, why not be Ranchek's father's wife for him? It's not so hard to say no, no sports car; to watch him sulk, knowing I'm right. To go off to bed for another night of the resentment that passed so easily for love.

No, I won't do it. I won't. I can but I won't.

If you loved him you would.

Yes.

You don't love him.

That's right. I don't love him.

Ranchek chose that moment to say, "I've been thinking—"

"I don't love you." Hearing the words spoken they didn't sound as true as when she said them to herself. "I don't love you. I want you to leave."

"He left?"

"Before midnight. He said, Where shall I go? I said, I don't care. Go. He said, can't I stay one more night and find a place tomorrow? I said, I want you out tonight.

"He went into the bathroom and stayed a long time. I pounded on the door. It's late, I said, you have to go. I'm sick, he said, sick to my stomach. The way he said it made me angry again. Go, I said. Get out of there and go. He came out with his toothbrush and razor. He took one of his new suits out of his closet. A shirt, I shouted at him. Take a clean shirt. He said, I'll stop tomorrow on my way to work. I said, I don't want to see you. Come at noon and take what belongs to you.

"He said, We can still be friends, can't we? Yes, yes, I said. Go."

I left Dawn alone and brought chairs to the table as she served our salad. We ate and talked about our jobs. When she was back at the sink with the dishes she said, "I think I've made it sound easier than it was." I adjusted the light to shine again on her hair. "At the time I wasn't stopping to think, but just the same I've never done anything harder. I knew when I said it that something important was ending for me. I could never take him back. That's what Ranchek would love, to be sent away and then called back. He'd love the tears and notes. Telegrams, phone calls. I know how he is. But I understood last night that if I told him to go I'd never agree to see him again."

"For your self-respect."

Dawn smiling looked serene. Ranchek had made her laugh so often and smile so rarely. "Girls at the bank come to me and ask how to tell if they're in love," she said. "I've got an answer for them, nothing to do with losing their virginity. It's when a girl has lost her self-respect and she's glad to be rid of it."

"Yours came back."

"Yes." She scrubbed at the last pan. "At least with virginity, once you've lost it, it's gone for good."

Soon after that, Dawn loaded her paraphernalia into a brown paper bag and left for her apartment. I called Ranchek at City Hall, where he was working late.

"Dawn was there? What did she tell you?" he demanded. "Nothing." "I know you won't believe me, but it's true that she threw me out." "It's no business of mine." "You think I used her while I was out of work and then as soon as I got a job, I left her." "That's the way it looks, doesn't it, George?"

Over the next weeks Ranchek fretted intermittently about securing a divorce, but it turned out that Tijuana marriages are legal in California only when registered in the couple's home county. Or so a law student told Ranchek, who was not disposed to inquire further. He was sure Dawn hadn't filed the papers and considered himself a free man.

Dawn must have reached the same conclusion, for when I stopped at the bank sometime later she had polished and restored to her desk the engraved plate with her maiden name. "She knew from the start we weren't legally married," said Ranchek, aggrieved. "She kept me as her plaything. And when I got old and started to lose my hair, she threw me out with nothing but a fine-toothed—"

"You have no complaint," I said. "None."

"I gave her my youth."

"It miscarried."

As if by sleight of hand, Ranchek's pensive expression gave way to a glower I recognized as his third most baleful look, the one usually reserved for breaches of public decorum.

✤   ✤   ✤

Every Wednesday and Friday that spring, Ray Morella rose early and left the house, not fully awake, for an art class at the university. I had heard about his paintings but I hadn't seen one, and Jeanne's appraisal was tentative. But Morella was no poseur. If he didn't have confidence in his work, I was sure he wouldn't delude himself by enrolling in the course.

It happened that on the first Friday he was gone, Ron Cooper called, entirely a coincidence, since Jeanne hadn't told him about the classes, and Ron, who called very seldom, had never timed his calls to the hours Morella was away. Jeanne boasted about having a jealous husband, but Ray seemed to take it for granted that a reconstructed Southern woman might enjoy talking occasionally with a Negro man.

Ron had just finished reading a book Jeanne must read and he wanted to drive right over with it. Had her husband been home, Jeanne would have told him to come, and Ron would have pulled up to the house with gears grinding and left his car idling in the driveway because it could be hard to start. He'd have shaken Ray's hand with pressure that was firm but not contentious and handed over to Jeanne the autobiography he admired so keenly. Within five minutes Ron Cooper would have been driving back through Laurel Canyon, out of the frowning white Valley.

But Ray was gone. Jeanne felt the black receiver weighing heavily in her hand and couldn't say the natural thing. How strange to be nervous with Ron when from the first time he spoke to her he had made her feel unfettered and free. "I was on my way out," she lied. "But I could meet you at the coffee shop on Ventura Boulevard."

"That's fine."

Jeanne drove her white convertible west into the sun, and as she squinted she thought, Did I bring my brush? I'll have to do my eyes again afterward. Afterward. She wondered, Why was I determined it shouldn't happen at my house?

Ron was waiting for her. That meant he had driven to the Valley before he called, positive Jeanne wouldn't hesitate to invite him over. He wasn't at all handsome today. In the harsh light his skin looked green. His eyes as they recognized her were timid. Their look made Jeanne angry with the Valley, this coffee shop. With him.

She was ready to plead an appointment and take the book and disappear. But he stood up for her, sat again to his left and patted the place he was making for her. It was an entreating pat and Jeanne yielded, sat, drank half his cup of coffee. When he asked her to come to a motel with him, she stood and walked briskly to her car on the side lot. Because of her hair she kept the top up, but the window on her side was open a few inches and Jeanne lifted her face toward the opening and said, "I'll follow you."

Was Ron relieved? She realized that he might have thought she was stalking away offended.

The clerk at the first motel did them a favor. As Ron opened the office door, he snapped off the vacancy sign and pretended to be busy at the switchboard. Both Jeanne and Ron felt much better then. Down the street the man was quiet but civil. Jeanne walked ahead toward the cabins. Ron went back to his car and waited there until she was inside with the door shut.

Jeanne had never believed this was going to happen, and wasn't disappointed that Ron coming through the door did not excite her in any conventional way. After the many years with Ray, her body still trembled whenever he reached for her. Ron only led her to the double bed, folded back its green rayon spread and pressed her down without a sign of desire. Jeanne felt her dress climb up her thighs. She let it bunch there, knowing it would wrinkle. Ron lifted her body and moved it slightly so he could lie beside her.

They embraced and stretched their bodies together. Ron tasted her mouth and smoothed her hair. After a time he unbuttoned his shirt very carefully and found the zipper that ran the length of her dress. He eased her slowly out of the top, the skirt, and draped it on the back of a chair near the bed. His own trousers he inched along, over the sharp curve of his buttocks, peeling them down like stockings, until with a quick shudder he could kick off his shoes and thrust the rolled pants from his ankles.

Back by her side, he guided her mouth to his chest and clasped her there until Jeanne took his dark nipple between her teeth. He sighed and stroked her head. He pulled her up with no urgency and kissed her and laid her head back on his breast. Resting there, she felt perfectly taken care of, and more maternal than when her son had been put in her arms. This man was her child, she was his little girl.

Without haste he unhooked the strap at her back and brushed away her underclothes as effortlessly as he had taken her out of her dress. She lay next to him, naked except for her stockings. In the pale light from behind the window shade he was brown, dark brown, and purple, and at the groin white, where his cotton shorts concealed him.

Until this afternoon Jeanne had hated making love with her stockings on. In several beds she had sat forward and pulled them off while at her ear a man muttered, they don't matter, leave them. Nor had she consented to be naked in a room until the man had taken off his clothes. She was afraid to be seen and fondled by a man who could pull himself away and leave, and never tell her why. Here with Ron she didn't have that worry. He would know and do what she wanted; he would want the same. She turned to let her small breasts rest upon his ribs and nuzzled softly on a nipple as it toughened under her tongue.

At last, with a careless motion, he rubbed down his white shorts and swung onto her. She watched him above her, smiling into her eyes. A mild sensation stirred inside her and she ran her hand down his long back. She received him, and when he fell forward she took him into her arms and let him bury his face in her hair. He stayed with her like that for many minutes, still moving as he kissed the edges of her face.

When he tumbled to his place beside her, Jeanne wanted to ask him not to dress until she came back from washing. It made her awkward to come from a bathroom and find the man already into his shoes. But at that moment she didn't care to hear her own voice, and she only took her stockings off and hung them with her dress. Ron nodded mock-solemnly at her as she turned in the doorway. Twice she stopped her washing to look out, but he was waiting on the bed, smoking and humming softly.

Jeanne left the bathroom naked. She watched to see that he was seeing her as she gathered up her clothes deliberately and began to put them on. When her hair began disappearing beneath the white nylon, Ron drew her back to the bed and kissed her at that place. The warmth of his breath was a mild pleasure. She didn't pull away. The instant ended and she was in her dress. "Stay there," Jeanne said aloud as she went to unlock the door. Ron watched her leave, still naked on the bed, not reaching for his shirt. Her last view of him was stretching until the light pads of his feet touched the blond footboard. He smiled, without regret, smiled as though he liked her as much now, and in the same ways, as when they came into this room.

Driving home Jeanne hardly knew what she felt. It was not the luxurious aching from a night with her husband. Ron had demanded no exertion. When he covered her, it had been a commitment no greater than when he took her hand for the first time. From their first meeting, Jeanne had sensed in him a strong feline streak, nothing to disturb her, something that had let her go with him today. Caressing his body, running her tongue over him, not between his legs but chastely at his heart, doing that today had made her this man's equal and reassured her about all men. How, or why she needed reassuring, Jeanne could not have said.

Driving along the route she had traveled for a month, Jeanne no longer had to watch for street signs or count the seven motels she passed before she turned into the driveway of the one Ron had chosen. Hands full with the steering wheel and her mind free, she could speculate this day on whether or not she was an adulteress.

The word brought back an afternoon when she and her best girl friend, finished with jacks, had snuck down the Old Testament from its shelf. They understood none of the archaic words, but they tingled to cadences hinting of wickedness. Adulteress: she could smell the Bible's leather binding on that hot day. The word was too grandiose. But if not that, what? She had never been a wife, not now, not even when she

173

married for the first time. Not wife, and absolutely never spouse. Parent? Sexless, speaking only of legal responsibilities. Mother? Charged with emotions beyond anything she felt for Sonny.

She could not be Ron's lover. It was being used carelessly these days but the word was masculine. Nor was she his mistress—too feminine and dependent. Paramour? Obsolete. Hopeless, anyway, with its echoes of paramount, blackamoor. For two people in bed at least twice a week, friend was coy. Mate was right for Ray, nobody else. With him, she felt mated. Concubine? See the honeysuckle, Jeanne sang to herself, and the concubine.

Back home they'd have words for her. She pronounced several of them aloud as she turned into the parking lot and shut off the ignition. Those old words didn't excite her anymore or touch secret reserves of guilt. They were simply the wrong words.

✹ ✹ ✹

Always before, Doug Goodwin had left for Tennessee late at night but had timed his return to enter Los Angeles before noon, as though to prove he could face the city at its brilliant worst. Before his latest retreat, I had mentioned that pattern to him, and when he came back after a month he arrived at midnight and called from a bar in Santa Monica: "Drive on out and I'll stand you to a nightcap."

I found him in a booth next to a pool table where two girls in sweatshirts were finishing a game. Sometimes the clicking of balls or their swearing made Goodwin stop talking until they were quiet. He had contracted gonorrhea on this latest trip, he said, and the doctor at home had forbidden liquor for ten days. But Goodwin couldn't sit in a bar without drinking, and he was compromising with beer sipped very slowly. Taken that way, he complained, the malt turned sour in his mouth and hit his belly without the icy crash and shiver.

We were an ill-assorted pair, me so deeply tanned I believed my skin could never again fade to the dead white of Goodwin's face. He seldom went willingly into the sun, and he looked the more drawn after driving all day and night. One lock of hair still tumbled onto his forehead, but the strand had thinned so much that to suggest carelessness it had to be conscientiously pressed in place. It was not impossible that if the girls at the pool table had been disposed to notice men, they might have looked first at me.

I was moved to tell Goodwin about my hesitancy years ago with the French prostitutes, and when I finished, he was chuckling. "You had to go all the way to Bordeaux to discover women, Brad?"

"To discover whores," I said. "For women I had to come to California."

"You can explain the difference?"

"Why so glum? Because you can't do the two things you like best?"

"What makes you say that?"

"If you picked up this thing back home, I assume that from the time you went to a doctor, four, five days ago, you haven't been—"

"You're a good man, Brad."

"How many times, then?"

"Three. Twice in El Paso, once in Tucson."

"Why?" I felt the crabbed, smug side of myself, the Friends' creature, rousing from his long sleep and using my eyes to stare incredulously across the table.

"Why not?" he asked negligently.

"Do you hate them that much?"

"That's what they say, isn't it? That if you get around to a lot of women, you either hate them or they scare you."

"I used to think that," I said. "I don't anymore."

"If you complain," Goodwin said, "about having to do something that another man wants to do, he's got a right, hasn't he, to say, Just who asked you to trouble yourself in the first place? I feel that way whenever I read about a man saying how hard it was for him to write his book. I want to say, Don't think you've got to do it on my account. So if I sit here complaining about having to make love, you can say, Look, I got a knife right here—all your troubles can be over."

"I don't have a knife."

Goodwin smoked cigarettes to the nub and his fingers were stained with nicotine. He never succeeded, either, in digging all the factory grease from under his nails. He held up his dis-colored hand and grimaced. "I look at this sometimes on a woman's leg, and I think it's dead. There's no feeling in my fingers. Then I move it up and touch her, and she's like all the others. When you're a kid, you think they're going to be dif-ferent, different sizes, colors. But they're the same and my hand doesn't change when it touches them. That's when I feel tired. I'm ready for it, I don't want to stop. But I'm tired.

"There's been a lot of times I haven't liked the woman, or I don't know her, could hardly remember her name. But I've got to start saying something and it's always the same: You're good, you're beautiful. All that time she's not listening to me, she's hearing some cowboy from a movie she saw ten years ago. She only wants to get it over with so she can go home and think about it and make it better than what I can give her. She'll remember that I said her name when I didn't even know it. Six months go by and she remembers feeling this big explosion when nothing happened at all.

"Sometimes I think of all that and I get mad. I think, Why should I be working so hard? Just being there under me, she thinks she's doing me a favor. But what do I really get out of it? She'll go home and remember this guy that had her, she'll make my face better, she'll forget about the two teeth I'm out at the back. That's what she gets—a chance to lie to herself about what she remembers. But I don't want to remember. I never can, anyway. I don't remember anything about ninety out of a hundred. So it's easy to start wondering if I haven't been the one who was used, when the whole world thinks it's the other way around. You think I hated those women in El Paso, but I wasn't really trying to hurt them. At the back of my head, I guess I was thinking, Well, if a couple of them get the clap now and then, they'll know anyway it was no movie."

"It's better to be a late starter," I said. "I still think they're doing me a favor."

"They are." It was a joke straight f.om the Army, when we had to insult each other.

A fortyish bar maid had come to announce last call, and she saw the bottle Goodwin had laid on its side, toying with it as he talked. With a simper she asked, "Spin the bottle?"

"Sure," Goodwin said. She gave it a tap that whirled it twice and landed its neck exactly between Goodwin and me. "Pay up," she said, pursing her lips and bending over to Goodwin's mouth.

✠   ✠   ✠

Doug Goodwin's words came back on the afternoon I was unbuckling my belt for an injection to cure my own wound. "Have you been promiscuous?" the elderly doctor asked me.

"No," I said.

"Then you know who was responsible?"

"No."

My answer annoyed the doctor and he lectured me on my duties as a citizen. I shouldn't try to shield the girl, he warned me. Nor should I try to punish her.

Punish her? For giving me a damaged gift? It could have been one of several girls, and I would remember all the evenings long after this ugly red sore had disappeared.

I left the clinic without trying to explain to this upright man with his hypodermic needle that none of it mattered.

Not an occasional disease for me or an abortion for Goodwin's women. Not my disappointment when one girl moves on or the night of tears for another girl who persuaded herself I'd never leave.

My nights were not beautiful or sordid; not a cataclysm, not a revelation, not a test. They were pleasant nights with willing girls, and as the crusaders passed beneath my window I was deaf to their slogans: Keep sex holy. Keep it hidden. Find yourself in sex. Lose yourself. Liberate or prove yourself.

Even had I been tempted to letter my own banner and raise it high, I couldn't expect to rally an army with the cry, It doesn't matter.

🙢 🙢 🙢

The small house Robert Rorke had rented was in Studio City, a suburb that spills over the hills behind the Hollywood Bowl and into the southeastern San Fernando Valley. The front of the house looked out on a few outdoor sets from the old studio where an eighty-minute Western had been ground out every week of the nineteen-thirties. The front lawn was enclosed by a picket fence—a token gesture of privacy, just as the decaying rose arbor in the back had been a half-hearted concession to romance.

Rorke had taken the house unfurnished. By the time I got around to calling on them, he still had bought no more than the bed, a half-acre of coils and ticking, so vast that from their respective corners two contenders could flail and swing and never touch gloves.

With the lobster thermidor that evening Faye served up yet another girl, pink and jolly this time but an actress nevertheless. Though I met prettier girls shopping for lettuce in Hollywood, this Meredith seemed good-natured, and I counted on her presence to save us from bickering, since she was a spy from the world that considered Faye, with her bungalow and working husband, the true Hollywood success story.

Working Rorke may have been, but from the hints he dropped there were difficulties developing at his office. He knelt across from me on the dining room floor and talked about joining the Peace Corps or, after twelve civilian years, taking up his commission again with the Army paratroopers. I wondered if he had run into a stock analyst even surlier than he was.

Waiting on us, Faye scampered in a ruffled red apron between the kitchen and the dining room and missed most of Rorke's fantasy. What she did hear she treated respectfully.

When she had us settled for demitasse on cushions in the living room, Faye told Meredith her plans for decorating the house, what styles in furniture she was considering, what shops in Beverly Hills and San Francisco would supply the fixtures and materials. Rorke indulged her fancies as courteously as she had listened to his, and none of the four of us mentioned the incompatibility of olive drab at Fort Bragg and plum-colored vinyl in a verdant suburb of Los Angeles.

Margo Stein was nobody's concept of a sentimental woman, but when she enrolled again at the ballet school four years after pregnancy had put a stop to her lessons, her eyes clouded over and she had to blow her nose. Margo returned to class with no hope. Stiff and heavy as she was, she doubted she could qualify for the chorus in a mediocre company, and her teacher didn't encourage her to set her sights that high.

Their very futility made the lessons precious to Margo. She loved the afternoons when she deposited Jacob with a neighbor and drove over Cahuenga Pass into Hollywood. She didn't envy the girls in the class five years younger than she, slight, nervous girls who mooned after the teacher and lived a month on his praises. For their part, these girls treated Margo better than the classmates four years ago who had been her age. They, Margo's contemporaries, had seemed to find her presence in class demeaning to them. They had made her feel that by daring to study ballet, clumsy as she was, she exposed the rest of them to ridicule.

The new girls understood that Margo had no ambition beyond being allowed to continue in the class, and to them Margo's heaviness turned her persistence into something admirable. Pushing on with her exercises when they knew she wanted to collapse, Margo impressed them, and her coming back to ballet as a housewife reassured those girls who had vowed that husband and family must wait upon a triumphant debut. You see, those unswerving young women told themselves, motherhood is not everything. For that heavy young woman it was not even enough.

I saw the Steins at their new house in Van Nuys during the first month Margo was dancing again. Telling me about the class and the way she could accept her limits, she was alight with pleasure. Billy listened as though he were hearing it for the first time, very happy for his wife and grinning less than usual.

Autumn came, went, then those foggy gray days that pass in Los Angeles for winter. I escaped on vacation to Mazatlán, where I was less rapturous than Rorke, probably because I stubbed my pride on a girl from Cincinnati who made me realize that Southern California girls did not speak for the nation and there were still women in the middle of the nineteen sixties who thought it was entered in a cosmic ledger how many men they slept with.

I was into my second week when Lonnie Chapman wrote to tell me that an automobile had run through a red light and struck Margo in a crosswalk. Her leg had been broken and she would be in a cast to the thigh for at least three weeks.

It was Lonnie, too, reading my notebooks a few weeks ago,

who pointed out that if I were writing fiction I'd have to elim-
inate Margo's accident. Coming so soon after she had returned to class, her bad luck seemed unbelievable.

❦   ❦   ❦

With Ranchek unwed again in every place but Mexico, we
met occasionally for dinner as we had when I was new to Los
Angeles. In those remote days I had waged a campaign to sell
marriage to Ranchek; this time around it was he who testified
for the married state, not in anything he said but with a dolo-
rous air that argued eloquently against bachelorhood. Restless
and tentative, he seemed perched perpetually on a curtain rod,
ready at the first invitation to flutter back to his cage.

Whenever he spoke of Dawn, which was often, he bathed
her in nostalgia. "She was a remarkable woman, wasn't she?"
he'd say, looking around the restaurant as though anything
else in skirts was a female impersonator.

"She's not dead, Ranchek. I spoke to her the other day."

"Where is she living now?" He had been shredding a paper
napkin, but to prove his indifference he stopped and looked
squarely at me. "Los Feliz, I suppose? Or Compton, out near
her brother?"

When she moved, Dawn asked me not to give Ranchek
either her new address or her unlisted telephone number. She
was sure that one night, too drunk to restrain himself, but
sober enough to dial, Ranchek would call. She didn't say so,
but she was afraid that if she had just finished her usual
whiskey nightcap, she might not bolt the door in time, or
want to.

Ranchek's lachrymose moods didn't stop him from inviting
out the girls around City Hall, plain jolly secretaries who
laughed at jokes he had rehearsed for five years on Dawn.
They stayed weekends at his apartment and drove off Sunday
nights, leaving Ranchek with a bleary feeling of discontent.

He found something lacking in them all, and I remember particularly his complaint that one girl wasn't intelligent when he meant, rather, that she didn't meet his requirements in temper or pride.

※   ※   ※

When Margo Stein's leg mended improperly, she was returned to the hospital to have it broken again and reset. Her frame of mind as she lay in a six-woman ward was ambiguous, even to her. She was not bitter or afraid of pain. She might have been marking time, except that once she left the hospital, there was nothing to anticipate. Her leg could heal, the second cast be removed, and no change would come into her life with the cutting away of the plaster.

Margo believed in nothing. That was her belief: no fate or afterlife, no benevolence at work here below. Yet from the day of her accident she had been visited by a sense that she was owed a debt, and since no higher power was looking after her, the debt had to be her own, to herself.

One evening Lonnie Chapman visited her in the hospital. Margo was glad he came by himself, not with her husband or Rose Weiner. Lonnie brought a pound of caramels, candy that made Margo's silver fillings ache, and she was angry about his choice until she remembered that Lonnie didn't have to know what kind of candy she liked. Billy had to know; Lonnie didn't.

The year she graduated from high school, Margo's thoughts had not been so different from other girls'. But while they let their fantasies linger, Margo, more from pride than guilt, drove hers away as quickly as they came. "Isn't that boy adorable?" the other girls whispered. "Isn't he cute?" Margo, who knew that the boy would never look her way, answered fiercely, "No! He's stupid! He's nothing. I say he's shit." Her habit had made Billy's proposal easier to accept.

Now here was Lonnie Chapman, one of the boys she had ridiculed, Lonnie who had become her husband's best friend, standing at her bedside with a box of candy. He hadn't brought it because she was beautiful and he desired her, only because her lameness excited his pity.

Margo was capable of throwing his candy back at him. She didn't. Lonnie was seeing life clearly, as she tried to do, and pity was what she deserved. What she couldn't bear were the lies he began to tell: that her leg, with pain leaping from her toes to the joint of her hip, was healing perfectly, that soon she'd be better than new. If visiting hours had not ended, Margo might have screamed, except that Lonnie would have expected her scream and understood it and with real compassion would have told the story to Rose Weiner.

※   ※   ※

Lonnie's visit to the hospital left him depressed. Something in Margo, he said, was desperate to fly, something in the universe was determined she would not.

"Even at your worst," I said, "you were never that mystical. It's Rose's influence. No games, no games, you said. But here you are playing at the oldest one."

Lonnie was too euphoric to take offense. "Playing," he corrected me. "Not playing at. Credit me at least with complete capitulation."

※   ※   ※

The coincidence did not escape Jeanne Darling that both her husband and her lover shared a fondness for art. When she had first met Morella he told her that growing up in Chicago he had painted in Saturday classes at the art institute and he sometimes regretted not going on with it. She took his confession lightly, thinking back to the erotic poems she had written to while away her virginity. But when he enrolled at the university, she was disconcerted. Coming less than a year after their marriage, she took this sign of restlessness as a reflection on her. She tried to act pleased, though, and exerted herself to admire his paintings.

Ron Cooper's work was easier for Jeanne to appreciate; she admitted that Ron's selling a dozen of his sketches might have influenced her judgment. Neither man had shown signs of an artistic temperament, neither expected to live by his brush, and their practicality comforted Jeanne. She was profoundly afraid of failure, not so much for herself as for the men around her. That included her son. She tried to hide it from Sonny, but when his grades were due she worried until she had the card in her hand. On those rare occasions he brought home less than perfect marks she had to bite down and swallow to keep from scolding him.

Now that she and Ron Cooper were meeting regularly at a Valley motel, Jeanne spent less time with him than during the weeks he had left her at her car without a kiss. He no longer invited her for those evenings around a café table, hers the one white face, to listen as black men quarreled over strategy, old hurts, the future. Ron never explained Jeanne to the others and no one had remarked on her. Very few black women joined the sessions. Those who did were tall, moody girls with bosoms as boyish as her own. They nodded when Jeanne took a seat.

With every reason to feel uncomfortable at the table, she never did. Perhaps because all that was expected of her was to be still. Their indifference freed her from the burden of being herself and she became invisible. Her lack of importance, existence, made Jeanne more light-headed than if she had been the center of attention. And she never forgot that Ron could see her. Even as he argued against a challenge from across the table, he could appreciate the variations in her reticence.

For weeks now he hadn't suggested that she join them.

When Jeanne asked about men she had met—Ernie, with his medallion of a spider embalmed in clear plastic—Ron said Ernie was fine, just fine.

🎌   🎌   🎌

Learning to care for Rose, Lonnie Chapman got a bonus: she gave him the excuse to extricate himself from his vows of poverty and chastity. But why Rose when any woman would have served? I suspected it was her firmness that appealed to Lonnie. Rose had a stance, a sense of being rooted to a spot of her choosing, that Lonnie for all his strength and suppleness couldn't match. She walked straight up and down, hardly moving at the pivotal joints, and conveyed with her doughty small body the integrity Lonnie had tried to achieve through philosophy.

In his company, Rose was fond but far from adoring. She let Lonnie know that he attracted her and that, although the attraction was a welcome surprise, she would have been equally determined to have him spindly or astigmatic. On the subject of sex, Lonnie had, after all, stated his case: it was so absorbing to him he had tried to swear off entirely. With fervor like that, Lonnie could afford the arid streak in Rose that had discouraged less passionate men.

On the street, Rose was the opposite of Jenny Black, who went pale whenever Josh's eye lighted on another girl. Rose encouraged Lonnie to notice lovely women. Passing a beauty she would say briskly, "Attractive," a word to convey that she knew Lonnie could have such a woman, that by choosing her instead, he had ratified her values. United on a higher plane they could patronize more obvious charms, though I had a hunch that Lonnie, like most men, didn't object to a touch of the obvious.

Rose, who taught high school in East Los Angeles, must surely have despised Lonnie's job as much as his parents did, but she was patient and never critical. Her waiting tactic proved itself within six months of their meeting when Lonnie decided of his own accord to return to the university for a doctorate. He would pay his way by teaching in the afternoons at the Valley college. I happened to be with them when Lonnie made the announcement, and Rose took it calmly, as though he were transferring from one parking lot to another.

"All that philosophy lived so conscientiously," I said. "Gone."

"You can't live by a philosophy," he said, as though it had been my idea to try.

"Will you start eating meat again?"

"I've lost the taste."

"Your other tastes—?" I thought better of it and stopped.

"My other tastes survived intact," he said. Rose, being modern, knew when an old-fashioned response was appreciated and she blushed as best she could.

When Lonnie signed a contract to teach in the Valley, it seemed likely he would encounter Josh Black. But three weeks before the start of the fall term, Josh and Jenny packed their belongings into their old station wagon and decamped for Arizona.

Ranchek and I had volunteered to help them pack, a simple job, it turned out, since Jenny was not one for hoarding. Old clothes, worn-out toys, even, I was displeased to learn, the letter I had written from New York six years ago heralding my arrival, everything was consumed and thrown out. If Jenny had never succeeded in making her living room more cheerful than her garage, she kept them equally uncluttered. "Why are you going?" I asked Josh.

"Money." As chief security officer on a larger campus his salary would be two thousand dollars more than the Valley college could offer him. I wanted to inquire after his career, but the word would have sounded like a taunt. "How about acting?"

"Hollywood will get along without me." Josh's rare moments of humility invariably came out snide.

"They've got a very good drama department there," Jenny called from the kitchen. "Josh can star in their productions."

Ranchek looked up from the baby's crib he was trying to collapse. "All the avant-garde work is being done in colleges," he said. "It's curtains for the commercial theater."

"Squeak, squeak, George," called Jenny, who had seen his act. "Squeak."

"Squeak, squeak," Ranchek added. "They've gone to Cinerama."

I packed linen in soup cartons and glassware in tall oblong cigarette boxes. From the back of the hall closet Black dragged out his green Army jacket with its arm patch of a tricolored fleur-de-lis. The coat still fitted through the shoulders, but he couldn't get the middle button closed. The brass on the lapels had tarnished to a deeper green than the fabric. "I haven't worn this for six and a half years," Black said.

I had been listening for a note of pain as Josh talked about leaving Los Angeles. In the Army neither modesty nor superstition had stopped him from treating fame as his foster mother who was readying a room for him on the West Coast. "Look me up in Los Angeles," he'd tell gawky recruits. "I'll fix you up with a movie star."

If success had been that lavish in her promises, could Josh be leaving now without bitterness? He picked up the leather scrapbook with his one review and I watched for his expression to soften, but he tossed it into a box with their other books—a green-backed copy of de Sade, *The Joy of Cooking*, two hard-cover reprints by the Arizona Senator who had lost the last Presidential election.

I said, "Where you're going, Jenny's politics will be popular."

"Populist?" cried Ranchek from behind the drapes he was disentangling.

"I don't think Jenny will get involved in all that again," Black said. "Will you, honey?"

Jenny popped into the doorway, her limp brown hair hanging straight, her forehead and cheek smudged; glowing. "No, I'm going to stay home more." She didn't explain how, short of chaining herself to the water heater, that would be possible. From the time eight months ago that her women's study group had dissolved in schism, the Blacks so rarely went to the theater that Ranchek claimed Josh had starred in one more play than he had seen. For a long time Josh had done their grocery shopping on his way home from the campus.

Jenny called from the kitchen that a lucky aspect of the move was its timing. Their elder child was about to start school, and now she wouldn't be torn away from her new friends. To that I argued what I was coming to believe: that the greatest gift parents can give their children is an unhappy childhood; adult life forever after is an agreeable surprise.

Black protested loudly, Jenny again dropped her perfunctory cleaning to debate the point, but Ranchek, swathed in the drapes he had brought down, preempted their attack. "My sister used to shout at my mother that she hadn't asked to be born," he said. "But was that true?" Ranchek's sense of high seriousness set his jowls aquiver. "Is not the sexual urge, that force so strong it overwhelms all resistance, is that not the celestial prompting of a billion voices pleading to be born?"

"No," I said.

"No, George," Jenny agreed. "I really don't think it is."

"Could we have a show of hands?" I had withdrawn long before from Ranchek's games, but when he called for the nay votes, the Blacks each dutifully raised a hand. Sadly Ranchek counted the tally. "One in favor, two opposed, one abstention. I want everyone in the chamber today to know I do not consider this vote a defeat and that I fully intend to resubmit the measure at an appropriate time in the near future."

"That will have to be in Arizona, I'm afraid," Jenny said. "With the cost of moving, it's going to be a while before we'll be getting back."

"That's right," Black said.

I knew as we stuffed the last bits and ends into a box that this wasn't the time for the questions I longed to raise with them, and I would never have another chance.

With Josh, I wanted to penetrate his bravado and ask when he had really given up. Had it happened at the same moment he first dreamed of being a movie star? As the prospect raced his pulse, did a fatalism assure him he would never come close? Or did Josh have what he had claimed, strength to look himself over and decide he wasn't good enough? He might say it; could he mean it?

With Jenny, no matter how eagerly she promised to play the game, I would never get an honest answer. Still I wanted to try: Have you ever believed in the talent you've praised so loyally? Or does leaving here today make you an honest woman for the first time in your married life? If, by a fluke, Josh did succeed, have you known he would use his new confidence to leave you? Do you see that he blames you for what is happening today? That he will never admit to surrendering now that you've evacuated him? Are you doing it to spare him? Were you absolutely sure he would go on failing? Or are you taking him away to hide him and keep him failed?

It led, my interrogation, to the one question I cared about: Have either of you tried to answer these questions for yourself? I suspect you haven't, and if not, why should I want to force you to look at your lives? If you can blunder through your large decisions, why am I angry that your instincts protect you? When I was younger my greatest hope was that everyone on earth could be happy. It was an adolescent wish I have outgrown. But for all its sentimentality, it was more sensible than asking them to be honest.

"Here's the bottle Doug brought us last Christmas." Josh held up a dusty bottle of Bordeaux rouge from a vineyard near our old camp. "No use trying to take that." While he rummaged around for a corkscrew, Jenny unpacked four glasses with a faint suggestion of bad grace. Even this bare reprieve for her husband she took as a defeat.

⚑　　　⚑　　　⚑

For more than a month Ray Morella had been getting a slight headache late in the morning. He felt fine when he got up, and he ate breakfast and read the sports page with a clear head. But at the hour he would ordinarily go into the bedroom and take up his paints, a cloudy pain, less sharp than persistent, began forming behind his eyes. Then his eyes would grow sore at the sockets and ache when he rubbed them. No tablets helped. Ray could only go back to bed and wait for the pain to lift. Lying on top of the covers, he shouted to Jeanne that she should call the restaurant and tell them he was sick again.

The year the restaurant opened, when Ray and his partners had parceled out their hours, he had asked specifically for the late shift, and many times since then he had shown up with ailments worse than this dim buzzing in his head.

But lately Sidney, whose wife was divorcing him, had installed himself permanently at a corner table where he stayed until closing time. He had been Ray's best friend at high school, the man whose uncle back East had arranged the loan that got them started, and until the divorce he had never taken more than two doubles. But lately he was not quite drunk and never sober. When Jeanne called, Sidney had already spent enough time in the bar to be morosely sympathetic. He forgot that two days ago, five days, seven days, Jeanne had called with the same story. "Don't let Ray worry about a thing," Sidney said. "I'd be here anyway. The important thing is for him to get well."

Ray knew, without going to a doctor, what his trouble was: he painted badly, and worse than that, badly in a style he didn't like. His visions might glow and shimmer, but when he raised his hand to capture them, he could only daub dark brown paint in thick ugly squares. Once in front of Jeanne he had thrown down his brush and shouted, "I want to create beauty," and Jeanne had been touched by his daring to use the word.

Ray got his headaches and didn't need therapy to tell him they were connected to a sense that he was failing. If that was simple, this was less so: when Jeanne had called Sidney and after Ray napped fitfully for an hour, he awoke with the headache gone. He should have left then for the club, but with the excuse already made, he went instead to his latest canvas. Ray disliked painting by artificial light, but he switched on every lamp and fixture and painted until Jeanne knocked on the door to say it was time for dinner.

What Ray couldn't explain to his wife was that even at his lowest point, when his arm fell back of its own discouragement, he lived while he painted in a way he never felt at the restaurant or the pool or smoking in the garage. In the throes of a new headache, burrowing his face in his pillow, Ray thought: Painting means so much to me that I don't want to do it. These headaches let me hold back until I'm so nervous that something pushes me into the room and I have to pick up a brush. Holding back until five or six o'clock at night, I manage to be painting all day.

With Jeanne, Ray talked about the headaches as only a physical ailment, a nuisance. But she could see for herself the stack of ugly canvases growing larger in the fourth bedroom, a room that Ray had jokingly called the nursery until Jeanne asked him, please, to stop.

***

Dawn became engaged to the manager of the bank across the street from the one where she worked, but she didn't wear his ring. "I hardly know him," she said, when I asked her why. "The third time he came to my apartment he handed me this ring and asked me to keep it while I decided whether or not to marry him. It's home in the drawer in my bedroom. I guess I'll give it back to him next week."

"You're not in love?"

"I don't even like him." Below the neck, Dawn's light pure laughter could become an obscene spectacle, and today our elderly waiter was giving her his solicitous attention. "It was easier for me to take the ring than argue about it. I don't think he bought it for me, anyway. The plush on the box is crushed, and the setting is straight out of the ads five years ago. I think it was an investment for him, and he likes to have a girl hold on to it so it's not going to waste."

Whatever her complaints about this beau and others, Dawn seemed to be enjoying their attention after the years with a man as unromantic as Ranchek. They took her to the movies, brought her flowers, drank four rye and gingers and told their life stories. As she listened, Dawn was marveling at how restful life without Ranchek could be. It was nice to be alone again, and with these sober harmless men she was.

***

Jeanne Morella wanted to believe she had fallen in love with her lover. On the days she was slack with herself, she could almost make the idea plausible: Away from Ron time certainly passed slowly. She endured empty days and tedious slow weekends for the moments she would be in bed with him. Lying beside him, she felt something different from anything in her life and she longed to elevate that difference and call it love.

It couldn't be sex, or not sex alone, though the afternoons would have lost their meaning if Ron stopped wanting sex with her. One afternoon he had been content to kiss and fondle her, and during the drive home Jeanne was quite ready to weep, except that freeway traffic was heavy at that hour and she'd have had to pull off a ramp in North Hollywood and sit sobbing by the curb.

From the time she had divorced Sonny's father, Jeanne let casual acquaintances, men like the one who did her hair, or the girl who mimeographed her column, regard her as more practiced about sex than she really was. The deception suited her, like the new styles, the shorter skirts that flattered her slim figure, and walking along Wilshire Boulevard in Beverly Hills, Jeanne saw nothing preposterous in believing that a hundred former lovers trailed in her wake. At less buoyant times she had to admit the number had been one-tenth that amount and that even today there was much about her hours with Ron Cooper for which experience hadn't prepared her.

The silences she had taken as proof of their intimacy sometimes could embarrass her, and spunky though she might be, she babbled from nerves, saying any foolish thing to break the quiet, until Ron laughed and laid a finger on her lips.

One afternoon he had driven her to his apartment in a building near the Baldwin Hills reservoir. The neighborhood was mostly Negro and entirely middle class. A procession of neat sedans was parked along the winding curbs. As Ron turned the key to the front door and stepped back for her, Jeanne felt herself becoming terribly prim. She went to the ivory-colored couch, sat with her knees pressed tight and let Ron mix the drinks and serve her. She heard her false voice as she thanked him. Horrified, she listened to her shrill exclamations over his sketches, his stereo, the view from his balcony.

Before she married him, Jeanne had treated Ray Morella's apartment as an extension of his character; it was good enough but needed a woman's touch. She told him where to put the chairs, what kind of cleanser to buy, how to defrost a refrigerator, and Ray deferred gladly, happy she cared enough to criticize him.

Ron's apartment was not at all connected to him, but it intimidated Jeanne and she wouldn't have dared to suggest a change. In his bedroom she had been startled to find a poster of a Negro hero. As they made love she winced under those sad deep eyes. But if she told Ron she'd been surprised, Jeanne knew that in this hateful new voice of hers, surprise would come out as disapproval, and he would jump nimbly from the bed, pull out the thumbtacks, roll up the heavy brown face. All the while he'd be laughing at her protests and explanations, and she was sure that when she left he wouldn't put the poster back again, though they both understood that the visit had gone badly and she wouldn't be returning.

At the motel on Ventura Boulevard they tried to get the same small room at the back of the court. After their fourth or fifth appearance the manager started to save it for them. The window opened to a foothill that was nearly perpendicular to the building. Since they were isolated in this court, Jeanne persuaded Ron to leave the shade up. She liked to see the grass, green from the March rain, and the yellow blossoms of the weeds. Even the candy wrappers sunk in the mud sparkled when they caught the sun.

By May, dry days and a bleaching sun had sucked the greenness from the hill, and left a tangle of stubby brown stalks that reminded Jeanne of her husband's paintings. "Look out there," she said to Ron one afternoon. "Look at the hillside, the way it's framed by the window, and tell me whether it doesn't look like a picture to you." Ron glanced where she was pointing and shook his head.

Whenever they crossed the threshold of this room, Jeanne became shy with him again. As an hour passed next to him, touching his body, her courage came back and she could start telling him the thoughts she had stored up since their last time together. Some stories she repeated from one week to the next because they were a pleasure to tell. When she had really imposed on his tolerance and told the same thing three times or more she was ashamed and said she was sorry and Ron laughed and held her closer.

He had let his hair go long. Jeanne liked the way it made the size of his head match his body, but she hesitated to say much since the style had a political meaning, one that might eventually exclude her.

He grew a mustache, and she liked that less. It was a barrier between his mouth and hers; like Ray's, it left the taste of rope on her tongue.

It was uncanny the way Morella now chose the nights she had come back from Ron Cooper to slide over to her side of the bed. But his expertness at making love, that wonderful secret she had kept from the world, was beginning to look to Jeanne like another of his failures. I must do it this way because I cannot be gentle, that became Jeanne's new interpretation of his ardor. He was manly enough to excite and ravish her, but he lacked the strength to kiss her eyes or listen to her voice. True, it had been her wish that he not be soft with her, but it was one more proof of weakness that he never disregarded her wishes. Jeanne debated, pinned beneath her husband, letting him thrill her, whether or not to file for a divorce.

❧   ❧   ❧

When the Rorkes divorced, it was Faye who hired the lawyer. He then handled the proceedings for both of them, a simplification made possible by Faye's decision not to ask for alimony. Calling to tell me she was leaving, Faye sounded apologetic. "He hasn't hit me again," she said. "It's not that. He's really been sweet and trying very hard. But you know, Bradley, it just couldn't go on."

When Rorke called later I didn't tell him I had already talked with his wife. Being around newspapers had taught me that at the worst of times people found solace in announcing their own disasters. "It's better this way," Rorke said. "You can't walk down the street without seeing a dozen good-looking girls. Sooner or later—"

"It's lucky you didn't go ahead with the furniture."

"There's only the bed." Rorke's voice cracked. "I'm letting her have—"

"I can take the afternoon off," I said. "Let's drive to the beach."

"I'm all right." To regain his composure, Rorke pushed a button on his desk and let me dangle on the line while he dictated a brusque business memo. When he came back, he said angrily, "I'm going to a shrink tomorrow. It can't hurt."

The end of the nineteen sixties was in sight, and consulting a psychiatrist had come to seem like some quaint throwback; so did calling him a shrink when the national mood was toward expanding the consciousness. I asked if he had told Faye he was planning to go.

"She's the one who suggested this guy," Rorke said. "It's the one she went to when she first came out here. I don't know if she told you about that. She had a rough six months. For a single girl this can be one hell of a hard town."

Yellow scraps of wire service copy were piling up on my desk, but I let our conversation limp along. Finally a buzzer sounded at Rorke's elbow and he let me know he could spend his time more profitably on another line.

⚜ ⚜ ⚜

Leonard Morris Chapman and Rose Esther Weiner were married near Westwood in a fashionable temple that looked like a battleship run aground. It was one of those weddings easy to satirize, but Lonnie survived it looking elegant in his dinner jacket, and he could put on a black cap without the nervous wisecracks Billy Stein kept making. Rose wore a gown that suggested white sweater and skirt; tennis shoes beneath its hem wouldn't have looked out of place.

After the services, fruit punch and sandwiches were dispensed at the banquet room of a nearby hotel, and when the receiving line had processed the guests, I offered Lonnie my congratulations. "You look happy."

"Very happy," he said. "Foolishly happy. I've been wondering why, and I think it's because today I got my license to be selfish."

"I heard you promise to devote soul and body to your wife."

"Yes, but listen." An idea did for Lonnie what his motorcycle did for Billy Stein. He wanted to gun it now and watch me admire its power, speed and optional fittings. "What was making me most unhappy? It wasn't my own life, it was the suffering around me. I told you about the fellow down the street who came back with his legs blown off. I couldn't stand to think about him. But if it happened to me I knew I'd be all right. For myself, I could take anything.

"But not the misery, the pain everywhere, all the unhappy people. I got to feeling that if I saw one more picture of the war, I'd walk to Washington and shoot the President myself.

"Then I met Rose. Since then I haven't had time to worry about the man with no legs. I read the paper now the way everybody does. I don't see the photographs. Rose is all I have time to worry about. Making her happy matters, nothing else, and I can do that. Selfishness, happiness—until today I didn't see that they were the same thing."

"What does your father say to that?" I had met the elder Chapman, meaty and handsome, proud today of a son rescued from a fate worse than dissipation.

"I am my father," Lonnie said. "And I agree with me absolutely."

When bride and groom had slipped off for their week in Big Sur, Billy Stein and I walked to the lot where my new red convertible and his motorcycle were sharing a parking place. "Is Margo sick?" I asked. "She made this match. She should be here taking bows."

"Margo's in San Francisco for the weekend." I had no reason to look surprised or dubious, but he added, "Visiting friends."

When Margo Stein confirmed her reservation on a morning flight (Jeanne Darling told me lately), she had already decided to take a cab from the house to the hotel in Hollywood where she could catch the airport bus. Several times Billy offered to drive her, but he did not insist, and Margo was determined to arrive at the airport alone, with only her purse, her lightweight plaid bag, and a magazine tucked under her arm. She especially did not want Billy by her side. At the boarding gate she didn't want him kissing her goodbye.

According to Margo's timetable, the flight would take less than an hour. She would be settled at her hotel before lunch, her two dresses hung in a closet so that the wrinkles could fall out. Or if the packing had left real creases, deep puckering, she could have already sent them for pressing, all before noon.

The airline ran planes to San Francisco on the hour, and from the expressions of the other passengers in line at the gate, the trip had become only an airborne subway ride. Most men were in business suits, several carried briefcases. Three were wearing hats.

Margo climbed the boarding ramp slowly. The stairs seemed steep. Once she winced and paused when a pain flashed the length of her leg. She was still limping slightly when she chose an aisle seat near the back. She was tempted, this being her first flight, to sit by the window and watch the city disappear. But she couldn't be sure that the sight wouldn't scare her or make her sick.

With only a little pressure she could slide her bag under the seat and she took that as a good omen. If there hadn't been room, Billy had told her to unhook it, let it fall open like a clothes bag and ask a stewardess to hang it for her. Margo was glad she didn't have to do that. It would have brought Billy for an instant onto the plane with her. And Margo wasn't sure either how to behave with these stewardesses and their hired cheer. For the whole time I'm away, she told herself, I am not going to talk to another woman.

Weekend traffic had crowded the plane and every place around Margo was filled. The man who took the next seat smiled and held out the inside section of his newspaper, but Margo shook her head. She was careful not to return his smile. She did mutter something, though, that he might have taken as thanks. She waited until he was absorbed in the front page and then stole another glance. He was gray haired and his nose was swollen with purple veins; she could have been more polite.

Over the months Margo had planned this trip, she had conjured up a handsome seatmate who would chat with her all the way to San Francisco. At the airport he'd suggest that they share a taxi; hotel room; bed; life together. She knew nothing like that would happen and she warned herself to be on guard against the man who did sit next to her. Everything about this trip was going to frighten her—and truthfully, now that it was under way, she was more scared than she had ever been in her life. It would be tempting to settle for the very first man, the man in the next seat, whoever, whatever he was, simply to spare herself the agony of searching later tonight. Whoever he was, he wouldn't be the perfect man she had imagined. He would be some ordinary salesman who would destroy, if she let him, her reason for making the trip. Margo had boarded the plane praying that the man in the next seat would be perfect, and positive he'd be nothing better than barely good enough.

She intended to have a drink on the plane. Scotch and soda was what she had seen herself ordering, a drink she had never tasted but one that sounded enlightened. From her infrequent parties, Margo calculated that she could risk two drinks without getting drunk. One on the plane would be a good way to relax, or, if circumstances had been different, to invite conversation with her seatmate. After she was settled at the hotel she could have one vodka and tomato juice with her lunch. That was a drink she had sampled and liked.

A man, it was true, could materialize at lunch, but that possibility hadn't figured in Margo's imagination. If nothing developed on the plane, she was sure she would have nine dead hours on her hands until men began drifting into the bars downtown. She was writing off the cocktail hour. The kind of man she wanted wouldn't be slouched in a lounge at five o'clock, throwing back salted peanuts, rinsing his mouth with dry martinis.

Margo watched the stewardess push the liquor cart toward her. None of the men in the row in front was having a drink and neither were the three across the aisle. "You, Miss?" the girl asked her. "Would you like a drink?" Margo couldn't speak. She shook her head. The man looked up from the stock quotations and asked for a Scotch on the rocks, and Margo almost said, "I've changed my mind," but then the girl was gone. I didn't speak to her, Margo thought. That much is still going right.

They landed and Margo, stepping off the plane, was struck by the brightness of the sky. Skies at home were never so blue and clear. She thought: Part of the funk in which I have been living has not been my fault. All the same, she wished the sun wasn't shining.

Margo had pictured San Francisco and New York as much the same, with overhanging parapets that turned each street into a dark alleyway. Life on the sidewalks would be too dirty and busy to miss the sunlight. Real cities were permanently at dusk, a time Margo loved for the way it liberated her and let her believe, standing at the kitchen table, opening cans for dinner, that life might not be over.

She had seen herself in shadows today, but Margo stood in the sun on the sidewalk in front of the downtown air terminal. People were crowding her on all sides, more bodies brushing against her than she could count in a week on the barren streets at home. More foreign faces, pimples and blotches, hair in odd places, strange lengths. Beards. On every face, glasses. But not with dark lenses—clear glass that let her see runny red eyes. White, sick, white, white skin. Ugly, Margo said to herself. I have come all this way to be where everyone is ugly.

She almost ran back into the terminal to catch the next flight home. But what could she tell Billy? Whatever she said, he would be pleased, even if he believed that she had come here to see spoiled Rebecca Mills and her pork-faced husband. Even if he believed her story he would sense a little of what had happened and know he never had to worry again.

She would stay. Five years from now on her thirtieth birthday, when life was over and no succession of orange sunsets could revive it, she would not let herself be sick with regret. Whatever fears she felt today, she would go ahead, so that at thirty she couldn't cover herself with reproaches. To Margo the image of herself in five years was implacable. It drove her forward. This is like saving money for my old age, she thought. Today I must invest a memory to draw on later. Only I can do it. Sons and daughters can send their parents money, the government can put a check in the mail every month. But what I miss today no one can give me afterward.

Margo remembered the names of several hotels, all expensive, and although she had the money she was afraid their clerks would not permit a lone woman to return at midnight with an unregistered guest. Planning this trip, brooding over it, had caused Margo five recurring nightmares. One had the hotel's detective pounding on her door.

Down the slight hill from the terminal, almost at Market Street, she passed an entranceway with a hotel sign peeling off the door. A faint black arrow pointed to the registration desk one flight up. Margo took each step slowly. Her leg was hurting again, and, besides, she didn't want to be out of breath for her confrontation with the clerk. She was ten weeks pregnant.

The lobby was only a dark hallway with two chairs and a couch upholstered in green imitation leather. A cigarette urn heaped with butts and dirty grit separated one chair from a deskstand. Behind the desk a bent old man stood making notations in a ledger. "Yes?" he said, not looking up.

"I want a single room. With bath."

"For how long?"

"One night. Two. I'm not sure."

Margo was wearing her maroon suit with its prominent seam at the bustline, but she had only brushed her hair into bangs, thinking she could experiment all afternoon in her room toward a more sophisticated style. Now in the mirror behind the desk, she saw herself looking young and wide-eyed, cute in a way she hated but might ease her past this man now and later. The clerk still did not look up, but he crooked an arm behind his back, snagged a key from the rack and pushed it toward her. With his other hand he boosted the ledger to the counter. He laid a ballpoint pen next to Margo's wicker purse. "Sign."

For weeks, Margo had mulled over a signature, but she stood here now without a name prepared. If she used her own name and address, couldn't the clerk or somebody, the man she came back with, try to blackmail her? If nothing that bad happened, wasn't it possible that the hotel mailed out advertising? A letter thanking her for her business? It was bound to arrive on Billy's day off, when he prowled the living room all morning and pounced on the mailman at noon.

But what if the trouble was another kind? The man tonight has pulled a knife and she must run to the desk for help. Police come. How does she explain registering under a false name? She cannot very well act the respectable housewife then, or the innocent tourist who stumbled by mistake up that flight of stairs.

She signed "Margo," paused, put a "t" after it, hesitated again and made the last name "Swann." The register called for a home address, but the others before her had written "L.A." or "N.Y.C." Margo dittoed the "L.A." on the line above hers. The room was four dollars, with another dollar deposit for the key. Margo paid with one of the nine five-dollar bills she had saved over the past five months. The clerk, not raising his eyes to inspect her round clean face, pointed down the hall.

Margo had imagined her room vividly. It would be one of two kinds: Lavish and dimly lighted. French windows opening to a panorama of the bay and the bridge. One rose in the bud vase on the leather-topped writing table. A pink marble tub sunk in the center of an immense bath. Or this room.

She hung her dresses at an angle to fit the shallow closet and opened the adjoining door to find a small toilet. In one corner, a rusty shower head poked out of the wall without a curtain to keep water off the towels and toilet paper. Margo covered the chipped glass tray beneath the mirror with a towel and laid out her black toothbrush, silver comb, and the three bottles and jars she had brought. She hadn't packed the can of hairspray because tonight her thick hair must feel soft, not starchy.

The room looked into the second floor of a garage across the street. From the bed Margo watched the cars swerving around the corner of a ramp and vanishing in darkness beyond the railing. She had considered driving up here. She drove well, and sometime during the seven hours she might have picked up a serviceman hitchhiking. But she remembered hearing, didn't she, that they could be dangerous? More interested in her money, or the car, than in her body? Left naked in a ditch, covering herself with one hand while she flagged down a truck: that wasn't one of Margo's nightmares. It could happen and she would survive. But it shouldn't happen the first time, and she had decided to fly.

Now it occurred to her that if she had driven she might have been parking her car at that garage in a few hours. Automobiles jammed together in darkness fascinated Margo. Mysteriously, they beckoned to her. She leaned forward on the bed, trying to see the faces of the attendants, but their long dirty white smocks put her off, and she didn't like the way they hustled and ran up the ramp.

Should she go to a movie? Looking for a hotel she had noticed several theaters, lewd lights flashing in the sun, that advertised either three Hollywood features made before Margo was born or the new skin films, writhing bodies in black lace. Not that if she went, Margo expected to watch the screen. She had heard that lone women were accosted in theaters; hands brushed their knees and crept slowly upward.

If that happened to her, Margo would be tempted to count it and that decided her against going. She could easily spend the afternoon in a theater and come back to the room convinced, whether a man had groped her leg or not, that she had accomplished what she came for.

She lay back on the cotton spread. It smelled of disinfectant. She lifted out the pillow so she could spread her hair on its gray linen. From the ceiling directly above her, a corrugated pink plastic shade hung so the bulb caught the sun and threw pink glints across the closet door. Tonight I will reach to this cord and extinguish that pink light, and as I do it a naked man will be lying next to me. The thought didn't make her burn today as it had on afternoons at home when she flung herself down during the boy's nap and dreamed about this very day, with its night stretching ahead of her.

She was here. But where she had felt fire, Margo was numb and cold. At home she could reach down and touch an emptiness so vast that she knew she would die if it weren't filled. She had to be nailed to the ground, something had to enter and pin her down and give her weight. If not, the burning as it spread through her body would leave only ash, to blow away. What she needed, the substance, she couldn't give herself. Trying, she only brought the sense of emptiness back more strongly, and the fire rose and Margo could smell the singeing of her skin. This was death, this flaking of her flesh into gray powder. This was disintegration. On the worst afternoons, Margo on her bed could feel the cremation of her body.

Billy was considerate and loving but he couldn't help her. Margo liked him, was happy when she could please him; she never displeased him on purpose. But Billy was ignorant of the flames she felt. At the moments they were joined, her void proclaimed itself to Margo and she rode out her passion empty.

Her consolation had been the prospect of being here with this night awaiting her, though a voice warned her that since she had already imagined tonight so perfectly, anything that happened, even what she had imagined, would disappoint her. Going out to live your dream, the voice told Margo, you only imperil both your life and the dream. Stay home. Refine your night of pleasure in your mind.

Another voice, a better friend, said that of course she must go. Your vision lifted and sustained you only because you believed you would make it come true. Accept it as a dream and you have lost it. Better that it break in pieces than it dry, like everything else in your life, and drift away. Already when you debated with yourself whether to go, the images were fading from your mind. To recapture them, you must say: I am going next month on the fifteenth at nine o'clock in the morning.

Propped on an elbow, Margo leafed through the magazine she had bought for the plane, a woman's monthly, with pictures of pie and chocolate frosting dripping off the pages. Pastries had never tempted Margo—she gained her weight on potatoes, butter, salty gravies—and the articles were equally foreign to her taste. She read, disbelieving, a column devoted to letters about children's problems from women who didn't seem to hate their sons.

Whenever Margo read a news story about a woman, usually a divorcee arrested with her lover, who beat her child bloody or locked it overnight in a closet, she felt a stirring of kinship. But for these women who looked to a magazine for advice on bedwetting and poor appetites, Margo felt contempt. They had to be, they must be, lying. Their children were as maddening as hers. Their letters were more lies, exactly right to print next to these photographs of chiffon pies as they never were. Margo threw the magazine down.

She was hungry. At home this morning she had hardly touched the eggs she fried. For the first time in her life, she had scraped bacon, on which she could make a meal, down the disposal, but only after Billy had left the table so he wouldn't think she was sick and ask her to postpone the trip.

Now her appetite had come back. Yet she didn't want to leave this room, where her plan seemed so much more plausible than it had on the sidewalk. Still, by going downstairs now, Margo could satisfy herself on one detail: Must she turn in her key each time she left the room? Or could she keep it in her purse? Obviously it would be simpler tonight to lead a man past the desk if she didn't have to stop for her key. The night clerk was bound to be someone different from the old cripple on duty now. If he saw Margo and a man walking confidently down the hall, why should he think to check the register and see that she had arrived alone?

Margo slipped on pale pink slippers, wrong with her maroon suit, but since the accident the one favor she could do for her right foot. When she stepped forward, even in low heels, nerves turned inside her ankle and sometimes cut so deeply she had to kick off the shoe and groan as she massaged her ankle.

The door to her room locked from outside. As Margo bent in the gloom to turn the key she listened for an answer to her metallic scratching as it sounded through the corridor. No one stirred behind the other doors. Too bad; if the man she needed were staying at this hotel she'd have less trouble getting him into her room. But nothing moved in any of the rooms, and to herself Margo predicted that when she did hear a noise it would be old lungs rasping over a wash basin.

The same clerk, head bent, did not look up. Margo carried her key past him and down the stairs to the street. He doesn't care who I am or what I look like, Margo thought. In a way, that was good. But if he had studied her face and with a cluck of the tongue gone back to his bookwork that would have been all right too. As she had rehearsed it, Margo's script allowed her one moment of hauteur to meet any disapproval in his face.

Across from the hotel a cafeteria advertised a choice of German plates—ribs, veal, sausage with sauerkraut. Margo crossed the street and went inside, where the light was dim and a green window shade warded away the sun from the serving table. She took knackwurst and potato salad and found a table for two.

At home, Margo pretended never to diet and ridiculed finicking ladies with their broiled fish and peach slices. When she and Billy went to dinner at someone's house, Margo loaded her plate with rich foods. When even the men were ready to quit, she took a second piece of cheese cake.

But alone with her son at noontime she ate less than he did. Not diet meals or small portions: complete starvation. Iced tea, grapefruit juice, anything to punish her body for its rolls of pink fat. If the fat could be pummeled away with her fists, Margo would have done it. She had the urge to cut off one large slippery overhanging roll with the electric carving knife Billy's uncle had given them for their wedding.

Riding to the airport, Margo had agreed not to rein in her appetite this weekend. She would have two days of indulgence. But when she took a forkful of potato salad, it tasted sour, and the knackwurst was hardly cooked at the center.

The noon crowd had gone and the restaurant offered only one possibility, his face pale but strong, sitting two tables away with a small boy. If that man were by himself, Margo wondered, would you settle for him? If you would, how could you approach him? He'd finish his meal, get up to leave, and you, halfway through this cold pink sausage, might look over and smile but he wouldn't even see you. Ah, she consoled herself, but this is not a bar, at night. Tonight the man and I will each have a drink in our hands to mellow the world.

While she was watching, the man put on glasses to check the menu, and Margo sighed with relief. The angle to the bridge made his nose look puffy. As he lowered his head to read, his jawline was lost in jowls. If only every man had warts or an expanse of bald head. If all the rest were seventy-five like the desk clerk and stooped with rheumatism, or so fat their suspenders quivered on their guts. Billy then would be the beautiful exception and Margo could be content with him. But in such a world, why would Billy Stein marry her?

Back in her room Margo was nauseated, and tired from the flight of stairs. She pulled off her suit and fell across the bed in her slip. She looked at her wristwatch and let her arm drop before she realized the time hadn't registered with her. She looked again. Two o'clock. She should have brought her transistor radio. It was small enough to tuck into a corner of the suitcase, and Margo had put it out next to the toothpaste, intending to take it. But it was a gift from Billy on her birthday last year; it had come with a card, "Love from Jacob and Daddy." The boy had pranced impatiently around her legs as she tore off the gift wrapping and drew the radio out of its carton, and then Margo hadn't exclaimed enough for him. "Do you really like it?" Jacob kept asking. "Sure," Margo said, wishing she could shriek or coo like other women. "Sure, it's fine."

She should have flown here at sundown, dropped her bag with the room clerk, headed for the nearest neon lights. With each lagging daylight minute she felt her resolution weaken. First it was: I must sleep. A minute later: I must get up and look around the city. Billy will ask what I saw. Margo looked at her watch again, again when thirty seconds had passed. She threw her left arm to her side and held it rigid so she couldn't see even the thin black watchband.

Then it happened that, wanting to sleep but not tired, trying to get up but pressed back by weights too heavy to resist, Margo felt a sudden warmth come over her. For the first time her body trusted this bed and gave itself up. The arm with her wristwatch went limp and she couldn't have brought the force on her elbow to raise it. Gradually this lassitude reached her brain. She felt it cresting until her cells were awash, and on their surface a dream collected. Margo, watching it form, was happy to be awake and to be living in her dream. The picture she saw made exact sense but not in ways Margo needed to explain. Everything happening in her mind escaped and passed before her eyes many times larger, but no larger than she had become. When all that had been in was out, she herself expanded until everything that had got out was safe again inside.

Afterward she slept. The sleep was sleeping, no more than that, and when she woke she remembered the waking dream, so different from her fitful naps at home.

⚜   ⚜   ⚜

Before her bus left for the airport the next morning, Margo hurried through a department store looking for a present for her husband. It couldn't be something marked "San Francisco," and that ruled out most of the paperweights she saw and the other ornaments for his desk. She boarded the bus empty-handed, but in a bookstore at the airport she saw a new edition of a dictionary that Billy had been wanting.

The minute she paid for it she was sorry, and carrying it onto the plane she called herself a dumb cow. Today, when she was feeling so fondly toward Billy, she should be bringing him something better, a book of poems, a romance.

By the time the plane took off, Margo had unwrapped the dictionary, run her fingers over the smooth pages and fitted her thumb to the indented index and decided she had made a good choice after all. In this sentimental mood of hers she might have taken another book, and written something on its flyleaf that would embarrass her when Billy read it and arched his eyebrow. This six-pound package in her lap had saved her that. She could not very well inscribe a dictionary.

⚜   ⚜   ⚜

Twice a week I would spend my lunch hour inside the building on Spring Street that looked like a grain elevator but served as main branch of the Los Angeles City public library. There I began to notice one of the receptionists at the information desk, a girl so contemplative and serene that to ask a question seemed a violation of her rich inner life. She was tall, with long black hair twisted in a braid, and she hid the soft roundness of her shoulders beneath dresses of peasant black. With a job that kept her seated for eight hours, she was spreading to fat, though her skin was neither creamy nor pink but white in the way skimmed milk or fluorescent light is white—that is, faintly blue. Her brown eyes, though startlingly wide-set, appeared because of her meditative cast to have been put in her face solely for decoration. Her soft voice carried memories of a mountain drawl.

I expected that a young woman so inert would grow old at her post, sinking each day a little further into her hips until, twenty years from now, she would be all tranquil haunch. Once again I was wrong, for on a rare visit to the library Ranchek saw this girl, recognized her potential and set about to marry her.

I met the girl two weeks after Ranchek had made her acquaintance, and he handled the formalities with a poise I would not have suspected. The night before I had forgotten my copy of Sartre's autobiography at his apartment, and after dinner I drove to Hollywood for it. Since Ranchek had told me he would be working late, I ran my fingers over the top of the door frame until I found his spare key. I let myself in. The room was faintly illuminated from a streetlight and I could pick my way among his Danish modern furniture and head for the bedroom where the book would surely be on his desk where I'd left it.

At the bedroom door I clicked on the overhead light. Ranchek and a girl sat up in bed, exactly as in the randy cartoons of my boyhood; she even pulled up the sheet to cover her breasts. "I came for the Sartre," I said.

"Words fail me," said Ranchek. "I'm afraid Pearlann isn't through yet. Am I right?" Without any idea of what he was talking about, the girl nodded and tried to yank more sheet from under his leg.

"I'm sure she can finish tonight," Ranchek continued reasonably. "Would that be all right?" I nodded as dumbly as the girl had. "Then," Ranchek said, "we had better get back to it. Would you mind turning off the light on your way out?" I struck the switch and retreated.

From that night on, Ranchek referred to Pearlann Johnson as though she herself were printed matter. When he took her to dinner, he talked about checking her out and returning her later to the stacks. He sighed over her supple binding, the ease with which she slipped from her jacket. He inspected her font, caressed her epigraphs, deplored, affectionately, the size of her bibliography. On an occasion when she was overdue, he worried to me about penalties and fines.

"At least," he mused one day when he was talking himself into love, "she was not uncut at the time I met her. That proves she wasn't designed exclusively for display. Not," he added hurriedly, "that she was dog-eared."

"Try saying what you mean."

Initially, Ranchek's sideburns had been discreet, but lately they had become two immense battalions of hair surging down his cheeks and sweeping in a pincer movement to threaten his small mouth. "I mean that while she may never have been on the charts, she wouldn't have been remaindered."

"Are you going to marry this girl?"

"We could be a matched set, don't you think?" Ranchek answered. "Promoted properly, with a publication-day party. Boxed, of course, in three bedrooms in the Valley. You don't think suggesting it to her would be vanity on my part?"

"It will be your second marriage."

"Yes." He bobbed his head. "I'm having second thoughts."

"But you're going to ask her?"

"I'm tired of browsing."

My regard for the academic life had dwindled year after sun-drenched year to the point that I considered Lonnie

Chapman's going back to the campus as much a surrender as
Robert Rorke's putting himself in the hands of a psychiatrist.
I tried to be tactful but Rose smoked out my feeling and
scolded me for it. "You think," she said, "that by the age of
twenty-eight a man should be done with formal education.
Lonnie should be too proud to take notes on what another
man says."

"Is that what I think?"

One burden Rose assumed with marriage was speaking for
her husband, though she kept a sidelong watch to see if he dis-
agreed or wanted to talk for himself, and when he did she
kept still. Usually Lonnie nodded to whatever she said, which
allowed him as a married man to be more isolated than in the
days he lived alone. He could meditate now for hours in full
view of company while Rose fended for him, and when she
was out of the room, I told Lonnie his example convinced me
that every Trappist should be married. He made a depreca-
tory gesture and waited for Rose to rejoin us.

She came back primed with new arguments: "When a man
needs help, he sees a doctor. When he wants to learn, he goes
to school."

To end the subject I asked Lonnie directly, "Is it hard to
adjust to the routine again?"

"No," he said, "it's as though I was never away."

"That may be what I meant," I said, but softly, hoping not
to provoke Rose to another half-hour talk.

From my vantage, their daily routine seemed stupefying,
but I must say they seemed happy with it. Lonnie rose at six
to study for two hours before he drove Rose to her high
school. He retraced twelve miles to the university, ate lunch
at a drugstore in Westwood and made an even longer trip to
the Valley for afternoon classes he taught on writers he was
studying each morning.

Back at their apartment, he would help Rose fix dinner, his
pride, as he tied an apron over his gabardine trousers, ostenta-

tious. Dishes done, he corrected student papers until bedtime.

A reformed rake is an irresistible target, and I enjoyed hectoring him. "Dogma was the single thing you condemned," I said, "and as a teacher you've installed yourself in the last stronghold of the Inquisition."

"Someone has to set standards," Rose said peevishly. "You're saying that all opinions have an equal value."

"I've heard that case put very convincingly."

"By a fool," she retorted. "Or a fraud."

"Or both," I said. Lonnie had been amused by his wife's rising temper. For the first time in the evening, he agreed with me.

⚔   ⚔   ⚔

Robert Rorke's divorce became final about the time I moved farther north on the beach, to Malibu. He consented to make the longer trip, but when he arrived he was more sparing in what he confided about himself. He acted as though any loyalty I might have developed for Faye made me a less trustworthy friend.

A man recently divorced often harbors that suspicion. He introduces a woman to his friends, dotes on her, shows her off, solicits compliments on her behalf. He marries her. At the break, he returns to those same friends demanding they say categorically that she was no good. Everyone knew it but him.

I couldn't slander a pretty girl who had erred, in my opinion, only by marrying Rorke. When I made no answer to the gibes and curses he threw out, Rorke looked on me as tainted: I was too soft to give up my good opinion of a wife he had the fortitude to get rid of.

Our reserve deepened when Rorke began talking exclusively about his bouts with the psychiatrist. Probably I should have mustered a more convincing show of interest. But even when I had broached the idea of therapy years ago, every analytical insight had already passed into the public domain. They were in the air we breathed, adding sometimes to the haze, and I thought a man should raise his head and inhale those elements he needed, not shut himself in a closed room to exhale endlessly and never suck up what was floating freely, within the reach of children.

One day, appropriate to nothing, he said, "Why does a woman bother to get married if she doesn't want a man?"

He had to wait for his answer while I strained out what I knew from what I was supposed to know. "For the same reasons a man does."

"Marriage is finished."

"Men who say that get married before the year is out. Isn't that what your doctor guarantees you?"

"My shrink says he's not a marriage counselor," Rorke said. "He's told me a lot of people come to him for the courage to get a divorce."

"I don't understand that. If you're unhappy enough, doesn't that give you the courage you need?"

"You're right. But," Rorke added, with the crushing solemnity I still took as a joke I was missing, "not everybody is lucky enough to know when he's unhappy."

Writing to me had probably been a chore Jenny Black dreaded and put off from week to week. But wives wrote the letters, it was the code of the Midwest, and when Josh prodded her I was sure Jenny hadn't suggested he answer my letter himself. Finally, screwing up the gaiety at her command, she had composed this bit of fiction, something to travel well among their friends in California.

"The air is wonderful." That, coming in the first paragraph, made me wonder how she had prolonged her letter dutifully to the bottom of the page. But the school where their daughter had entered kindergarten was good for three paragraphs. The moon on the desert, too beautiful for words, was worth two.

Right now Josh's job was so demanding that he hadn't been able to investigate the campus drama society. But Jenny knew it was only a matter of time before he'd be playing leads.

Ranchek and Doug should forgive her if she asked that this letter be shared. All of us mired in L.A. should visit the Blacks in God's country.

⚜   ⚜   ⚜

With Ranchek bedding down with Pearlann at each of his ample opportunities, Doug Goodwin was the last of my friends still free for nights of beer drinking or trips across the Mexican border. In ten years, nothing much about Goodwin had changed. I could visualize him during the next twenty years, hair grizzling, skin mottled, as he moved on every few months to a new job and tavern.

Changing jobs so often, Goodwin never became a supervisor. He stood at his bench or machine earning good pay but liable to layoffs and strikes, and to deductions from his check when he drank all night and didn't report the next day.

In the Army, I had been drawn to Goodwin by the discriminating way he read. I was at the height of my own bookishness, and I approved his culling the post library for the better novels and nonfiction. For several years after we were released, he kept up the habit. But when he picked up a book now it was likely to be an adventure story, while at the same time, the women in his life got coarser every year, and less a challenge.

One night when his DeSoto broke down, I agreed to drive him to a drugstore in Van Nuys where he was to meet a woman at seven thirty. "Why did she want to come to a drugstore?" I asked.

"I don't know." I knew. She was either married or under age, and the woman who came out of the doorway was more than old enough. She reached the car while Goodwin was midway through his cumbersome process of getting out. To look lankier than he was, he exaggerated his stiff movements until he looked like a stranger to automobiles and the other contrivances of a city. Watching him perform for this woman, I thought how sure a man must be of his body to act graceless and know it would enhance his appeal. And I wondered how much time would pass before he would only look arthritic.

⚑   ⚑   ⚑

One sunny morning very close to noon, Jeanne Morella put a sheet of blank paper into her typewriter, and prepared to begin her column. She laid her fingers on the keys, ready to strike down, but she couldn't remember what day of the week it was.

Annoyed with herself, Jeanne pressed her memory to say whether it was Tuesday or Wednesday and found that she didn't know the day of the month, or the month itself. Or the season. It's May, she said. It's October. Outside the sun was shining, the day was fair. No clue from that. Feeling foolish now and a little panicky, Jeanne concentrated on the year, but that, too, refused to come.

She knew her age. She knew the year she'd been born. Adding the two she reached the current year: thirty-six plus thirty-two. It was not a form of arithmetic easy on her vanity. But doing the addition calmed as it depressed her. The month came back: April. The twenty-third of April. Tuesday. A backward way to tell time. Given a choice Jeanne would have forgotten her age and remembered the day of the week. Thirty-six. Everyone told her she looked thirty at the very most. Everybody said that. Ron Cooper was thirty. Did they look the same age? No. She looked older.

Across her hard curved hips the skin had begun to pucker very slightly. In the sun the day before, noticing how the flesh above her bikini had wrinkled together, Jeanne had jumped to her feet and smoothed her skin with sun-tan oil until the tiny creases went away. Sitting back, she arranged herself so the tanned surface wouldn't bunch or crack.

On principle, Jeanne didn't worry about her age. But as she watched it work on her, she wondered why these small marks weren't making her the more determined to hold Ray. That would be the sensible reaction: Ray never noticed what the years were doing to her. If she were a girl friend coming for advice, Jeanne would tell herself not to be a fool. You're not getting any younger, she'd say. Cliché or not, it was still the best way to bring a woman to her senses.

But Jeanne's trouble was exactly that. She expected to go on defying the law that compelled her to get old. And so far she had got away with it. Who was freer than she? Or looked as good? Or handled men better? For the past fifteen years she had rehearsed how to be a woman, and none of the practice counted because it didn't show. Now it showed. At the pool, on her hips. There had been no years of grace. Time had ticked away, and it was only Jeanne, pretending not to hear, who said it hadn't.

Ron Cooper was not the man to set the clock back for her. Try as she might, Jeanne had never been able to mislead herself about him. Ron's concerns were more important than hers, and placidly, calmly, she knew she was losing him to his work. Their afternoons had become rare; he was busy. It was no excuse. He was very busy. Jeanne had seen him on television, the six o'clock news, looking so strange that without his name beneath the picture she would have flipped the dial past him.

Their next time together she tried to talk about the program, but he waved his hand and laughed. Perhaps it was too serious to share with her. If that was how he felt, Jeanne could believe he was right. No matter how truthful she was, she might say the wrong thing. Nothing insensitive or crude; a half tone off pitch.

Watching Ron on the television screen, Jeanne had to accept the other gulfs between them. If she tried—one example —to explain how she felt about the creases on her hips, Ron's response, whatever he said, would be meager.

✦   ✦   ✦

Ron Cooper was scheduled to speak before a conference of black leaders and I went to hear him, knowing nothing about the state of his romance with Jeanne. Since she hadn't spoken of him for six months, I assumed they were no longer meeting. The last few years of riots, fires, murders, and lootings had brought groups like Ron's more attention than their decades of petitions, but Ron himself was being pulled two ways within his own movement. His speech that day suggested that he leaned toward the conciliatory faction. His enemies said Ron's moderation explained his regular appearances on television.

When the conference adjourned, Ron and two friends accepted my invitation for a drink in the garden lounge of the hotel. Since the last time I had seen him, Ron was even huskier and in fuller command of himself. As a speaker he had turned to assets both his fumbling hesitation and the tendency of his voice to turn tremulous and crack. He could rumble along like a preacher, pause, stumble over his harshest indictments and end on a pained vibrato that was an appeal or a threat, whichever the audience wanted to hear. To me Ron sounded like a good man pushed past his limit.

Both his friends were shorter than Ron and lighter-skinned. They indulged us as we talked about the Army.

"That reminds me, Brad," Ron said at one point. "I keep forgetting to ask you. You ever see that little blond school-teacher you were running around with?"

"She's married, living in Denver. I got a letter from her last month."

"She's married but she still writes you letters?" His attempt at a suggestive tone was only perfunctory. Even without what Jeanne had told me, Ron was clearly a man whose ruling passions were other than sexual.

"It was the first letter in years."

In talking, I discovered that Ron felt warmly toward Ranchek but only a glancing pity for Doug Goodwin. "Doug's still putting away beer and making it with anything that's ambulatory?"

"Yes," I said. "But the friend I haven't seen for a while is Jeanne." Since that day on the picket line we had never mentioned her name. "I guess she's fine."

"She's a fine woman." Ron repeated my adjective to mock it. But he stopped combing at his new mustache with the edge of his finger and said to all of us, "A man's got to wonder, don't he, why he was born at one time instead of another. Not that I'd want to have been born earlier. There wouldn't be much percentage to that. But I wonder where we'd all end up thirty years from now if we were just being born tonight, down at General Hospital."

The younger of Ron's friends, a drummer, was entranced by the idea. "Shit," he said happily, in two syllables.

　　　　🏴　　　　🏴　　　　🏴

Three weeks or so after that, Jeanne Morella, who had been waiting for a day when Ray felt good enough to go to his restaurant, fixed his favorite lunch—omelet with cheddar cheese and green onion, shelled peas, a glass of white wine to wash down the creampuffs she had bought fresh that morning.

After he had eaten, Jeanne followed him into the bedroom where he painted. For ten minutes she stood watching as he mixed colors. Ray didn't like her there, but if she neglected to come once every week or two, her indifference upset him more than the interruption.

"I'm going to have that one framed," Jeanne said, pointing to a canvas he had propped against the couch. "I want it over my desk."

Ray was pleased and he scowled. "No, it's no good. This next one will be better for you."

Another day the temptation would have risen in Jeanne to shout at him that everything he touched was rotten. If she could admit years ago that her horoscopes were frauds, Ray should be made to face a few truths of his own. She wouldn't say that now, even if he were staying. Jeanne had stopped saying what she thought. Her lover had made her shy.

Shy! She with the laugh that blared through school dances. She would never forget the night the band stopped playing and everyone stared at her. She, whose mother had warned her from the age of eight against her booming whiskey voice. Not too shy to say anything in the world over coffee to Billy Stein. But tongue-tied with her lover. And lately with her husband. Because she didn't want to hurt Ray? Or give Ron the chance to hurt her?

Ray went off to the Strip. A little after midnight Jeanne arranged herself among the pillows in their bed to doze until he came home. His voice roused her. "What's the matter? Couldn't you sleep?" He leaned over to look at her in the dim light. She knew he'd think she stayed up because she wanted him. He was hurrying with the buckles on his boot. She had to speak now.

Ray listened, holding his trousers upended by their cuffs. When Jeanne finished, he went to the closet, brimming with her clothes, and rustled through the skirts and dresses for a wooden hanger. The muscles of his naked back stood out, white but sinewy. His biceps looked powerful. He may choke me. Jeanne was exploring that thought when his shoulders shook and she heard him cry.

It did not unnerve her or weaken her will. Hearing the sound she didn't believe it, as she had listened to him describe his headaches without ever believing he could feel pain within his head. What was there inside Ray real enough to hurt him? His desire? But Jeanne had handled his desire for herself. It didn't exist inside. It only hung on him, more hers than his.

She heard the sobbing and wondered if he was breaking down. For weeks he may have been having a breakdown. It was one more dramatic word, like suicide. Nervous breakdown. She liked turning the phrase over in her mind, and she watched with interest as his shoulders heaved.

He stopped shaking. He kept his face turned toward the rack of dresses.

Jeanne was still looking at him when she saw his back. Not its whiteness or its muscle. She saw it, the back itself, saw it and sprang from bed to stand behind Ray and wind her arms around his neck. She wept with him, she from fear, pulling his shoulder blades back to her body, trying to obliterate the sight of his back. Ray misunderstood the gesture and for a moment he thought she had changed her mind.

In the course of one eventful Saturday both George Ranchek and Faye Tayne proposed to give matrimony another chance. I planned to leave Faye's afternoon reception in time to drive to the Baptist Church in the Antelope Valley where Pearlann's parents would bestow her on Ranchek. But the Friday night before, a neighbor of my mother's maternal aunt called from Spokane to say that the old woman had collapsed and died at a downtown bus stop. Since I seemed to be her sole living relative, would I please come to handle the arrangements?

Whenever I had calculated my freedom from a family, I had never taken this woman into account. Gaining and losing her in the same phone call seemed unnecessarily abrupt. All the same, I flew that night to Washington and negotiated a modest burial.

Walking away from the cemetery in the fog, I thought how often Ranchek had said, "It's fine being single when you're young, but what about when you're old and alone?" That same spirit may have led my great-aunt to get married sixty years ago; yet on the day she died she had been a widow eighteen years. However dismal the prospect of dying alone, it was beginning to strike me as a small price for the privilege of living alone.

Tuesday morning I was back at work. Reveling in a perfect alibi, I was waiting for the first lull to call Faye and apologize for missing her wedding. My job of late had developed into something not quite serious: I spent most of the morning writing headlines. It was an art form highly valued by the publisher since an intriguing banner sold thousands of extra copies at the newsstands. The country had already entered upon its horrific years, and it may not have spoken well for my character that I could take each grisly fresh calamity and compress it into the five or six words that would most stun the eye.

I had finished condensing an airline crash when I reached Faye at her new husband's house in Bel-Air. My perfect excuse proved too pat to satisfy her since I had never mentioned a great-aunt. Only when I suggested lunch that same noon did she begin to forgive me.

Half an hour past the agreed time Faye materialized at the reservation desk, looking like a re-creation of her former self from more ethereal and expensive stuffs. The auburn hair was pale blond, close to no color; her fitted suit was spun from fiber so fragile it shouldn't have been expected to survive the afternoon. She was borne to my table by the captain and a sleek waiter, who stood by as she kissed my cheek before they enswirled us in pink tablecloth and napkins.

"Philip wants me to invite you to dinner." It was the first thing she said when we were alone.

Not a chance of it, I promised myself. Social obligation cannot possibly extend to a friend's first wife's second husband. "I'd like that," I said.

Faye and her bridegroom were leaving that weekend for two weeks in Caracas, and she retained her touching faith that I could answer any question about Venezuela, from coups d'état to wholesale jewelers. Two fast vodka gimlets and she still wasn't convinced of my ignorance. "Enough about Latin America, Mrs. Ernst," I said. "Tell me about your new husband."

She provided the unimportant details: Ernst had been married twice before. He was thirteen years older than she, a film producer admired for bringing in his product below budget. She left only one piece of information for me to deduce: once again Faye had married a man she didn't love. Presumably he could further her career, but my impression was that neither of them cared about that. "Philip is clever," Faye concluded.

At the wedding she had met the groom's Hollywood friends for the first time, and if she'd had an illusion left, they dispelled it. "One man asked me if I had settled on the size of my alimony," she said. "Philip's friends were betting on how much I'd take him for. With the first two wives they bet on how long the marriage would last. With me they wanted to try something new."

Philip expected any wife of his to entertain a great deal. "I've already bought hostess gowns and I'm having six sets of pajamas designed by—you don't care about that sort of thing, Bradley, but, really, the best designer on the West Coast. I'll have boys in red coats running up and down our canyon parking cars while I receive guests standing by the grand piano."

"Grand, indeed."

"You really must come to my first open house. Say you will! Let me make up for those dreary afternoons in the Valley. Do you remember that awful house? All we had was a bed. Everybody had to sit on the floor."

"I didn't mind."

At my tone Faye took my hand. "Don't try to make me ashamed, Bradley. This time I'm happy. Believe me."

One lock of hair had shaken free across her forehead and she reclaimed her hand, heavy with its square diamond, to brush the curl back. There are few things a woman does more gracefully, and I decided Philip Ernst would spend his money well. Faye sought my hand again. "You're such a romantic, Bradley," she said. "Marrying for anything but true love is tragic, you think. But women aren't like that."

"Except," I said, "that one day a young, handsome man will—"

"And you have no imagination! No man has," she added to soften the blow. "I'm young and pretty, so when a young man comes along, I have to fall in love with him. What if I don't happen to be that way? Who writes the plays about young wives deceiving their husbands? Men! Unimaginative, romantic men. Men who can't believe a woman might need something that lasts longer than love. I've found Philip to take care of me. Nothing would make me hurt him."

The wisp of hair had fallen forward again and I brushed it back among the other ashen strands. "I'll be your fourth husband."

"Third, you mean."

"No, he's the one who will pay for all this meekness."

"You don't believe me."

"Do you like this new husband of yours?"

225

Unhesitatingly: "Very much."

"Better than Rorke?"

She pondered, intent, I think, on being truthful. Then she decided simply to smile. Her wisdom teeth had been pulled sometime before the wedding, or some other adjustment undertaken, and the full curve of her mouth was no less dazzling than before, though more conventional.

※　　　　※　　　　※

In his first term back on campus Lonnie Chapman allied himself with the roiling and impassioned element and wrote incendiary manifestoes of the sort that prescribe Armageddon as a social tonic. Except for the fierceness of his tracts, Lonnie didn't match my picture of a revolutionary, but he had never been satisfactory, either, as an ascetic.

One trouble was that both he and Rose were gleaming these days with tough brown health. She liked tennis and they played each morning. By the end of the summer Rose was darkly freckled, giving her, until she launched her sermon on guerrilla war, an urchin's sooty charm. Lonnie, too, talked hotly about endemic injustice. I told him that he never sounded tentative now or mild.

"I had been burying the best part of myself," he said. "Anger is a great strength. It's when we bring our anger to bear on crimes of society that we're at our very best. I was expecting tolerance to save the world and it couldn't even save me. Look around at the world. There's only one legitimate response and that's anger."

"And hatred?"

"And hatred," Lonnie agreed. "Why deny it? Why pretend you can rise above it?"

"Not even immersed in selfish pleasures?"

"You're always trying to hold me to something I said a

year ago. Maybe pleasure is enough for you. Mine comes now from trying to help."

We were on the Valley campus batting balls over a net. At noon the temperature was already over one hundred and even Lonnie was not fanatical enough to insist on a real game.

We had traded a few swipes when he deliberately whacked the ball hard and low. I swore and jumped aside.

"I was reminding you how close anger is to the surface," Lonnie called. "I was trying to hurt you."

"For my own good."

"A lesson."

When we had slumped off the court I asked him whether he and Rose saw much of the Steins. "Margo is pregnant again," he said.

"I heard."

"Rose and I should have children." Sprawling on the grass in his white shorts, Lonnie looked fit, and Rose was a handsome woman. On every test of intelligence they would score high. They were in love. Yes, they should have children. Whose upbringing would be, I reckoned, unenviable.

"I want five sons," Lonnie continued, "in all sizes. With one daughter with pink ears to nibble on."

A vision loomed of Rose presenting her lobe for a small bite, and I was glad all over again that with enough determination we can avoid learning about each other's private tastes. I said something of the sort to Lonnie, who was slightly affronted. "Of course we do everything," he said. "What's wrong with that? We're in love. Rose and I aren't ashamed of anything we do. She'd tell anyone who asked her."

"Margo?"

Lonnie was sitting cross-legged juggling three tennis balls, another of his gifts. "No, not Margo," he admitted. "Margo's the kind of woman no one tells the truth to. It's too big a responsibility."

"Is the sun hot for you?"

"No, I'm right about her. I used to brood over ideas like that back in the days I thought people, individually, were interesting."

※   ※   ※

My inclination was to ignore the light knocking at my door. It was well past midnight, and the low moan a few seconds later could have been a night sound off the sea. Beside me, though, the other figure sat upright. "What's that?" she said.

"Nothing."

"You've got to go and look."

"It's nothing."

She was out of bed and to the door, a bustling girl who was more self-reliant than I preferred. I pulled on my pants and brought a robe to cover her.

The cottage fronted a cove at Malibu, but the noise had come from the back, close to the highway. Glenda was peering out from around the door as I wrapped her in my robe. "There's someone on the beach," she said. "You've got to go down there."

I sighed, slipped the latch and walked to the end of the garage where rickety wooden steps led to the beach. The night was overcast. The moon, which made the waves iridescent other nights, was nowhere in sight. At the bottom stair, I tripped over an object prone on the sand. When I caught myself on my knees I heard someone groan beside me.

It was Ray Morella, bare to the waist and sopping wet. The groan was his attempt to say something. "What?" I asked.

"Can't get back."

He let me raise him to his feet. By hooking him under my arm I could drag him up the stairs. He tried to help, pressing his heel down to make contact, but it skidded and bounced off every step. When I had pulled him into the house and let him fall on the bed he looked to see who I was. His eyes were glazed and his long wet hair stood out like spikes. He didn't notice the girl watching from the doorway. "Call the police," she said.

"He's a friend of mine."

Ray was repeating, "Can't get back."

"What's wrong with him?"

The edge to her voice made Ray blink. He pulled himself up and began to explain excitedly. "Chicago was on fire. I saw the headlines. Chicago in flames. I went out the door. I couldn't see the fire. I went into the water." He winced and closed his eyes. "I can't get back."

"Do you know who I am?" I asked.

"I know."

"Listen to me, then. Down the beach in Venice I saw a lot of people like this and they all got back. You will too. Try to relax. This could be nice for you. Chicago isn't on fire. Not since the cow. You remember the cow?"

He laughed. "The cow."

"We'll get you out of your wet clothes. You can lie on the bed and listen to music. All right?"

"The water!" He tried to get up, but it took very little of my strength to hold him down. "You can hear the water," I said. "Listen to the waves. They come up under the porch, you can hear them breaking. Do you hear? And the long sigh when they go out again. Do you hear it?"

He lay back contentedly. "Yes."

Their flaring wide cuffs made his corduroy pants easy to pull off. His shorts were wet, but out of deference to the disapproving eyes in the doorway I left them on. His feet were bare. "Where are your boots?"

"I threw them in the ocean. My wallet. I took out the cards. I threw everything in the water. The money."

"It's only paper."

"I'll remind you of that in the morning," Glenda said. She thought me ungenerous, and with her I may have been.

"I see you," Ray said, as though to reassure her. "I know where I am. This is Brad's new place. But I can't get out."

"You'll come back. Look at me. You're sure you will."

"I'm not sure." The voice that answered was a child's voice. "I don't think I can." He had stopped shaking from the cold, but with another spasm he grimaced and bared his teeth. He seemed very remote from me. Glenda said, "I'll call a doctor."

"No! Don't!" He was ready to run naked out to the highway. I went back and pressed his shoulders down again. "She won't. She wants to help you. Where was the party tonight?"

"Up the road," he said. "Past the colony."

"Was Jeanne there?" The last I'd heard they were separated and Ray was living with his married partner in Coldwater Canyon. "No, she wasn't there."

"Do you want me to call her?"

"No."

The girl was spinning the dial on the bedside radio but nothing was right. Piano inventions on the classical station made Ray uneasy; the throbbing electrical music was interrupted by commercials that made him thrash around the bed. I kept repeating that he was already feeling better, but he wasn't hungry and wouldn't eat the eggs Glenda scrambled.

By four o'clock both she and I were yawning after each sentence and I felt stupid from lack of sleep. "You'd better go home," I told her.

"I'll stay." Her temperament fitted her admirably for moments of stress. It was during evenings of music and idle talk that her competence could seem so predatory.

"You'll go. Here are my keys. I'll pick up the car in the morning."

"Come after eleven then," she said. "That will give me time to have it washed."

"Nine o'clock," I said.

She dressed in the bathroom, a show of modesty I wouldn't have expected from her. When she came out she kissed me and then, in one of those errant gestures that keep a man involved despite himself, she bent over the bed and kissed Ray's forehead. "You're going to be fine."

"Who are you?" he asked innocently. "You're beautiful."

"Find out for me," she said, "exactly what he's on."

"Good night."

"Eleven o'clock," she said as she disappeared out the door.

I pulled the mattress off the twin bed and laid it across the bedroom threshold. To leave, Ray would have to step over me. "I'm going to sleep now," I told him. "We'll leave the light on. If you want anything, wake me."

The sun was already coming up when Ray pushed on my shoulder. He was crouching alongside me, wrapped in a patchwork quilt from my bed. "Hey," he said, "I'm sorry. You got a right to be mad."

"There'll be other nights. How do you feel?"

"I don't know. All right." His hair had dried in long shards that hung forward across his face. The pupils of his eyes were still small and bright, and he smelled musky from the sea. "What am I going to do?" he asked.

"You'll be fine. I told you."

"I don't mean that. What am I going to do about everything? I sold my share of the restaurant. That was the party last night, the guy who's buying in. Now what am I going to do? What about Jeanne?"

"You're divorced?"

"It's final next month."

"Do you see her?"

"Not much. The kid doesn't like me. You know." He got up, and I followed him to the porch that overhung the ocean. The first rays of sun had lit the water to a brighter blue than the sky. Looking at the reflection it was easy to think that the

231

sea had become air, that we were floating through space, and the sensation reminded me that this morning an American space team would be maneuvering near the moon. Very soon the television networks would carry a live broadcast from the capsule making its practice run for a first landing next summer.

Ray fell on a lounge chair. With the blanket, his impassive face and his hair sticking up like black feathers, he looked like a brave who had drawn too deeply on the pipe. "I didn't see anything last night," he said. "Just the dark."

"Too bad."

"It's nice here. But the sun hurts my eyes."

"Don't look at it." I led him back to the living room, where he flopped belly down on the couch. The quilt hung on him now like a toga. He pressed his bare feet against the screen of my television set. "Look!" His face was hanging over the edge of the couch as he stared into the gold nap of the rug. "Look!" he repeated.

"Are you going to be sick?"

"No, down there. Moving. It all moves."

"Very possible. I don't have a vacuum cleaner."

"It's making patterns. Look. Look." He was awestruck. "You should see it."

I stood over him. "The green stain is crème de menthe. The kind of girls who drink it spill it."

"It all moves. The forms fade into each other. Look." He stared at my face. "The hair on your cheek," he said, still awed. "The blond hairs go up and down, and some of them slant in toward your mouth. They're forming patterns. The ends of hair along your cheek."

I reached past his legs to snap on the television set. "You've done me a favor. I'd never have been up early enough to see this."

Ray paid no attention to the wavering picture forming on the screen. Two hundred thousand miles away three men were trying to link vehicles and their effort was being relayed around the world. Four hours from now I would drive downtown to celebrate their achievement in three words and perhaps, given its majesty, an exclamation point.

I said, "Incredible, isn't it? You can see the inside of the capsule."

Ray did not raise his head; in fact, his chin dipped closer to the carpet. He was lost in the movements below him. "Look!" he said again, his toes splayed against the face of the capsule commander.

At eight thirty I called Jeanne, letting her understand only that Ray was slightly ill. Without hesitating she offered to come for him. Ray by that time had stopped talking entirely, and when Jeanne came into the living room he looked uneasy. He let us lead him out to the highway and settle him in the back seat. Jeanne locked all four doors.

She had thrown on the clothes nearest to hand, and I saw that, uncorseted, her flesh formed a small pouch in the yellow slacks. Her blouse was stained with coffee. I liked her without makeup, preferred the natural pink of her lips. "Thank you, dear, for everything," she said, when I got out of the car on Olympic Boulevard. "It was lucky he was near your house."

"Goodbye, Ray," I said to the knotted shape face down in the back seat. "Yeah," he answered faintly.

"He can stay with you for a couple of days?"

"It's his house," Jeanne said. "I've always told him that."

It was a generous attitude, especially since the California courts had ruled otherwise, but I didn't know then what a godsend Jeanne considered my call.

She hadn't changed her mind about the divorce, it wasn't that. She rejoiced at regaining her own name, or more accurately the name of her first husband. Without overestimating its value, she prized her independence. Yet the fact was that she missed Ray.

After Ray moved out, she and Ron Cooper still met at the motel. There was no reason now that he shouldn't come to the house. Except that Jeanne worried that when he drove up the curving driveway, entered through the heavy brass-bound door, walked past the French windows to admire her patio and the pool, she would find herself standing with her left hand raised to her neck, as though she were wearing pearls.

When they saw each other, then, they rented the room on Ventura Boulevard. Ron knew about the divorce but never asked about it. Long ago, their second time together, he'd made a passing remark about her husband that could have been an invitation to compare them as lovers. Jeanne didn't know how to persuade Ron that she preferred him, though Ray was the more accomplished. She changed the subject, accepting that Ron would misunderstand. After that, he never mentioned Ray. Once, though, she thought he may have insinuated that Jeanne was not the peak of his experience either.

Ron was gone two and three weeks at a time now, speaking at colleges and churches, and often he had to rearrange or cancel his times with Jeanne. One day he called only twenty minutes before she was due to meet him to say he couldn't make it; maybe tomorrow. She had gone back to the bedroom to hang up her linen dress when a word spoke itself out loud: "Reprieved."

Jeanne, who despised married women who complained when their husbands wanted them, made herself repeat it, "I have been reprieved."

Why feel that? She had no better way to spend the afternoon. In another hour Sonny would come from school, but they grated continually on each other these days and he would head straight for his room. On the coffee table, unread, sat two novels that would not be moved until she took them back to the lending library. She could write to her mother back home, thank God, in Georgia. Or take a walk outside where an elderly Japanese was tending the lawn. Once in a great while she joined him on his gardening days, pulled up weeds from between the russet-colored flowers, and let him tell her mischievous stories about a Western actor who once owned the house.

Jeanne had no reason to feel reprieved, and less cause, when Ron called back ten minutes later to say he could get free after all, to tell him she felt a slight headache coming on.

Jeanne did not expect him to call the next afternoon, but when he didn't, she was disappointed. Two nights later a friend from her first marriage, a man, came into town from Atlanta and invited her to dinner. Knowing nothing about Ray, neither the marriage nor the divorce, he expected them to spend the evening as two unrepentant Southerners and talk of old times, old friends. For the first half hour Jeanne ground her teeth, but with the drinks she relaxed and at the door she let him kiss her. Safe inside she wanted to run to the telephone and call Ron Cooper to hear his voice.

The next time she saw Ron, Jeanne had girded herself for certain risks. As soon as he slid away and was lying beside her, she began to probe. Yes, Ron answered her, he was paid full time now. Where the money came from he neither knew nor cared; two banks and an attorney kept the books.

To everything she asked, Ron replied easily. Jeanne wanted to make it harder. She urged him to reminisce about growing up in New Jersey, and to oblige her he told a few stories— things he had put out of his mind ten years ago. But Jeanne had read accounts of childhood in Harlem and Mississippi, and Ron's routine humiliations, flatly told, didn't move her. She herself had been as badly bruised, raised a white girl in Georgia. Not that Ron asked for sympathy. He was being courteous and Jeanne wanted more than that.

They spent a longer time in the room than usual. She was

ready to let him go if he looked at his watch, but he seemed to have time for everything. Jeanne set the trap she had prepared on the drive over: she mentioned again her attempt at suicide. The year before she had told him every detail, but today Ron received the story as new to him. He even responded with the same words he'd used a year ago: "What would you want to do that for?"

All the time I've lain next to him feeling transparent, Jeanne thought, I was as opaque as he was today, answering my questions. What's happened to the millions of words I've spoken in this room? After all those words, what picture does he have of me?

He was half-dressed, Jeanne was smoothing her seamless hose. "Ron?"

"Yes?" Whenever they were about to leave, he took care not to sound distant or rushed, and their partings were always more affectionate than the nervous embrace when she arrived.

"The first time, do you remember? Why did you ask me here?"

He sat next to her on the bed and took her in his arms, cautiously, because she was dressed now and Jeanne, in her afternoon dresses, conveyed against her will a worry for the wrinkles he might be causing. "I asked you because you were beautiful."

"A lot of girls were younger and prettier."

She could tell he was at a loss. He tried again. "I asked you because you were gentle," he said. "And good and kind." With Jeanne, he usually could suppress the orator within him, but in his confusion it was that voice that took over. "You were the sweetest girl I had ever known," he said, and catching the rhythm, continued to woo her with love talk, while Jeanne, hearing him out, felt her heart sink with each inappropriate adjective.

From what Goodwin vouched about his latest girl, Donna was indistinguishable from her three hundred predecessors, women who came and went, valued, like the marten and the mink, for a few square inches of pelt. If Donna was different it was because she bore the liability of four children from her first marriage. Over the years that he had courted divorcees with small children, I had never heard of Goodwin arriving with so much as a pack of gum in his pocket.

This new Donna was a secretary at the plant where Goodwin joined radio aerials to automobile fenders. Telling me about her the first time he said only that she was a nice girl, his standard tribute for women he had got to bed.

A minute later, though, he'd found a way to quote her opinion of a film they had seen together and her view of the possible candidates for President. It was then I bothered to ask what Donna looked like.

"She looks like me."

I met her and found that Goodwin was right. She had the same prominent cheekbones that recessed the eyes, the thin curving nose that split a face cleanly and called attention to the symmetry of its halves. Her chin was cleft, but that's no asset to a woman, just as men rarely benefit from dimples. Her hair was the brown color of Goodwin's and, owing to the style, almost the same cut.

Their striking resemblance did not make them an attractive couple. At his side Donna, with looks essentially masculine, called attention in Goodwin's face to any signs of softness.

For three months Goodwin spent every night with her and then one Friday noon he took off for northern Oregon. This time he carried no passengers, and so far as I knew, none of his eight brothers and sisters lived there. In due time a post card arrived with a scribble about getting away to think things over. On the pretext of asking for his address, I called Donna.

She sounded surprised to hear from me and unenthusiastic.

"I don't know where he's staying," she said. "The letter I got was from Portland."

"How long do you think he'll be gone?"

"I don't really know." Behind her desk she was a good deal more composed than the night I met her at Goodwin's rooming house.

"If there's anything you need—" I let the sentence hang.

"No, thank you," she said. "Doug is the one who needs help. But he'll have to work it out for himself."

I said goodbye gladly. However much she might look like Goodwin, this girl didn't sound like him or like any of the others. Either she was a mistake from which Goodwin had escaped or the culmination he was trying to avoid.

※   ※   ※

My memory of the placid girl at her library desk gave me reason to expect my first evening with the Rancheks after their Hawaiian honeymoon to be a restful few hours. Certainly I anticipated nothing worse than colored slides of Oahu after dinner. Through connections at City Hall, Ranchek had discovered a condemned three-story house near the new Music Center that rented cheaply because its fate hung suspended. The house was theirs week to week until they heard the wrecking ball on the roof. Pearlann had furnished the first floors with wedding presents and scraps from her family's garage.

I had scarcely toured the house and found a chair in the vast beamed library when my expectations for the evening collapsed. "Pearlann," Ranchek said reproachfully from behind the mahogany bar, "there's no Scotch."

"Don't blame me, George," she said. "How was I to know you liked it at lunch in your milk?"

"Take my advice," Ranchek said, with rue that sounded heartfelt, "never judge a book beneath the covers."

"I'm tired of that joke," Pearlann said sharply. "I never did think it was funny."

"Never marry a girl from the Bible Belt," Ranchek whispered. "I thought I was getting Song of Songs and every night it's been Revelations."

"Oh, you!" Pearlann said over her shoulder. "Just stop it!"

Ranchek stopped but only to introduce a counterpoint: "Wonderful meal!" he said over the last helping. Pearlann was a bride and may have thought he meant it. "It's good to have macaroni after those months of eating out. And with Dawn, you remember," he said to me, "it was all chicken breast, breast of lamb, tuna breast on toast—"

Pearlann's normal, pretty breasts seemed to shrink to nothing. "George!" she said. He looked innocent. "A figure of speech," he said.

"Just stop!"

"Quite right," Ranchek said. "No use trying to cleave to the past. Heaven knows Dawn couldn't have made macaroni like that, with precisely the right—"

"It came from a jar," the girl said defensively. "I was working all day and I got home late. You didn't tell me we'd have company for dinner." She remembered me and added apologetically, "There was nothing else in the house."

"Don't give it a thought," Ranchek said magnanimously. "A wife has many duties more germane than keeping house."

She looked resentful and blushed, leading me to wonder if their marriage, despite its extensive trial demonstration, was as liable to malfunction as everything else produced lately in the country—like their new washing machine that had taken to flying open and covering the back hall with suds.

"Tell me about Hawaii," I said.

"We missed our plane," Pearlann replied. "George forgot the tickets, and by the time we drove back to the airport we had to go on standby for the midnight flight. We got to the hotel in time for breakfast."

From his place at the head of a long unvarnished table, Ranchek beamed at her. "Pearlann was a good little scout," he said. "She never complained at all. Until just this minute."

The girl was covered in confusion. "Anybody can forget," she said. "It was fun, really. We got to fly over the islands with the sun coming up. The other way we would have missed the view."

She was willing to maintain that mood for the duration of my visit, but Ranchek interceded. "The washing machine!" he said, snapping his fingers. "I meant to call about it right after lunch. Now we won't be able to do the wash tomorrow."

"Oh, George!" Pearlann Ranchek wailed, vertical lines of exasperation forming between her brows that were unlovely to me but not, presumably, without their appeal.

＊＊＊　　　＊＊＊　　　＊＊＊

Within the same week I made a point of calling Dawn at the bank. I knew she would want to hear about Ranchek's new wife but might have scruples against asking. For several months I had kept in touch with Dawn exclusively by telephone and then the calls diminished too. Seducing a friend's wife in a city with half a million available women rarely justified itself, and though the rules for ex-wives were less stringent, I knew Ranchek would hear about it if I courted Dawn and be hurt. Or be funny.

I felt safe enough in accepting Dawn's invitation to dinner since we would spend the evening talking entirely about her former husband. She set the time and gave me directions for reaching her new apartment. The carefully guarded address turned out to be in a landlocked section of Los Angeles that is named—inaccurately in Spanish, defiantly in English—Mar Vista.

Dawn's pink stucco building, faced with green flagstone

and built in the classic penitentiary style, surrounded an empty pool that made an echo chamber for three children scuffling at its deep end. Dawn's apartment at the back faced the carport. As I came up the walk she was stooped in the door holding tight to the collar of a huge police dog. "Now, there," she soothed the animal as it strained toward me, "don't growl. Go lie down in the kitchen. That's a good girl. Go on.

"That's Dolly," she said as I slipped in the door. "You haven't seen her, have you? But you don't like animals." Dawn prided herself with remembering, along with birthdays and anniversaries, the crotchets of her friends. My dislike was entirely for the effect cats and dogs had on the people who owned them. It was more prudent, though, to say that no, I didn't much care for animals.

"Oh, Dolly's different," Dawn assured me. "She's so funny! Two minutes before the alarm goes off in the morning she jumps on the bed and sticks her wet nose in my face. She wants me to shut off the alarm before it rings, and if I let it ring anyway, it's as though I haven't trusted her. She sulks all the rest of the day."

The great dog had slunk back to the living room and lay in a proprietary mound at Dawn's feet. "You're a silly dog, aren't you?" Dawn asked musically. The animal bared its teeth equivocally and let a prodigious tongue unroll to the floor.

Dawn looked good. She had lost weight everywhere but in her bust, and she had become resigned to that special burden. She moved with the confidence of a woman who knows she may attract only fetishists but knows equally well that to them her appeal will never diminish.

In my avuncular role I asked about romance in her life, but Dawn had none to report. A married man from the bank drove to Mar Vista every week or ten days, but otherwise Dawn turned down invitations to dinner or the movies because, she said, Dolly was waiting at home for dinner and a walk around the block. It seemed unfair to keep a big dog like that cooped up all night simply to go out with men she didn't much enjoy.

卐   卐   卐

For years, despite Billy's fondness for Jeanne Darling, Margo Stein had resisted meeting her, but now that Jeanne was volubly bored and unhappy in her divorced state, Margo relented and asked her, with me, to dinner. "She couldn't be matchmaking, could she, my dear? After all this time?" We were driving from her corner of the Valley to the Steins' less stately one.

"You're an eligible divorcee again."

"Did we ever go to bed together?" Jeanne relied on questions like that to keep her reputation in bad repair.

"I'm sure I'd remember."

"What's the name of their new baby?"

"Radhu," I said. "A name from Hindu mythology. Radhu Stein. The boy is named Jacob. He must be about eight."

"I know Jacob. Billy brings him along when we have lunch. Radhu. Radhu." She turned over the name appraisingly. "Radhu Darling. What do you think?"

"Gilding gold."

"When I was a girl my name was Jeannie May Willis," she said. "Horrid. Then after the war those civilian jeeps came out with advertising about how on back roads it went further, faster than anything else. You can imagine! But I guess being named Fell was no treat."

"That's the doggerel to live down. And on the East Coast a girl who'd threaten to charge me with felonious assault. I haven't heard that out here."

Jeanne had not spoken about Ray. When I called for her there had been no sign of him, except that in the living room she'd hung one of his less repellent paintings over the fire-place. What that signified I didn't know.

"Margo's lucky to have had a second child," Jeanne said. "I'm thinking of adopting one. They're letting women alone take them now. I could get a black child and give him a good home."

Her fantasy would come true on the day Rorke rejoined the paratroopers. But when she repeated the idea at dinner she got warm support from Margo Stein. "I'm glad I could have the second baby," Margo told her. "It was like getting a second chance."

Margo had parted her black bangs and brushed them back. The height of her forehead gave new and mature definition to her face. With Billy as she served him and listened to him talk, Margo was solicitous. With me she was as indifferent as when we first met. She liked Jeanne immediately, though I could think of many reasons why she shouldn't.

When the women turned from children to husbands, I overheard Jeanne say, "I don't mind saying there are times I miss Ray."

"I was lucky to marry Billy."

He tried to carry on his banter with me, but his round face insisted on wrinkling with pride. Margo realized we had heard her and she stared at me, daring me to scoff.

After dinner Billy drove us to the Hollywood Bowl, where a rock group from San Francisco was going to lay waste to twenty thousand teenagers. Billy had been given the tickets, which were so hard to come by we were morally obliged to use them.

Ranchek claims the Bowl is suited only to Fascist rallies. But the music that night was loud, even good. At least the audience shouted after every number and stamped its sandals. The air was sweetened by more than pine needles, and huddling there against the slight chill was a fine way to spend a summer night. Only Margo, whom I'd taken as spiritual kin to the children around us, looked uncomfortable. She turned down Jeanne's offer of a brown cigarette and clung to Billy's arm in a way that, were she anyone else, I would have called matronly.

⚜   ⚜   ⚜

Mergers and realignments had befallen his company over the years, but Robert Rorke survived them all and, though his title and rank changed regularly, went on juggling portfolios. Now the firm had asked him to head its new branch office in San Diego, and after reading entrails with his analyst, Rorke was ready to go. The psychiatrist not only endorsed the move, he told Rorke he needn't consult another doctor when he got there, so it was as certifiably sane that Rorke came to bid me farewell.

"You ought to get out of here, too," he said, sticking a finger in his drink to pull out an invisible foreign body.

"Out of this house? Out of Malibu?" I hadn't been there three months.

"Out of this city." Rorke listed the undeniable drawbacks to life in Los Angeles. "Nobody in his right mind," he concluded, "would hang around here."

"I hope you've told your doctor that."

"He says getting away will take care of my problems once and for all. I'm supposed to join a golf club, get a big apartment on the bay and buy a closetful of new clothes. All that's important to me, he says."

"Without his bills you'll have money for it."

"Best money I ever spent," Rorke said, proceeding to give me reasons, not entirely insulting, why I'd benefit from the same treatment. "Any man who hasn't married by the age of thirty-two needs it," he assured me.

"I don't have the money." It was the only excuse people accepted these days for my not doing what I didn't want to do.

"Well, yes, it was pretty expensive," Rorke said indulgently, as though he had bought a yacht.

Before the year was out, an engraved card arrived in Malibu announcing Rorke's marriage to a young woman I had never met. A page from the San Diego paper had been enclosed and it identified her as a welfare worker among Mexican day laborers. From the picture she was a nice-looking girl but no beauty—unplucked eyebrows, natural lashes, the kind of girl I'd once been resigned to marrying. She wore a simple blouse and her expression, in this photograph taken before the wedding and the honeymoon, was pensive.

⚜   ⚜   ⚜

I had finished daubing my shoes with black polish when a rap at the door got me to my feet. It was evening. Behind the muslin curtains in the bedroom the light was fading. I passed the chest of drawers with its large square mirror and saw that the glass was streaked with dust. I ran my fingers through my hair and pulled the door shut on the bathroom and the steam still seeping out after my shower. As I did these things I felt that years had already passed and I was remembering them. I knew somehow who waited at the door.

"Hello, Brad," she said.

"Hello, Ann."

"You didn't answer my letter."

"Come in."

"You're dressed up. You're going out."

"Come in."

She pressed past me in the narrow hall. In ten years, she hadn't changed her perfume, and she still wore blue. But my hands didn't reach for her hips; too often in the past she had shaken free. Now I could almost believe that she was waiting to feel my hands move toward her. It may have been only that the hallway was dark and she had to pick her way carefully toward the windows that looked out on the ocean.

"It's beautiful." She stood, her lovely back to me, watching the waves. Nothing could have persuaded me ten years ago that as we watched the sun set side by side I would feel only ill at ease.

"Sit down."

"You're going out."

"No." I pulled the white telephone on its long cord into the kitchen and began to close the door.

"You don't want me listening?" Even before she saw my face she regretted saying it.

"Not while I lie," I said. "I'm too good at it."

When I came back to her she had moved to the couch and scanned the water with eyes that looked blank to what they were seeing. Her face was unchanged. The skin beneath her eyes had been dark, even at twenty-six, and the eyes themselves were as sad then as now. Her body had acted on me with a force that made touching her irresistible. It was the same body.

"Where is your son?" I asked.

"With my mother."

"And—" I couldn't think of his name.

"In Denver."

"Is he unhappy?"

"I've been a good wife." She raised her sad eyes to smile. "I am a good wife."

"I didn't know how to answer your letter."

"Anything would have helped."

I had never heard that tone from her. It was I who had done the pleading, and she who was kind, often; and ironical and impatient.

"How did you get to Malibu?"

"A man on the airplane gave me a ride."

"Where are your clothes?"

"I left them in a locker at the airport. I thought I might be going back tonight." I didn't say anything and she said, "I don't want to go."

"You can stay here."

She got up and came to where I stood and put her arms around my neck. I held her in my arms but did not pull her close. "I loved you, Brad." That lie took all her courage. She didn't dare say she loved me now.

"I loved you more than—" I couldn't think of a comparison.

"Do you know what I'm going to do? Before we say anything else?" Disengaging herself she became again the woman I knew. "Since you gave up your dinner for me, I'm going to fix you a meal."

"We'll go out." She was already in the kitchen addressing the open refrigerator. "What do you do," she asked, "buy one jar of everything in the market?"

"I buy what I'm told," I said. "Every cook doesn't have the same specialties."

"This many cooks have been in your kitchen? Who in the world wanted pickled celery hearts? Or don't gentlemen divulge that information?"

"I've stopped worrying about what gentlemen do."

"That sounds promising." It was too early for that and we both ignored it. From the freezer she drew out two steaks in frosted cellophane envelopes. "How about these? After the gourmet dishes, I'll enter the competition with meat and potatoes."

"Anything."

"No, Brad," she said. "Not anything. I'm going to give you what you want, but you've got to help me. I don't even remember if you like steak."

"I like it. And baked potatoes. They're in the bottom cupboard. Somewhere on the second shelf there's sour cream."

247

"Thank you," she said. "Go in and sit down. Read. If instant bordelaise and sautéed artichoke could manage out here, I can."

I did as she said except that I didn't read. Numbly, with a book open on my knees, I pondered emotions like triumph and elation. Setting the table, she passed behind my chair, not speaking, humming low and tonelessly. I wanted to play a record but any song I chose would be a comment, and I understood why her humming had no tune.

"There," she said. I went to look. The table was crowded with platters and serving bowls. If she had seen the candlestick holders and the yellow candles from past evenings she had left them on the shelf. Tonight's could have been any meal midway through our tenth year together. The ordinariness of the plates together with my dulled silverware touched a chord, and as I seated her, I kissed her pale blond crown. "I'm glad you're here."

"And glad I came?"

I sat across the table and took up my fork for the salad. "Tomato and onion."

"It's what we always had at that café across the road from the gate. What was the name of the old woman who ran it?"

"Madame—I can't remember."

"I hope this steak isn't as tough as hers used to be. Do you remember the night your friend—the Negro boy—"

"Ron Cooper," I said.

"The night Ron lost a filling? And he kissed Madame—Biloux, her name was—because it meant two days in Bordeaux getting it fixed."

"Ron's in Los Angeles. I see him sometimes."

"They were happy times," she said. "I know that better now than when I was there."

I chewed my steak. The silence began awkwardly but smoothed out into a quiet several minutes. "You've changed," she said at last. "I'm not sure if I passed you on the street I'd recognize you. You look much, much older." Her sad eyes still fought her bright smile, and as always the smile lost. Once their conflict had made my stomach knit. "That's meant to be a compliment," she said.

"You look exactly the same."

"How can you know? You haven't had a picture."

"I'm sorry I did that."

"I hadn't realized how many you had taken until the mailman brought the box. Didn't modesty ever make me ask you to stop?"

"I took a lot when you weren't looking. Or asleep."

"Yes." She closed her eyes for a second as though to watch our scenes replayed. "George Ranchek wrote to me once, just before the wedding."

"Ranchek? Why?"

"Asking me to reconsider. He said your friends were afraid you'd do something—rash, I think he said."

"Ranchek has always been a fool."

"He meant well."

"Of course he didn't."

"Were you that upset?" she asked softly.

"If I was, I didn't ask for sympathy."

"I wonder why I went through with it."

I felt myself getting angry. I might no longer be that wretched boy, but I owed him more than to sit calmly and review his hours of pain. "Because you loved him, I suppose."

"Loved him?" She was surprised and looked away from me to consult with herself. "No, it was never that."

"It was long ago," I said.

"Brad," she said, "am I dead to you?" Those eyes, expressly meant to weep, had never shed tears for me to see. Now they grew large and dim. Surely we owe a kindness to the ones we loved and love no longer. "You're alive," I said. "You're here. It takes getting used to."

"I want to hear everything." Often she had tried to pass off extravagance as vitality. "We'll go and sit on the porch and watch the stars. Remember the porch behind the school? You liked to sit there."

It was cold but we went out. A sea mist quickly settled over us and took the faint curl from her hair. I told her what I was doing, she talked about what had happened ten years ago. "Do you remember?" she would ask, and usually I had forgotten.

After dinner, she had looked for coffee and found instead my canister of marijuana and the cigarette roller Jeanne Darling had given me on my last birthday. "Make one for us," she said.

"Is it a good idea?"

"The best I've had since I got on the plane this afternoon."

"I don't smoke much," I said. "It's one last deference to my conscience."

"I remember your conscience." She took a freshly rolled cigarette and sat so her head touched my shoulder without resting on it. "I've done this once or twice," she said.

"High in Denver."

"No, you can be very low in Denver. Ask me."

I didn't. Her letter had given me a clue—another unhappy marriage. She could take three hours to tell me about it and when she finished I'd still say everything but what she came to hear.

"Are you tired?" Only ten o'clock, and I had even dredged up the Blacks' New Year's Eve party eight years ago.

"I am, a little."

We went into the bedroom. As I turned back the spread she laughed, an easy spontaneous laugh that, coming then, disconcerted me. "What?"

"I remember the night four of us—Doug Goodwin was with that French girl—were having dinner in Bordeaux and you were going on about responsibilities—I'm sorry, Brad, but you did go on sometimes, you know. You did. And Doug said, 'The only thing a man owes a woman is clean sheets on the bed.' "

"You agreed with him."

"To tease you. You were getting solemn."

"I remember." The French girl's test had come back positive that afternoon.

She stayed a long time in the bathroom. When she came out, my yellow beach towel was draped off her shoulders like a sarong. I made room for her beneath the blanket and turned off the light.

Over ten years, the strongest memory I had kept was of her shivering when I touched her, a slight withdrawal, as though she were stepping away from her body and leaving me the abandoned flesh to hold. I had made excuses for her then: I said the pitch of my own excitement would have left me disappointed with any response she made. I may have been right. At least, tonight she astonished me with the pressure of her need. I kept pace, for the sake of the boy who loved her.

I held his memory in front of me, as Faye said Rorke imagined other men's faces. I used the thought of his rapture at this body to stimulate myself, this body freed tonight from all suggestion of disdain.

But of course without that reserve, without the flinching or the drawing away, she was not the same woman, and the boy observed her eagerness with distaste. He had depended on her for slight signs of apathy or resignation, he with his attic full of old guilts, and I could see him more clearly now, forever talking of responsibility in hopes no one would mention pleasure.

And this was pleasure. Let the boy turn his face if he must. He lost this woman. I've got her back and I can keep her. If I want her.

I fell asleep. Perhaps she did. I had said nothing to her. I hadn't kissed her when I finished. At three o'clock I awoke wondering who was with me. I put out a hand but I couldn't identify any recent woman—no plaited hair, or legs so short they hardly reached my knee, or breath heavy with cinnamon. Exploring, I already knew the answer. But I had dreamed too often that she was with me like this and woke to find myself alone, or, worse, with another woman who stirred when I did and wouldn't let me slip back to my dream. One final touch, to make sure. But at the touch of my fingers, this girl, the dream herself, might awake, and if she does, I must be ready with my answer.

One time was nothing, hardly more than taking her hand or kissing the top of her head. But if she wakes now and I embrace her again, then I am saying that she may stay. I admit she hasn't lost the power that made me plead with her to share my life.

Twice tonight, and in the morning my verdict cannot go against her, or I have used her intolerably. We both know the laws of this court. She may be awake now, trying to guess at my decision before I pronounce it.

Her left hand has been covering her bare breast. Now it falls to her side and rests between us, touching me only with the heat a body gives out. At dinner I was pleased to see she hadn't taken off her rings when she boarded the plane. It seemed honest to come here as a married woman. I feel a sharp corner of her diamond graze my skin as her fingers arch back and their nails touch my leg.

It is now I must decide. Even to let her hand turn and cup itself on my leg would be to consent. If I am going to submit again to this woman, I will do it and not force her to make my decision for me.

The nails lie without weight. I have another moment to think.

I loved her once. With determination, perhaps I could love her again. Worry, again, whenever she fell quiet, watch for her warning signs of boredom, ask myself into the late hours whether I had given her what she needed. Beside her in this same bed, it could be my fingers that were the tentative scouts again, afraid to touch her thigh, convinced that if I did she would roll away, yet half persuaded this would be the night she would press herself into my arms.

I could love her, brood again when the world went flat for her, take her restlessness as proof of faults, not in her or even in the world, but in myself. I could return to the heightened state where every word, hesitation, look, silence, has a secret meaning for the future.

Love can teach us, I never denied that. I had learned much about myself and more about the limitless demands love makes. I met them once, but I was not I.

Love. I mistook it for life because it warmed my blood. A single squeeze of her hand pumped my heart to twice its size. But her same power could drain that blood, collapse that heart, until murder or self-murder appeared to me as simple choices rationally arrived at. Love came near to being my death.

Since then I have experimented with the synonyms for love—fondness, affection, attraction, desire. Lust. They have given me pleasure. More important, they've left my appetite and my reason intact. Only love trapped and impoverished me and poisoned me almost to death. I admit it was the great moment of my life. I don't want to repeat it.

Against my skin, the surfaces of her nails are slippery and cold. But she is turning her hand and the tips of her fingers burn me. I make a sleeper's noise and with the merest motion disengage my body.

      ❦   ❦   ❦

The next three days I stayed home, availing myself of sick leave I had accrued. I threw out every half-filled jar from the refrigerator and took the sheets and towels she had used to the laundromat. After two cycles of bleach and blue powder, her scent still seemed to cling to the pillowslips. Home again, I took the telephone off the hook. I don't know why. She hadn't called from the airport and wouldn't call now, from Denver. I began these notes.

By the fourth day I was sick of myself and wanted to go for a drive. But I was too orderly by far to back the car from the garage without a destination. I decided to ride to the Valley college and plague Lonnie Chapman about his new notoriety.

His photograph had appeared twice lately in the paper— Lonnie with a small beard that pointed up his chiseled looks— and I had written the caption. First "rebel leader," then, on reflection, "dissident spokesman." His faction was so distrustful of formal leadership that without a title or much experience Lonnie had begun to shape policy.

During the week I stayed home, students and teachers on his campus had called a protest strike, and Lonnie was listed again as a strategist, though this time photographs from the scene consisted of crowd shots, nightsticks and bleeding heads.

I set out for the college through Topanga, past wooden shacks and abandoned stores that made the canyon look like a mining village. At every bend, young hitchhikers extended their thumbs, and I picked up one yellow-haired girl traveling with a frail soft-spoken boy. As we rode through the scrubby brown pass, they debated whether to go along to the college with me. At last they agreed that the hostility on the campus might jeopardize their chemically induced euphoria, and I let them out at the onramp of the Ventura Freeway.

Their caution had made me smile, but when I turned on the radio I found their intuition had been sound. A news broadcast interrupted itself to report that rioting had broken out again on the campus and the National Guard was being alerted.

I had edited enough bulletins to know that "rioting" was a flexible word that could cover anything from manhandling a dean to armed insurrection. Too, I had been processing violence daily for several years, until sometimes ink from the galley proofs welled up on my desk like black blood. The prospect of a melee on the campus didn't stimulate even my curiosity, and I couldn't spend an hour with Lonnie if he was barricaded in a building. I took my time driving to the south edge of the campus and, since I was in no hurry, found a parking place on the first street I tried.

At the main entrance police cars were double and triple parked. Four large black vans with barred windows had been driven over the curb and parked on the lawn. Their back doors hung open toward the central quadrangle and I went off in that direction. At a passageway between the administration building and the gymnasium two wooden sawhorses were blocking the pavement and policemen in white helmets were clustered between them.

I made a quick show of my laminated credential: "Press." A trim young sergeant waved me through. "We're going to be clearing the library," he said. "They're trying to get a fire going in there, and the minute they do, we'll go in with the firemen. You better stay away from the steps and the side door."

I trotted down a path toward the crowd near the library entrance. From a second floor window, a bearded boy was exhorting the clean-shaven young men and pretty girls below, but he didn't have a bullhorn and what he was shouting was lost to me.

Police were lined up between the crowd and the steps, and if the boy at the window hoped for a surge forward he was disappointed. No one moved. A few young men waved to him; half a dozen girls tried to get an obscene chant going. Their alto voices were lilting and delicate before they died away.

The lunch hour caused students to shift ground and relinquish their places so that I was propelled gradually to the front where I spied Lonnie and then Rose, in the seventh month of pregnancy. I pushed gently toward them and tapped Lonnie's shoulder. "What are you doing outside?" I asked.

"Look who's here, Rose. Our side must be winning."

Apparently his first neat beard had not satisfied Lonnie's conscience, for he was letting the hairs run scraggly and free. No matter how poorly he groomed, his was a raffish face, and one I suspected he saw as a wall poster one day. Rose's print dress hung well below the knee and there looked to be colored beads sewed across the toes of her moccasins. In spite of those handicaps, all self-inflicted, she looked splendid. The roundness thrusting up from her belly gave her a softened, tamed look. She offered me her hand.

"The police are going in soon," I said.

"They'll wait until one o'clock," Lonnie assured me. "That's what happened yesterday at the science lab. There were fifty-six of us inside for three hours. Then at one o'clock the police came and took everyone away." If Lonnie derived an emotional jolt from these activities he was shrewd enough to conceal it. Rose looked very tired.

"That doesn't explain why you're not inside the library today."

"Our steering committee meets this afternoon. Anyone arrested now won't be back in time for it. What's happening today isn't important. It's something to do while we get our plans together."

"The police say you're going to burn books. You will have come full circle."

"We're not going to burn anything. But," he said, "we might do it sometime. If it's the best way to make our point."

That Rose didn't join our conversation seemed strange. I had considered her primarily responsible for Lonnie's activism, but now that she had had her husband locking himself in public buildings, she seemed indifferent to the outcome. At one point, when Lonnie said he was willing to go to prison for his beliefs, Rose smiled—a warm, perfectly fond smile; a smile all the same.

She agreed with me, though, when I said Lonnie's group should recruit more black students. "Try to find them," Lonnie protested. "Most blacks live thirty miles and forty years away from here."

"Do you know Ron Cooper? He's a friend of mine from the Army."

"I've heard the name. Pretty much of a Tom, isn't he?"

Rose interrupted. "I must go someplace where I can sit down."

"Okay," Lonnie said. "We'll meet you in the cafeteria as soon as they clear the library."

Rose took herself away without goodbyes. Her leaving was a signal to the band of students waiting to talk with Lonnie but not wanting to intrude. Three girls and two young men flocked around us, pouring out that hour's rumors. Lonnie listened and met their questions disingenuously.

At three minutes past one a police squad marched up the library steps, cracked open the glass doors, and jogged inside. Soon we could see scuffling at the upper windows, and a minute or two afterward, ten boys and two girls, all white, were dragged out of the library with their arms twisted behind them. One boy bled from a small cut on his scalp. Two others made a clenched fist with their free arms for the cameramen. "In the Army," I said, "that had a different meaning."

"Same meaning, broader scope," Lonnie said. "We're more ambitious than you were."

"The police clipped one fellow a little."

"A little, a lot, it's the same." I knew from his tone that Lonnie was bored and wanted to fence. "The instinct is wrong, whether it's hitting a man with a club or shooting him with a bullet. There's no measuring degrees."

"It's the same whether a man speaks rudely to his wife or beats her?"

"Rude to Rose? I wasn't rude. She understands that my attention is going to be divided these days. Your trouble is that you expect husbands and wives to be as polite with each other as you are to the girls you pick up for a night."

"What I expect doesn't matter."

"Don't worry about Rose," he said. "She's tough."

Diversion done for another day, we drifted with the crowd to the cafeteria where Rose was waiting at a table. An empty milk glass stood in front of her. As we sat down, those students who recognized Lonnie called to him, but he merely returned their wave and didn't beckon them over to introduce his wife.

I asked Rose how she was feeling. "I'm more tired than I expected," she said. "I wish this had come up after the baby so I could be more help to Lon."

Lonnie said promptly, "After the baby, you'll be home with him."

"You have the gender guaranteed?" I asked.

"Look at her," Lonnie answered. "Of course she's going to have male children."

"Like Lady Macbeth." Rose sounded glum.

"Its naïve of me," said Lonnie, "but I keep shaking my head when I think of Rose having this baby. Even a composer needs sheets of lined paper. But here's Rose, with nothing but her body, producing this baby and as many others as she wants."

"You made a contribution," said Rose, but Lonnie went on addressing himself to her full belly. "A dot, that's what I gave," he said. "It could have come out of a tube. No, it's the women who are amazing."

"Men and women aren't that different," she insisted.

"Of course they are." Lonnie couldn't have been more expansive if this had been office hours at the English Department. "Look at that swelling. Can you imagine me with the patience to walk around like that for nine months?" Tenderly he laid his hand on Rose's belly, with a suggestion that he was reaching past the walls of her womb to seal his compact directly with the ally inside.

    ⚜   ⚜   ⚜

When a controversy erupted at Councilman Blanco's headquarters in the last week of his reelection campaign, George Ranchek became the third and least probable of my friends to turn up in the headlines. On the morning of his news conference I took an hour off and drove to the Los Angeles Press Club, convinced, as behooves a friend, that however much Ranchek was in the right, he was about to make an ass of himself.

It had been a month since I'd last seen him, and our evening hadn't been a success. I had gone to the kitchen to mix my own drink, Ranchek to this day too sparing with his liquor, when Pearlann joined me at the sink and began to cry. "I'm so damned sick of it," she said as she sobbed. "Can't he ever stop?"

"No, I don't think he can."

Ranchek heard the commotion and came to investigate. "Have I injured my little wife's feelings?" he asked. "I was wrong about the telephone bill. You must call the Antelope Valley anytime you wish. We should just be glad your dear mother is still with us. Can you ever forgive me?"

Pearlann made a face and nodded, but Ranchek had pulled a ballpoint pen from his pocket and was scribbling on a paper napkin. "At least," I said, "you've given up that charade you played with the confessional." He handed the napkin to Pearlann, who opened a drawer and put it in with several others. "Now what's that?"

"My wife, for whom I left the one true church, being a Protestant," Ranchek said, "I can hardly do penance when I sin. So I have adopted the custom of her faith."

"And do what?"

"Make a substantial contribution to the building fund."

Pearlann had no chance for the rest of the evening. As I left them, the wrong side of my mouth was sour and stiff from laughing out of it.

The press conference was under way on the outdoor patio when I arrived, and to my relief Ranchek was facing the lights without his dark glasses. He had bought sunglasses with prescription lenses and wore them everywhere—to art films, bowling alleys, evening concerts at the Music Center.

More encouraging, Ranchek was sitting sedately, elbows on a white enameled table, and talking logically and grammatically. He reviewed the history of the councilmanic district, trying to prove it had been realigned to increase the percentage of white voters. Now, according to Ranchek, Blanco's professional campaign managers had passed out pamphlets that pictured his black opponent as a revolutionary whose election would set off new looting and arson. Ranchek said that both he and Blanco knew the accusation to be false and he had resigned this morning as field deputy to protest the tactic.

One television reporter hinted that Ranchek had resented outsiders being imported to run the campaign and had quit from pique, but he handled that adroitly.

"Do you have another job?" another man asked.

"No," Ranchek said without a quaver. "Until this morning I have devoted myself to the job at City Hall."

"Do you think the opposition might offer you a position?"

"Under the circumstances, I would not accept."

"Anything else, anybody?" The doyen had his eye on the Press Club bar. "Thank you."

The lights were switched off, the cameras, cords and heavy metal boxes hauled away, and the crews drove off to film Blanco's rebuttal at City Hall. Ranchek and I stayed behind at the white table.

"You did well, Ranchek."

"I didn't talk too fast?"

"You were fine. You really don't have another job?"

"I'll find something," Ranchek said. "But I had to quit. I may never do anything very good with my life, but I can try not to do anything too bad." Had he not risked a calf-eyed look at me I would have let it pass. Seeing his eyes widen, I forced myself to make one last protest. "I'm waiting, George," I said.

"Squeak," Ranchek began reluctantly. "Squeak. It gets harder the older you get. Squeak. The muscles get out of condition. Squeak."

Insisting had been a mistake. On the edge of middle age, we had to grant each other the right to talk sonorously, look grave, posture, bluster and perform. I relented. "You were very good today, George."

"Thank you," said Ranchek daintily.

"I'm back," Doug Goodwin's voice informed me.

"What were you doing in Oregon?"

"I got a job for a while. I drove around in the mountains."

"You had a good time?"

"About the same."

"You left in a hurry."

"It was Donna's idea. She asked me when I was expecting to take off again. I didn't know, so she said I'd better do it right away, that same night, and not come back until I was ready to stay."

"You're staying?"

"I'm back."

"Where are you living?"

"I'm on my way over to Donna's."

"She didn't want you overnight because of the children."

"We'll be getting married."

"Is that right? How soon?"

"I've got to get a job. And Donna wants to move out of where she is. I've got to save money for a down payment on another house."

"Congratulations. She must be an unusual woman."

"She looks like me."

⚑   ⚑   ⚑

Robert Rorke flew to Los Angeles on business and modulating his snarl to an approximation of friendliness called me to suggest dinner on the Sunset Strip. He chose the steakhouse Ray Morella once owned, and I agreed since at least he wouldn't be abusing waiters at my favorite restaurants. "I'll be bringing a friend of yours," he informed me but wouldn't say more. I expected a mutual friend from the East Coast, embalmed in a button-down shirt and striped rep tie.

If the club had changed since Morella sold his share, I couldn't tell it, for the lights were dimmer than ever. I was led to a corner and deposited at a table hardly bigger than a checkerboard. By the time Rorke came groping toward me, my eyes had adjusted enough to make out that a woman followed, her hand resting for guidance on his shoulder. He had seated her and maneuvered himself into a chair beside me before I saw her face. "Surprised?" Faye asked.

"Struck dumb."

With a snap of his fingers Rorke summoned a candle for our table. It was duly brought but with the wick implanted in a glass so darkly red that no light extended as far as our menus. For me all the candle did was illuminate Faye and Rorke from the hairline upward.

The choice of restaurant had been his, and Rorke insisted on our ordering the house specialty—steak smeared with yellowish paste—and washing it down with champagne from upstate New York. "I have a toast," Rorke announced when the ice bucket arrived. Faye instinctively raised her glass. I considered public toasts on a par with Ranchek's games, but I crooked my elbow and brought the rim of my glass level with my lips.

"To the next generation," Rorke proposed. Faye understood before I did. "Oh, Robert, that's wonderful!" She kissed him; at least their scalps met in the candlelight. "When?"

"Six months."

"That's wonderful! Bradley, isn't that wonderful?"

"It fills me with wonder. Congratulations."

Rorke overlooked our undercurrent of surprise. Even as he sent back the dinner wine and called for the piano player to lower his volume, he was bursting with contentment.

When the bill arrived I dug in my pocket but Rorke was adamant. "This is my party." The only fault he found with the evening was that it had come three years late. At that, he had reconstructed the recent past as best he could, omitting only the woman who made our celebration possible. "Too bad," I said, "that you didn't bring your wife."

"I came on the plane and she's never liked flying. Now, of course—" He broke off, the danger of a woman three months pregnant aboard an airplane too obvious to need mention.

"I'm sure she's a lovely girl. She looked beautiful in the picture." Faye in her magnanimity was artless and breathy. Throughout dinner I had watched the years falling away until she was again the sweet unsure girl who marinated fruit rind in her gin.

"Oh, yes," Rorke shrugged, "she's beautiful."

Faye had called for Rorke at his hotel on her way to the restaurant and they had come the rest of the way by cab. Now, as Rorke finished overtipping, I offered to take him back to the hotel and Faye to the side street where she had parked. I drove cautiously, muzzy from the various wines, but Rorke, who would ordinarily be drumming his fingers, was in no hurry. In fact, he said, he was not at all tired and was glad now he had bought a bottle of cognac to keep in his room. "Would you like to come up for a nightcap?" His tone said no for me.

"No," I said on cue. "Thanks."

I had pulled up the hotel driveway to where the attendants lounged in their metal lawn chairs. "How about you?" Rorke said, staring at the glove compartment.

"I'd love to," Faye said.

The next morning the shy girl was gone for good; it was the stylish Bel-Air lady who ventured to call. "You think I'm terrible."

"I believe in endings," I said. "We don't get enough of them."

"It was only for Robert," Faye said. "It meant a lot to him."

"I'm sure it did." To contradict her, I'd have had to confide more of my own experience than I was ready to share.

🐝 🐝 🐝

For the launching of his trattoria on Ventura Boulevard, Ray Morella gave a party for his friends and future patrons. He had deliberately applied for the state license that permitted only wine and beer on the premises and that, taken with the unassuming interior and low prices, would stamp the place as a family restaurant. As we shook hands he grimaced. "Back with the meatballs. What can I do? It's what I know."

He shouted an insult to a young television actor, a friend from the Strip, and beckoned him over to introduce me. Close up, the man was no more compelling than Josh Black, yet there he stood, known and loved, ready to accommodate the women who wanted their menus autographed.

In a starched and bouffant yellow dress Jeanne was acting as Ray's hostess, and I overheard him pointing her out to the actor as his wife. She slipped behind me while I was watching the actor oblige his fans. "If you ever saw television," she murmured, "you wouldn't be looking so skeptical. He's really quite good. But at least there's vino for you." She collared a boy with a tray of red and pale yellow glasses. "It's California tonight, dear," she warned me. "Stick with the white."

A dozen abstracts had been hung on the walls and I asked Jeanne whose they were. "I can't think of the name." She frowned to remember. "Ray found something by him on La Cienega and asked if he'd like to display them here. Ray wants to show a different painter every month."

"How about an exhibition by the owner?"

"Where people are eating?" She checked to see that Ray was far enough away not to hear. "No, dear, he's painting again, but it's about the same. When he stacks them in the bedroom it looks like a mudslide."

"Ray is back?"

"Of course. I thought everyone knew. He's back. But not for another marriage. We're not going to let respectability ruin it again."

"What do I call you?"

"Miss Darling, Mrs. Morella—it doesn't matter. Sonny's sulking, but at his age it's good for him to think his mother is a little wicked. It will give him that contempt for women that's so attractive."

The crowd had grown until we were wedged together amid checkered tablecloths and rustic wood chairs. A few couples were eating, but with the guests immobilizing the waiters, Ray had closed the kitchen. I was about to leave when the stir and murmuring near the door dropped sharply and, by craning my neck, I could see that Ron Cooper had come in with two friends.

One of them I knew, a blues singer from a club in Hollywood. All three were in black jackets, fuchsia scarves at the neck, dark glasses—an exotic eddy moving toward us through the wash of white faces. Jeanne and I went forward, but they cleared a path much faster than we could, and the five of us met close to our corner. Jeanne kissed Ron's cheek. "I'm glad you could come."

"You're looking good."

"Fat," she said.

"A little fat's all right. A little fat is nice."

Around us everyone was trying to listen but discreetly, and that meant the noise and laughter were rising again as Ray came to meet Ron. "Jeanne's told me you paint," Ray said. "Would you bring over some of your work? I'll hang them here when these come down."

"Thanks," Ron said. "Right now I don't have anything to show. I haven't had much time."

Ron and his friends stayed for one glass of red wine and then eased out in single file. Even among the eavesdroppers who understood that Cooper had come in friendship, relief was broad and obvious. Only Jeanne dimmed when they were gone. "What's wrong?" I asked.

"Does it show, dear? Nothing, really. I'll never get used to the way people pass in and out of my life. Even Sonny's father, when he calls from Louisville I like hearing his voice. I need to know that those years we spent haven't just evaporated. He really exists, somewhere." She said it smiling. "I was going to make myself into a beautiful vase filling up with the wonderful things that happened to me. And I'm only a sieve, like everybody else."

"You'll see Ron again."

"The way I did tonight." She laughed. "Oh, well."

Perking up, she prodded my elbow for me to drink my wine. "At the moment," she said, "I'm concentrating on Ray and praying that everything will turn out for him."

"To whom?"

"What?"

"Praying to whom?"

"To myself," Jeanne said. "I'm the one who can make the difference."

"Lucky Ray."

"We shall see, love. We shall see."

* * *

On the day I concluded that these notes had served their purpose, I typed them through, changing only the names and a few sequences, and took the result to Lonnie Chapman. For ten years I had been punctuating to the dictates of a linotype machine, and if I was to send the manuscript to a publisher, I wanted it examined first by a professional pedant.

Rose had gone out for the evening, and Ruth, their baby daughter, beautiful and unnaturally good, was asleep in the next room. While Lonnie read and commented, I intended to sit opposite him and read from another critic, Sainte-Beuve.

Marriage had wrought many changes in Lonnie, but it had not cured his ulcer. He brought a tall glass of whole milk to the table next to his chair and served me a glass of bitter port that must have been the gift of indigent students. Lonnie flipped the pages speedily, far too fast, I would have said, for comprehension. I wanted to remind him that it wasn't a student's examination paper, except that for Lonnie now all books were nothing else.

I treated my author more courteously, reading slowly, trying to reconcile the France I remembered—Basque farmers in black berets—with the lucid and elegant world on the printed page. In about half an hour Lonnie had finished. He shuffled the sheets back to the beginning and cleared his throat with a swallow of milk. "I've gone through it quickly," he said. "Now I want to read it again."

"Take your time." I was relieved that he had been leafing through to find the passages about himself. Vanity was easier to forgive than bad habits acquired at the university.

The second reading went so ploddingly, with Lonnie subjecting each page to the minutest scrutiny, that after another hour I reversed myself. "Hurry along, will you? I want to get back to Malibu before midnight." His reply was to go on turning the pages lugubriously.

I was nodding in my chair when he said briskly, "I'm done." I shut the heavy volume in my hand and waited. "It's too bad Jeanne Darling had to be Southern," he said.

"Yes, it is."

"Did Margo find a man in San Francisco?"

"She told Jeanne she did. Ramon. He worked in a cannery and was very handsome."

"Do you believe her?"

"I guess I do," I said. "It doesn't matter."

"How will you end it?"

"Doug Goodwin gets married next week. I thought I'd end with that."

He frowned speculatively. "You'll be his best man?"

"The Blacks will be in town on their way to Santa Barbara for a vacation. I told him to ask Josh instead."

"Goodwin agreed?"

"I don't think he cares much about anything these days."

"Not everybody gets married because he's worn out," Lonnie said. "Or because he's timid or bored or impotent or sadistic. Strong, normal, healthy, intelligent men and women get married every day. It's your bad luck you don't seem to know any."

"I took these friends because I've known them the longest. I could have used the others and the result would have been the same."

"You told Jeanne Darling you wanted to discover the essence of marriage. Did you find it?"

"Fear," I said.

"That's not true. Or if it's true it's so little true it might as well be false."

"I could only write about what I've seen."

As I spoke Lonnie was flipping through the manuscript to the point where Ann reappeared at my door. "You give yourself away here," he said.

"Ten years ago I would have married her," I agreed. "I changed in those ten years and the country changed. You and your friends talk about revolution. We've had one and I survived it. You're the casualty."

Lonnie's combativeness went out of him. He drank his milk to the bottom as I watched his unhappy face, feeling that without connecting I had managed to land a foul blow. "I'm going to tell you something," he said. "You'll find out sooner or later. It's nothing I'm ashamed of. Rose isn't here tonight because she's joined a therapy group in Westwood. I've promised to go with her when the summer term ends. There's nothing wrong with either of us. Our marriage is very, very happy. But by discussing it frankly we think we can be even happier."

"Most unique." It was the kind of donnish joke to make Lonnie smile, and he exposed his formidable teeth.

"I knew you'd manage to misunderstand," he said. "But since Rose and I add up to the one reasonable marriage, you'd be better off not mentioning the therapy. It would look as though you couldn't resist one last sneer."

"No games," I said. "Remember?"

"I grew up." He wasn't smiling now, his voice was sad. Perhaps I was intended to hear pity in it. "And when I grew up, I got married."

     ⚜   ⚜   ⚜

They tried first to reach me by telephone, but finding my receiver off the hook the Blacks wired from a town near the California border to ask that I meet them at a coffee shop in Santa Monica three hours before Goodwin's wedding. Plan-

ning their itinerary to cut motel expenses, they left their
house early to drive directly to the wedding and then north to
Santa Barbara, where Jenny's aunt had offered them her guest
room.

The coffee shop was large, mostly glass, with gray leather
booths and orange mosaic lamps. Lucky for me, it served
breakfast twenty-four hours a day. I had barely found a spa-
cious booth and ordered black coffee when the Blacks burst
through the entrance. Jenny smacked a toddling infant and
then rapped impartially with her knuckles on the head of an
older boy, who was shouting loudly that he was innocent. A
solemn girl followed at the rear. She had been making shush-
ing noises until she realized that she was only adding to the
uproar. She stopped and walked as far as she could behind her
family.

Jenny reached me first and took my hand between her own
dry palms. Josh lifted the younger boy to the middle of the
booth and settled the other one next to him. The girl was allowed to drift along and alight near her mother.

We adults congratulated each other on coming through the
last four years so well; my compliments, at least, were tendered in good faith. Jenny looked better than I'd ever seen
her. She was deeply tanned and in the rich brown frame of
her face, her eyes were startling. Whatever oils she used to
offset the desert sun had given her skin a dark even gloss. Her
figure looked ripe.

Josh tanned less becomingly. His pale skin mottled, his nose
peeled. But he had lost a little weight and no hair, and his
teeth, like Jenny's, looked as though he ate nothing but charcoal and other whitening agents. I was introduced to the children with their no-nonsense names: Jane I remembered, John
had just begun walking when they left, now James.

Josh had wired when he realized he'd lost Goodwin's letter
with its instructions for reaching the church in Canoga Park.

He proposed that we eat lunch together and he could follow me to the Valley in their station wagon.

"You'll find a lot of changes," I said. "Or have you noticed?"

"We drove down Wilshire so I could stop for a wedding present," Jenny said. "All the buildings! You don't see trees and grass anymore."

But both Blacks were more concerned with the change in Doug Goodwin that had led him to take a wife. "I never thought he'd do it," Jenny said.

"She must really be something," Black added.

"A lot of his girls have been better-looking. This one is pretty."

A waitress delivered my eggs, and cheeseburgers with french fried potatoes to the Black family. I was about to lift my fork when Jenny laid her finger on my wrist. "Would you wait just a second, Brad?"

Perplexed, I lowered my hand. Jenny leaned across the table and clasped the baby's fingers together. The other children had already folded their palms and bowed their heads. Josh was sitting with eyes lowered, hands in his lap. Jenny began to pray.

It was no singsong verse or short formality. As she asked blessings on our food, Jenny invoked freely the blood of the lamb and other gore the Friends had never introduced into their meeting house. As she gave each grim phrase its due, her expression was placid but resolute. When she reached the "Amen," her children echoed it and grabbed for their cheeseburgers.

"What kind of a church is it today?" Jenny asked me.

"No denomination. Goodwin wanted to get married downtown but she wanted another church wedding."

"They're prettier."

"Jeanne Darling—do you remember? She says a wedding

license should be issued only if the bride can prove she's pregnant."

Jenny winced. In their house the expression may have been "in the family way." "Isn't she the girl who was having trouble with that Italian?"

"They're fine now."

At their station wagon I proposed that Jenny ride with me, but she thought she'd better stay with the children. We set off, a caravan of two, with my convertible leading the way.

At the forlorn west end of the San Fernando Valley, Canoga Park consists of one immense air-conditioned shopping center and several thousand ranch-style houses where herds once grazed. Most families had spent their savings on the down payment, and they deferred planting trees or laying sod. On several streets we passed, children squatted to play, using the front yards of an entire block as their sandbox.

The church when it was built had been elbowed to the edge of its lot so that four-fifths of the property could be paved. Heat today had raised blisters in the asphalt, and the white concrete slabs marking each parking place looked like gravestones sinking in tar. "It is hot," I said as we got out of our cars. "Even for August."

"I hope the church is open," Jenny said. "I've got to get James inside."

"We're early," Josh said. "You take the kids in, and Brad and I will wait out here for a while."

Jenny looked dubious. "You said it's hard on the engine to keep the air conditioning running."

"It will be all right," he said. "Go on in."

I climbed in front beside Josh and let the cold air turn the damp creases in my trousers hard and brittle. Jenny and the children had been inside the church five minutes when Ranchek came hulking out a side exit. He was wiping his face on a woman's tiny embroidered handkerchief. I swung open the back door for him.

"Can you fit back there with all the suitcases, Ranchek?"

"Oh, yes. Don't worry about me." He greeted Josh and crushed down on something that tinkled and gave way. "I thought the wedding was supposed to start at two."

"What time did you get here?" I asked.

"Two o'clock sharp. A little later? At the very latest two thirty."

"I told Goodwin that if he wanted you as an usher, he'd have to lie. Is he inside?"

"No, but the bride is ready and waiting. My wife and Jenny are attending to her toilette." From beside his seat Ranchek hoisted a battered black case with Josh's initials in silver. "Here's your old makeup case! I haven't seen that since the Army."

Josh turned to look. "Jenny uses it now for her powder and lipstick."

"It's easy to see"—Ranchek was about to amuse himself hugely—"who wears the paints in your family."

The case had been resting on a copy of one of the radical tabloids that had sprung up in the last few years. Black pulled it out and leafed through the classified advertisements. "I've seen this back home," he said. "They must be kidding."

"I shouldn't think so," I said.

He read aloud an explicit request by one married couple for like-minded wives and husbands. "I was positive they were a gag. Are you sure they're serious?"

"They're serious."

Black read another, a loving inventory of the wife's anatomy. "This couple's our age," he said. "She's two years younger than her husband, too."

"Already you have a lot in common," Ranchek said.

"Seriously, George," Josh asked. "Would you ever answer an ad like that?"

Ranchek scratched his head at the one place that wisps of

black hair still intersected. "I've been invited to orgies, but I always come up with some limp excuse."

"Brad, you get around. What do you think?"

"I doubt that they start the evening with a prayer."

"Oh, you mean Jenny? That's new. She thinks it's good for the kids. No, really," he said. "It's funny they can get away with these. Maybe the police put them in as a trap." The idea cheered him for a moment. "Do you think so?"

"No."

"It would be interesting to answer one, just to see what kind of people they could be. You'd have to be careful, though."

"I can't imagine Jenny at something like that."

"No, you're right." Josh, after all, wasn't much of an actor. He realized he hadn't sounded convincing and tried again. "No, of course she wouldn't go for it."

Ranchek had found an ad for leather and chains. "Do you remember when Puss 'n Boots was a children's tale?" He sighed nostalgically. "And split beaver was a fur coat?"

When Goodwin drove up beside us, the green sedan he had bought for his honeymoon was badly buckled on its right side. On his way through Benedict Canyon two days before, Goodwin said, boys in a pickup truck had rammed into him and sped away. Police found the truck abandoned off a remote trail and traced it to a plumber who had reported it stolen in June. Goodwin probably couldn't collect on the insurance. He shrugged. "Anyway it runs."

For the ceremony he had bought a new navy suit, tight through the shoulders but with a bulge at the back of his neck. The trousers were short enough to expose his ankles in their black wool socks. He had remembered boutonnieres for us and stood cracking his knuckles as we pinned them to our lapels. "I guess we better go in."

The church's lobby was outfitted like a kindergarten, each

corner crammed with small chairs for Sunday school. We moved into the air-conditioned chapel, an oblong empty room with the only dot of color a red cloth across the altar. Two vases of lilies lent scant warmth to a plain gold-plated cross. Like the altar, the empty pews were of waxed blond wood. High windows of frosted white glass along the east wall confirmed the mood: it was a room for charity funerals. Ranchek looked around with ecumenical reverence. "Beautiful," he whispered.

Since there had been no time for rehearsal, Goodwin led Josh to the minister in his study behind the organ. Ranchek and I slumped down in the back row. "I was sorry to miss your wedding, Ranchek."

"Yes," he said. "Because of my public position at the time we had clergymen of all faiths officiating. The wedding march itself was performed by the accordion section from the Los Angeles Philharmonic."

"They're very good."

"Coming from a man with your ear, that's high praise."

In twos and singly the guests began to arrive. Occasionally an older woman would look questioningly at us, but when my headache kept me anchored and Ranchek didn't stir either, she'd find a place on her own. A pert blond woman poked Ranchek's shoulder, though, and he sprang to his feet and took her on his arm to the front pew. "Donna's mother," he whispered when he returned.

Unless my watch was fast it was now ten minutes past the announced time. Twice a husky man with a crewcut had peered from the study door and the third time made his way to the organ, where he pumped out a romantic song of the day.

Goodwin and Black appeared in the doorway, nudged forward by a morose bald man. From the back of the room Pearlann Ranchek and Jenny and her three children rushed down the aisle and stepped across us to the next seats. They were just ahead of the bride who was gripping a young man by the arm.

"Donna's father is dead," Pearlann whispered to me. "That's her brother giving her away."

During the bridal march tears had started running down Pearlann's cheeks and she reclaimed her handkerchief from Ranchek. As the bride's party met the groom's contingent at the altar, Pearlann snapped open her compact. Holding it down out of sight, she began repairing the damage to her eye shadow.

I caught the right side of my reflection in her mirror and smiled. The troublemaker, scourge, sickly lurking malcontent had been banished long ago and I could regard myself now in mirrors and polished silver without a shudder. If I had not been able to live by his ethic, neither could he match my endurance. I had watched him waste away, imprisoned in a body he reviled, pleading from behind my eyes; failing at last for lack of sustenance.

One seat past Pearlann, Jenny was staring anxiously at her husband. She seemed unnerved that he should be back on the boards, even in a supporting role. Black was incapable of standing still and performing the minor function expected of him. He had to listen to the minister, truly listen, and react, not quite mugging, but hawking a deep commitment. At the serious passages Josh tightened cord and fiber. When the charge grew sentimental, affectionate melancholy played over his features. The bride, by contrast, looked drugged and Goodwin dead.

Arguing with Lonnie the other night I had made every objection to marriage except the true one. It comes to me now as I watch Goodwin from the last row. All eyes are on him. No one looks back at me.

The minister is speaking of obligation and duty, and those

tarnished words still have the power to rally my spirit. Today Goodwin is being offered the chance to lose himself in something larger than he. It is never an easy offer to refuse and he will accept it.

He will leave the reception tonight before I do, take his bride's hand and draw her to his car. From the sidelines we friends and family will hoot and call after them. For an instant, as the car pulls away, we who cry out will feel desolate and envy the adventure that is beginning without us.

But the car goes a block and turns the corner. Our shouts are lost. The ringing in Goodwin's head abruptly stops. Everything in the car is quiet. He turns to look at his wife and she smiles. He smiles back.

His sense of drama has caused the minister to hold back the climactic oaths and let the organ pour out another lachrymose melody that passes at weddings for joy and hope. Goodwin had not expected this interlude. He looks over his shoulder to be sure the guests haven't grown restless and gone home. The bride, after swaying once early in the service, is holding herself taut. A half-veil obscures her resemblance to Goodwin.

"Where are the children?" I whisper to Pearlann Ranchek.

"At camp until after the honeymoon."

The Goodwins have reached their honeymoon hotel. I watch them register under their legal new name. To the bellboy and the room clerk they are unmistakably newlyweds, and as they are shown to their room they play their part. Goodwin becomes more nervous than he feels. Donna colors as the door to their room is thrown open. The bellhop whistles while he turns on the bathroom light and checks the air conditioning. For a minute, until he pockets his tip and bows out the door, he is their common enemy and makes Goodwin grateful for the girl's presence.

The door closes. Goodwin doesn't look at her. He feels her watching as he opens the suitcase and lifts out her dresses.

The skirts and suits are new and strange to him. When he faces her she is strange. She looks at him out of strange eyes. For the rest of his life, unless he breaks the vow he made today, her eyes will see him, all day and through the night when he sleeps. He knows only one way to close her eyes and wearily he reaches for her.

Not for me, that surveillance. I need no assurance that I exist. Blinding the eyes of my own weaker self took years. Now, if I must be seen at all, it will be from inside, from the position I fought to occupy and hold. I won't graft on other eyes to watch me, watch over me, set my limits and keep me forever the man I was on the day I married. Rather a thousand other eyes, for a night, than one scant pair for a lifetime. The prospect haunts me of those same eyes, watching, waiting, watching long after feeling has faded, glazing over but waiting and watching. Watching me to my grave.

The organist has segued to a second number and the minister looks at him over his shoulder. He seems surprised. Throughout the chapel the guests begin shifting on the hard wood. Only Jenny Black's children do not stir. Even the youngest, chewing the corner of a prayerbook, is enchanted by his father's showmanship.

At last the music stops. The organist folds his hands. To be sure another crescendo will not drown him out, the minister waits until the reverberations have died beneath our feet. His silence tells us the moment has come.

But then, to an appreciative smile from Josh Black, he stretches the pause past the time the rustling has ended. We wait, and wait. When he can prolong the hush no more, he speaks in a voice hardly less resonant than the organ:

"Wilt thou, Douglas, take this woman to be thy lawfully wedded wife? Wilt thou love her, comfort her, honor, and keep her in sickness and health; and forsaking all others, keep thee unto her as long as ye both shall live?"

I cannot hear Goodwin's response but it is appropriate, for

the minister now puts the same question to the bride. She answers firmly, "I will."

Goodwin, placing the ring, leans over to lift her short veil. I see his wife close her eyes to receive his kiss.

A Note About the Author

Born in 1933, A. J. Langguth grew up in Minneapolis.
He was graduated from Harvard College in 1955, and
has written for several magazines and newspapers,
including *The New York Times*. His first novel,
Jesus Christs, appeared in 1968. Mr. Langguth lives in
Los Angeles.

A Note on the Type

The text of this book was set on the Linotype in Janson, a recutting made direct from type cast from matrices long thought to have been made by the Dutchman Anton Janson, who was a practicing type founder in Leipzig during the years 1668-87. However, it has been conclusively demonstrated that these types are actually the work of Nicholas Kis (1650-1702), a Hungarian, who most probably learned his trade from the master Dutch type founder Dirk Voskens. The type is an excellent example of the influential and sturdy Dutch types that prevailed in England up to the time William Caslon developed his own incomparable designs from these Dutch faces.

This book was composed, printed, and bound by *The Colonial Press Inc., Clinton, Mass.*

Typography and binding design by *Christine Aulicino.*